I0574838

THREE TIMES A MURDER

THREE TIMES A MURDER

Once Upon A Crime Trilogy: Book Three

NOLON KING

STERLING & STONE

Copyright © 2022 by Sterling & Stone

All rights reserved.

No part of this book may be reproduced in any form or by any electronic or mechanical means, including information storage and retrieval systems, without written permission from the author, except for the use of brief quotations in a book review.

The authors greatly appreciate you taking the time to read our work. Please consider leaving a review wherever you bought the book, or telling your friends about it, to help us spread the word.

Thank you for supporting our work.

Chapter One

Seventeen Months Ago
Private Prison Cell, Undisclosed Location
12:03 a.m.

RULES WERE MADE to be followed, not broken. It was his job to punish those who did not comply.

Each step he took down the dark hallway reverberated off the cement walls, then returned in a thudding echo. But not just back to him. They went forward, too, announcing his approach.

His pace was slow, deliberate ... designed to herald his arrival. Give his prisoner time to make the appropriate adjustments. Prepare for the visit. Greet him accordingly.

Or suffer the consequences if he refused to comply with the rules.

And it was all about rules. More specifically, adherence to them. People ended up in prison because they violated social contracts and broke long-standing mores. Regula-

1

tions. Laws. It was a matter of discipline. Order. Mental fortitude.

In prison — in *his* prison — inmates had two choices. One, abide by the prescribed set of guidelines and serve their sentences with dignity. Or two, continue to buck the system and break the rules. He didn't recommend option two, as such behavior would be met with swift corrective action until they learned to behave.

He was young when his father taught him to obey the rules, so he knew compliance could be learned. If a child could do it, surely an adult could.

And if they didn't have such strength on their own on the outside, they would learn it on the inside. He'd make certain of it. There were plenty of teaching methods at his disposal. He ran his fingers along his cudgel, the wood warm under his fingers. This wasn't state-issued. No, sir. He'd made this one himself. Whittled it from a tree felled by his own hand. Shaped and sanded until it was smooth as porcelain and the handle fit in his palm like it had been poured in a custom mold.

His father taught him that skill, too.

"Stand at the ready, Prisoner 04091970."

He was twenty feet from the cell.

All his time as a guard at a state-run correctional institution taught him there were always inmates who thought they'd rise in the hierarchy if they rebelled, believing being mavericks would catapult them to the top of the food chain.

They were wrong. It was his job to prove it to them.

He stopped outside Prisoner 04091970's cell and looked inside. Clearly a lesson would need to be taught.

"Well?"

No reply.

"What is the penalty for prisoners who do not keep

themselves or their cells tidy?" He stood there, staring at Prisoner 04091970, waiting for a response.

But none came.

"Your list of infractions is growing, inmate. You are to respond when spoken to."

Yet the prisoner remained silent.

He shook his head. "When I brought you here, I was very clear. I gave you a set of rules and stated explicitly that they were to be followed to the letter. To do so means your time here will be easy on you. Rather, as easy as maximum-security imprisonment can be. But if you don't comply with the rules, what happens?"

Still, the inmate chose not to respond.

"Very well." He sighed. "If you want to do things the hard way, we'll do things the hard way. Your initial infraction is a violation of the personal hygiene rule. If you refuse to maintain your appearance, I will maintain it for you. And trust me when I tell you, I will not be gentle."

The threat lingered between them like the reek of a hard day's work. Something the prisoner was about to know all too well.

He unlocked the cell, the clunk of the mechanism releasing loud in the otherwise silent facility. When the inmate didn't respond in any way, he took a deliberate step into the small space.

"The second rule you've violated is ignoring prison personnel when you were addressed by your designation. But you already know that, don't you Prisoner 04091970?"

Still no response.

"Answer me!"

The inmate said nothing.

His fingers wrapped around the handle of his night-stick as his vision tinged red. In one swift movement, he yanked his club free of his belt, then his arm traced a wide arc through the air. Wood met skull with a satisfactory — yet sickening — thud.

Just like that, it was over.

Prisoner 04091970 was on the floor.

He was looking down in horror and fury. If his father had seen what he'd done, he'd no doubt meet the same fate. Or worse. There was a time and place for losing one's temper, and the workplace was neither the time nor the place. Certainly not when it caused more work. He'd only meant to scare, to threaten. Not to follow through. Well, always to follow through. Empty threats were pointless. But not to this extent. He wasn't to inflict this kind of damage.

Now he had a mess on his hands.

The cell would need cleaning.

The prisoner would need stitching. Maybe more than that.

And once he was finished, he'd have to address his own flagrant disregard for the rules.

Because rules were made to be followed, not broken. And it was his job to punish those who did not comply.

Chapter Two

CHELSEA WALKED into the station with a giant pastry box and a full drink holder balanced on top of it.

Jim rushed over to divest her of the four cups, though he didn't take his gaze off the box. "I hope whatever's in there didn't get crushed under the coffee."

Norm joined them. "I hope that's coffee from Hill of Beans."

Charlie was on his heels as they all followed her like baby ducks after their mother to the back of the room. "I hope you got cinnamon rolls."

She fought a sigh as she placed her burden on the table. "Nothing's crushed, Jim. I kept the coffee on the edge so the walls of the box would support the extra weight. Of course I went to Hill of Beans, Norm. If I'm treating, I'm doing it right. And yes, Charlie, it's not a real treat without cinnamon rolls."

As Charlie removed the lid, Jim surveyed the contents. "You got a variety of pastries. Donuts, fritters, scones, bear claws."

"Dibs on a bear claw." Norm grabbed one with his free

hand. He already had his coffee in his other. "Appreciate it, Sullivan."

"Yeah, thanks. You're the best." Charlie took his cinnamon roll and a cup. Both of them returned to their seats.

"So, what's the occasion?" Jim took a maple twist and his own coffee. But he didn't return to his desk. He waited for her to answer. His manners didn't extend to waiting for her to make her selection before eating, though. He took a giant bite of his pastry, then moaned as he chewed.

Chelsea shook her head. "I had to go to the big box store this morning for Dad. He gave me a huge list from his prepper group. This is my attempt at bribery. I was hoping you'd help me deliver it all later."

"Fair trade. In fact, I think I got the better end of the deal."

She smiled at him, glanced at the television set playing the news in the corner of the room — just weather at the moment, and it was a beautiful day for autumn — then she turned her attention to the pastries.

While she was looking over what was left of the baked goods, two sets of patrol officers came through. She smiled at the first one — her old partner, Neil Rafferty. But it was hard to keep her expression friendly when his new partner and his two buddies followed. Oliver Thompson and his lackeys Ethan Miller and Jeremy Berger had picked a fight with Jim in the locker room when he'd first transferred to Zone Four. She was still amazed that her partner won the fight when he was outnumbered one to three, though she should know by now never to bet against him.

Steeling herself for what was sure to be an uncomfortable exchange — at best — she grabbed her coffee and the last cinnamon roll then pointed at the box. "Hey, Neil. Nice seeing you upstairs for a change. You're all welcome to pastries. Get something before they're all gone. When Delfino shows up, he's liable to eat half of what's in there himself."

Rafferty grinned. "Chels, you're a lifesaver. I only had a protein shake for breakfast. Kayleigh has us both going keto."

"These are everything keto isn't."

"Thank God for that." He took the other maple twist.

Berger and Miller muttered something that almost sounded like thanks as they took donuts from the box, but Thompson just stood there sneering. "Did I hear you correctly?"

"That pastries aren't keto-friendly?" She arched an eyebrow. "Do you actually think they are?"

"Not about that shit. About shopping at a big box store for survival supplies."

"Let me guess. I somehow managed to mess up buying in bulk."

"As long as you know." He shrugged as he took a fritter from the box. "Though why you'd want to screw your old man like that is beyond me. But whatever. I guess we don't all love our family members the same way."

"Fuck off, Thompson." Jim wiped his hands on a napkin, balled it up, then tossed it into the trash a little harder than necessary. "You don't know shit about shopping, and you sure as hell aren't qualified to talk about how to express love for someone."

Thompson put down his pastry then stepped toward him.

Jim countered.

Berger and Miller each took an arm to pull their friend back.

Norm and Charlie appeared from nowhere and did the same to Jim.

7

Neil and Chelsea exchanged a look before their gazes bounced between the two angry men.

Davenport walked in and headed straight for them. "What's going on here?"

"Good morning, Captain." Chelsea gave him her brightest smile and held up the box. "Care for a pastry?"

He took a blueberry scone.

"Excellent choice, sir," Rafferty said.

"Uh-huh." Davenport stared at him, frowned, then looked at Jim. "Not going to answer me, Detective?" He looked at Thompson. "Officer?"

Both remained silent, as did the rest of the group.

"Okay. Maybe we should take this into my office for a more thorough Q&A session."

"Sir." Chelsea shook her head.

"What is it Sullivan?"

She pointed at the television. Her blood had run cold, and she couldn't manage to give voice to the myriad thoughts caroming through her mind at the moment.

A "breaking news" banner scrolled across the bottom of the screen as a journalist reported on a chilling turn of events.

"—en route from the state penitentiary to the hospital. Responding officers say the EMTs, guard, and driver were all found dead, and that was only possible if Fletcher had help on the inside. They've turned the investigation over to the State Police. Their spokesperson says Fletcher is believed to be armed and extremely dangerous. If anyone sees him, they are not to approach him but should call the authorities immediately. A hotline number is on the bottom of the screen if you have any information as to the whereabouts of the Grimm Reaper. We'll be following this story as it develops. Back to you, Tom and Maggie."

"Officers, get back to your posts. Now." Davenport's voice had developed an edge.

Rafferty, Thompson, Miller, and Berger were gone before the words were out of his mouth.

"Anderson, Paxton, start pulling any details you can that the news doesn't have. I want everything."

Norm and Charlie were already on their way back to their desks.

"You two," Davenport said to Chelsea and Jim as he started walking, "my office."

She was a step behind him. Jim was by her side the whole way.

The door wasn't even closed when she lost the tenuous hold she had on her composure. "He's out? He's *out*? He's supposed to be away for life. For *life*, Captain. Maybe they define 'life' differently at the state capital than they do in Steel City, but to me, life means life. As in, the duration of his lifetime. How did he get out? And more importantly, why didn't they tell us? Tell *me*?"

"Easy." Jim pulled her into his arms and held her tightly against him. She listened to the rhythmic beat of his heart thrumming in his chest, and it steadied her.

At least it started to.

Then she realized it was pounding faster than it should be, even if it was slower than hers. It also didn't help that she was hiding in his embrace and fighting off tears in front of her boss.

She shoved away from him and started pacing in the small room. "I'm fine!" But her voice was too loud.

"Well, I'm not."

"We're cops, Jim. This isn't a professional reaction to this news."

"We're also human. The Grimm Reaper held you captive. He almost killed both of us. And we're finding out he escaped on the news instead of from the prison, so we're also processing the fact that he could have gotten to either of us before we even knew he was out. It's perfectly natural to be a little freaked."

"Jim's right, Chelsea. But now that you two have had a moment, we need to talk next steps. I'm thinking protective details. He's going to be coming after you."

"No, sir." She shook her head. Maybe too emphatically, but he had to understand. "Fletcher's too smart. He's a master of disguise. No one will see him coming."

"It's not like he's traveling with a make-up kit, Chelsea," Jim said.

"But you heard the news. He had help. Couldn't have pulled it off, otherwise."

Jim rubbed his head. "So, what do you suggest?"

A knock sounded.

"Come in," Davenport yelled.

Charlie opened the door. "It seems Fletcher has been complaining of chest pains for the last few days. His so-called symptoms have been escalating. Because of his medical background, he was granted more frequent access to the medical ward than most people. And the doctor talked to him like a colleague rather than a prisoner. Grew a little lax. There's *chance* he *might* have had access to medicines that *may* have helped him mimic symptoms that *could* have fooled the doctor and made him think Fletcher *possibly* had a heart attack."

"Geez, Paxton. Enough conditionals in that statement?"

"Sorry, Captain. I'm just telling you what the doctor told me."

"Fucker's trying to distance himself." Jim pounded the desk. "Plausible deniability. He knows he screwed up and doesn't want the blame."

Chelsea shook her head. "Or he intentionally helped Fletcher. Who would know better how to fake a heart condition than two doctors?"

"That's a baseless accusation," Davenport said. "Especially against someone with impeccable credentials. At least, to this point. You can't go around saying things like that. Not outside this room, anyway."

"It's just a theory." She shrugged.

"A damn good one." Jim dropped onto the sofa. Then he stood up and paced again. "Once Fletcher got into the ambulance, he still had to overpower ... what? Four people, right?" He looked at Charlie.

"Three. One EMT, one guard, and one driver."

"That's not even protocol." Jim looked at Davenport. "What the fuck is going on over there? News said two EMTs, not one."

"Probably should have been two." Charlie nodded.

"Only one guard?" Jim asked

"That's not unheard of," the captain said.

"You're right, it's not. When the guard is in tactical gear and there's a second vehicle for backup if he needs it. The news didn't say anything about a follow car. Was there one?"

Charlie shook his head.

"Was Fletcher in ankle shackles?"

"Doc said there wasn't time. They didn't even have his hands cuffed together. One hand cuffed to the bed rail. The other hand was free. Ankles free."

Jim looked at Davenport. "Sound like protocol to you?"

"But one hand was cuffed, right?" Chelsea finally spoke up.

"What?" Charlie asked.

"He still had one hand cuffed. And even though the

guard wasn't in full tactical gear, he was armed. So you had a trained guard with a gun and an EMT who was fully mobile, as well as a driver who could have swerved all over the place to keep the prisoner off balance. All three of these people against a guy who was cuffed on a gurney. How did Fletcher overcome all of them? It doesn't make sense."

"He had help from the inside," Charlie said.

"Had to," Jim added. "Cops on scene already think so. The prison doctor is my bet. Had means and opportunity."

"Motive?" Davenport asked.

"We'll find it," Jim said.

Chelsea rubbed her forehead. Her temples were throbbing, and her stomach was about to revolt. "But he wasn't on the bus."

"Didn't have to be. He did his part back at the prison. Had to have given Fletcher whatever he needed for his best chance of getting free." Jim turned to Charlie. "What do we know about the crime scene?"

"Cuff on the gurney was either picked or unlocked. EMT was found by the gurney. The guard was found not far from him. Both throats were slit, no hesitation marks."

"Like with a scalpel, maybe?" His jaw ticked.

"I'm not an ME. Would be nice if we could get Nia to do the autopsy, but they'll never give us jurisdiction on the case. Might be able to get the photos for her to review, though."

"I'll put in a request for them," Davenport said.

"What about the driver?" Chelsea asked.

"He was found on the side of the road."

"Also with his throat slit?"

Charlie shook his head. "No. He was shot."

"With the guard's gun?"

"They're running ballistics now, but they don't think so."

"They don't think so?" she asked. "Are there rounds missing from his gun or not?"

Jim ran his hand through his hair. "That's how they know he's armed and dangerous. He took the guard's gun with him."

Davenport shook his head. "Not necessarily. If it wasn't the guard's gun, that means someone else was there. With another weapon. Or Fletcher somehow got on that gurney already armed."

"Yeah." Charlie sighed. "Sorry it's not better news."

A burst of maniacal laughter escaped her. "Better news? What could be better news than the serial killer who abducted and nearly murdered me escaped prison because he had inside help, slaughtered his transport officials, stole the guard's gun, and is now on the loose? Oh, and no one informed us? *And* we have no leads? Did I forget anything?"

"Chelsea?" Jim said. "It's okay. We stopped him before when we knew a lot less about him. We'll get him again. And this time, the whole state is after him."

"Yeah, Sullivan. Don't worry about it. He'll be back in custody before sundown," Charlie said. "You just wait and see."

"Why don't you take a few days?" Davenport started typing. "We can juggle the schedule."

"No. Why is it when things get tough, you guys always try to protect me? Just because I'm a girl — a *woman* — doesn't mean I can't handle myself. I'm a cop, same as all of you."

"No offense, Chels," Jim said, "but you just kind of had a meltdown."

"Who's the one who needed a hug when we came in here? Wasn't me."

He glanced at Charlie, then arched his brow at her. "You didn't? Could have fooled me."

"It's immaterial. What I need right now is a plan. I need to not be sitting here. I need purpose. Action. I need—"

"To get to the crime scene," Davenport said.

Chelsea looked at him.

"Both of you. Go. See what you can find that the first-on-scene missed. As far as I'm concerned, the Grimm Reaper was your case, so you're entitled to be there. Anyone gives you grief for it not being your jurisdiction, have them call me."

The way she felt, she almost hoped someone would start something with her and Jim about whether they had the right to be there. She needed to blow off a little steam and had no intention of calling Davenport to back her up.

"After you, partner," Jim said.

But she was already halfway to the door.

Chapter Three

IT SHOULD HAVE TAKEN about thirty minutes to get to the crime scene. Jim made the drive in a little over fifteen.

Chelsea didn't say a word the entire time.

He tried talking to her for the first five minutes. She refused to respond.

Tried music for the second five. He was torn between classic rock and modern country and decided country might be too depressing. She slapped the "off" button when Blue Oyster Cult's "Don't Fear the Reaper" came on.

An unfortunate twist of fate, but he couldn't blame her. He didn't bother putting on a different playlist.

They drove the rest of the way in silence.

The road was closed two miles from their destination, but when he flashed his badge, they were waved through.

The mobile crime unit technicians were loading their vehicles when they arrived. Jim and Chelsea donned booties and gloves before getting out of his SUV, then they approached.

A state trooper met them before they reached the

yellow tape. He sighed, the weariness evident on his face and the set of his shoulders. Probably had been through this drill a thousand times in the last twelve hours. "Gotta stop you there, folks, and ask you to move along."

Jim moved his jacket so the guy could see his shield clipped to his belt. "I'm Detective Jim McPherson of Steel City PD. This is my partner, Detective Chelsea Sullivan. We're—"

"Sullivan and McPherson? *The* Sullivan and McPherson?"

It was Chelsea's turn to sigh.

He let go of the tail of his coat and let it fall closed. "You make us sound like a sideshow act."

"Sorry. Didn't mean it like that. You're legends in this state. Probably across the country." He held out his hand, saw their gloves, then dropped it to his side. "Name's McCann. Cade. I followed the Grimm Reaper case. And then the Gomorran Society? That task force on human trafficking is doing amazing things. It's an honor to meet you both. You give cops a good name. We need some positive PR these days, you know?"

"We just did our jobs. And that's why we're here. Fletcher's out, and we want to put him away, same as before."

McCann glanced over his shoulder. "I'm really not supposed to let people contaminate the crime scene. Or even loiter here."

"We're not just 'people,' McCann," Chelsea said.

Again, he glanced over his shoulder. "I know you're not. As soon as the crime techs leave, I'll let you down there."

"Appreciate it." Jim nodded.

"Can you tell us anything the news hasn't reported?" she asked.

"The MCU techs would really be more helpful than I would. I've mostly been chasing away gawkers and gapers all night." He shook his head. "I don't understand it. The scene was grisly. Macabre. The stuff of nightmares. None of us wanted to be here. We'd all like to forget what we saw, but we never will. Yet dozens of civilians sought it out. And that was after we told the public it isn't safe to go wandering around the countryside right now. Why the hell are people coming here in droves, putting themselves and their loved ones in danger just for a look at something so vile?"

"You figure out how to stop a person's fascination with something so sick, and you'll stop violent crime," Jim said. "Then you'll be the one who's a legend."

"And we'll be out of jobs. Happily, might I add." Chelsea turned and watched the last crime scene van pull away. "Mind if we go take a look now?"

McCann held up the tape so they could walk under it. "Just don't take too long. If the investigators come back, they'll be pissed. At all of us. But I'm the one who'll take the heat."

"It would be a lot easier if they'd work with us," Jim said.

"Did you ask them to share what they had with you?"

"They weren't here when we arrived."

"They're good guys. They might be willing to work with you. But not if you sneak around behind their backs."

"We'll just take a quick look," Chelsea said. "You can give us their names and contact info on our way out."

Jim led the way down to where the techs had set up markers before photographing evidence. In some cases, it had been removed for processing. They had no way of knowing what those items were. In other cases, plaster molds had been made. He and Chelsea studied footprints and tire marks near the areas where the casts had been poured. She took pictures, which would have to suffice, but they wouldn't be as good as what the State Police had.

"We need to make nice with the investigators on this case if we want to get anything useful," she said.

He grunted. Making nice wasn't something he did often. Or well.

"You think that shoe print is Fletcher's or one of the vic's?" She pointed to a footprint in the mud. The only one they'd managed to get a clear photo of. All the others had been destroyed by the crime unit walking on them or taking molds of them for evidence.

"I doubt it's Fletcher's. I'm guessing it's at least a size thirteen. I'm taller than he is, and that print is bigger than mine. People's feet are usually proportional to their height. Do we know how tall the driver was? He was the only one who made it off the bus."

"People's feet aren't always proportional to their height. I'm only five foot four, but I wear a size ten."

Jim glanced down at her feet. "Holy shit, Sullivan. I never noticed. It's like you're walking on skis."

"Shut up, Jim. My point is, you can't make assumptions based on his height."

"Well, you dated him."

"Thanks for reminding me."

"My point is, even if you can't count on his height as an indicator … never mind." Open mouth, insert foot. Even if it wasn't a size thirteen, he was choking on it.

Her cheeks reddened. "Get your mind out of the gutter, McPherson."

"I just meant you knew him better than I did."

"That's not what you meant."

"You used to love to watch him work. Did he have big hands?"

"I don't know, Jim." The heat left her voice. "I didn't analyze his hands or his feet or anything else on him. I thought he was smart and kind and charming. The physical stuff wasn't important. Shame on me. Can we just get back to the evidence, please? Or whatever's left of it?"

"Yeah. Of course." He led her over to the ambulance. "Better check out the bus before they come for it."

It had been easy enough to dismiss the dark patches on the ground outside as variations in the soil instead of a pool of blood that had seeped into the earth. But there was no way to ignore the carnage that had happened inside the transport vehicle. Although the bodies had been taken away, the evidence of the murders was still blatantly evident by the crimson splatters on the ceiling, smears on the walls, and puddles on the floor. Spatter patterns were tagged for photos and would be analyzed to determine the angle of the arterial spray, but Jim already had a good idea of what had happened.

By Chelsea's wide eyes and pale skin, he suspected she did, too.

"I think we've seen enough in here."

She turned and left without a word.

They walked up to the road, following the path the driver took as he left the asphalt. The crime scene techs had tagged a long stretch of skid marks.

Jim sighed. "I'd convinced myself he managed all this in a few seconds. Some kind of ninja attack. Now I'm starting to think there was a longer struggle involved. At least as far as the driver was concerned."

"The two in the back had to be taken out fast. Otherwise, the guard would have stopped him."

"Unless the guard was in on it. That's the only thing that makes sense."

"But he killed the guard," Chelsea said.

"You think he's above a double-cross?"

She shrugged. "I don't know what to think."

"You're letting him get in your head."

"And you're not emotionally compromised?"

"Work with me on this, would you?"

"Fine." Chelsea crossed her arms.

"Yeah. That's open-minded."

She rolled her eyes.

"Here's what I think. Fletcher convinced the doctor he'd give him money or something if he helped him. So he gave him the keys to his cuffs and hid a scalpel somewhere in the gurney. He made sure not to shackle his ankles and only one wrist, then he told the EMTs it was too big an emergency to do it. Because Fletcher was 'unconscious' at the time, it wasn't that big a deal. Or so they were led to believe. If the guard was in on it, too, and I think he was, it made things that much easier for him. When the bus hit this stretch of road — practically deserted, no cameras — Fletcher slit the EMT's throat, who was caught off guard. Assuming he was quiet enough, the driver would have been unaware. The guard probably helped him by catching the body so it didn't make noise when it fell. Then Fletcher was free to unlock his cuff, at which point he dispatched the guard, who foolishly thought he was safe."

"No one could ever think he was safe around Fletcher."

"Relatively safe. Safe enough. Maybe they struggled, but Fletcher managed to kill him. That could be why the driver skidded for so long. There might have been a scuffle in the back. Then when the driver finally stopped, he ran. Fletcher chased him down and killed him, too. He'd have had the guard's gun by then."

"Except they don't think the driver was killed by the guard's gun."

"The prison doctor could have given Fletcher a gun along with the keys and a scalpel."

Chelsea shook her head. "That's a lot of smuggling."

"Well, we know — or think — this happened at an arranged place. Stands to reason there could have been someone else involved in his breakout scheme. They could have been waiting outside with a getaway vehicle. And a gun. If there was another weapon that took out the driver, it's the most logical way to introduce it into the mix."

She didn't say anything.

"Well?"

"It's the only theory we've got."

"But you don't like it."

"I don't like any of this. Doesn't mean it isn't plausible."

"So, you agree with me?"

"I agree it's a possibility. None of this matters. It's not like we have any evidence to actually go on. For that matter, it's not even our case."

"Yet we're here. Davenport sent us. We know Fletcher better than anybody. And if anyone's going to find him, it's us."

"Yeah, because he's probably coming for us."

"Doesn't matter why."

Chelsea rolled her eyes.

"Come on. McCann's pacing. We need to get out of here before he loses his shit."

"You can't blame him. He's sticking his neck out for us. And investigators can be jerks. They could make his life difficult if they come back and find out he let us walk the crime scene without their permission."

Jim took the lead on the way back toward their car. "What do you mean, investigators can be difficult? They're detectives. We're detectives."

"Look in the mirror. I rest my case."

"I'm a delight."

"You're something. 'Delight' isn't the word I'd use."

"What is?"

"I told you. Difficult."

"Why do I get the feeling that isn't the word you were thinking?"

"I don't use the kinds of words you're thinking."

"Ah. You might not say them, but I bet you think them."

Chelsea sighed and picked up her pace. "Trooper McCann." She pitched her voice a little louder as she closed the distance between them. "Thank you for letting us walk the scene."

"I'm sorry I couldn't be of more help." He produced a business card. "The investigators didn't leave me any of their cards, so this is mine. But I wrote their names and numbers on the back."

She removed her gloves, pocketed them, then shook his hand. "Much appreciated." Chelsea took the card then looked at the names on the back. "Danny Sherick's on this case?"

"Who?" Jim asked.

"Yeah," McCann said. "You know him?"

Chelsea smiled. "We've met. Anyway, thanks."

On the way to the car, Jim nudged her. "So, who's Danny Sherick?"

"We were in the academy together. He, Rob Morrison, and Neil—"

"Rafferty?"

"Yeah. They kept me sane. They said I was too serious and made sure I laughed at least once a day. Usually at their antics. Sometimes at myself."

"You are too serious."

"We work with criminals. There's not much to laugh at." She climbed into the car.

He folded himself into the driver's seat. "Think you can use your charm and convince him to work with us on this one?"

"I'll talk to him. But I can't make any promises. He's agreeable, but like I said" — she tapped the rearview mirror — "detectives can be jerks. We don't know anything about his partner, and he might not be the sharing type."

"Give him a call. Meanwhile, I think we need to go to the prison. I'd like to chat with the warden, the doctor, some of the guards, and his cellmate."

"If they'll talk to us. We're not officially on this case."

"Then maybe you should make that call now." He turned the key, put the vehicle in gear, then pulled out, engine growling and tires squealing. "Because I intend to talk to them whether we're officially allowed to investigate Fletcher's escape or not."

Chapter Four

CHELSEA PUT the phone on speaker then dialed the number on the back of the card McCann had given her. It was answered on the first ring.

"Sherick."

She hadn't heard that voice in years, but the rich timbre was instantly familiar and brought a smile to her face. "Danny. Hi. It's—"

"Chelsea Sullivan. Son of a bitch."

"How'd you know it was me?" But she knew. The recognition came as easily to him as it did to her, and by his tone, he was as happy with the reunion as she was.

"How'd I know? I'd recognize your voice anywhere. How the hell are you?"

"Fine, thanks. You?"

He paused for a moment. "How'd you get my number, Chels?"

But it wasn't a question he needed to have answered. He knew, and she knew he knew. She bit her lip. Probably should have taken a moment to rehearse what she wanted to say. But this wasn't any old detective from any old crime scene. This was Danny. She didn't have to practice a speech with him. They'd been nothing but honest with each other since the day they met. "A trooper at a crime scene gave it to me."

"I should have figured I'd be hearing from you. Hell, I probably should have proactively reached out. But we've been a little busy."

"That's why I'm calling."

"Yeah, I gathered. We're not turning the case over to you."

Jim glanced at her.

She shrugged at him as she spoke into the phone. "And I wouldn't ask you to, Danny."

"Good." The relief was evident in his voice.

"But I do have a favor to ask."

"What?" And just like that, he sounded wary.

"Can you just keep us looped in? Give us access to what you find?"

"That sounds a lot like us turning our case over to you."

"Come on, Danny. You know we know Fletcher better than anyone."

"I know he almost killed you. I know the last person who should be investigating him is someone with a grudge."

"I don't have a grudge."

Jim arched an eyebrow and muttered, "I sure as hell do."

"What?" Danny asked.

"Nothing." She smacked Jim's arm. "Look, I'm not asking for anything other than a professional courtesy. And it's as much for your benefit as ours. We know Fletcher better than anyone. Even your psych profiles can't tell you what we can. So, let's partner up on this. We can help each other. It'll be like old times. Quid pro quo. You scratch my back, I'll scratch yours."

He chuckled. "I fondly remember some mutual back-scratching."

Jim's lips quirked.

She smacked him.

"What was that noise?" Danny asked.

"I don't know. Road rumble. I'm in the car. So, what do you say? Will you send us what you have and tell your witnesses to talk to us? In exchange, I'll tell you everything you want to know about the SOB."

"SOB? My virgin ears can't take it. Might need to wash your mouth out with soap if you keep talking like that."

Her cheeks burned. "The teasing never gets old."

"Let me call you back in five." The line went dead.

"So," Jim said. "You want to talk about the mutual back-scratching, or—"

"No, I do not."

"Okay. Just thought I'd ask."

"Just thought you'd *pry* is more like it."

Before he could answer, her phone rang. It was Danny's number. She put it on hands-free. "Hey, Danny."

"Chels. I talked to my partner. We'll try it. But if you step on our toes, we're pulling the plug."

"That's fair. Thanks, Danny."

"We'll send you copies of what the crime techs found as the lab processes everything."

"Great. In the meantime—"

"*In the meantime*," he talked over her, "we want you to send us everything you have from the original case."

"Everything? That file is huge. We have *boxes* of information on Fletcher."

"Then I guess you have a lot to keep you busy for a while."

"Are you trying to give me busywork to keep me out of the field?"

"Don't be ridiculous. A history on Fletcher is vital to understanding what he might be up to now.."

"Ask me anything."

"We want a full dossier. We don't know what to ask because we don't know what we don't know."

"Fine. I'll have someone copy the files and send them to you. I'm not at the station right now."

"No?"

"No. I told you, I'm in the car."

"Where are you?"

"Out."

"Out where? Doing something related to my case?"

Jim shook his head.

She sighed and ignored him. "We're on our way to the prison. We want to talk with some people of interest."

"Like who?"

"Like people of interest. You're the lead investigator. Don't you know who's of interest?"

"You're already making me regret this back-scratching thing."

"Danny, he tried to kill me. Now he's on the loose. You know I'm not going to let this go. You can help me and we can catch him faster, or you can stonewall me and we can get in each other's way. Then guess what'll happen? It'll take us longer to find the monster and more people will get hurt. So, what's it going to be? Are we going to be at odds on this? Or partners again?"

"Dave and I left the prison half an hour ago. I'll call the warden and tell him to expect you. But Chelsea, I do want your case files."

"I'll get someone on it."

"And I'd be remiss if I didn't say I think you and your

partner are too close to this thing. You really should consider letting us handle this."

"Danny, the whole state is looking for him."

"True, but we're coordinating the search. And you two should be miles away. Probably in a secure location with a guard detail."

"Is that what you'd do?"

"Just send the damn files, Chels. I have to go call the warden."

"Better call fast. We're at Black Meadow."

"Of course you are."

"Thanks, Danny."

"Later."

She could practically hear him rolling his eyes at her as he ended the call.

When Jim pulled up to the guard shack, they both showed their IDs. While he was given directions where to park, Chelsea called Davenport, filled him in on their progress, then asked him to have a clerk pull the full case file on the Grimm Reaper and have it forwarded to State Police Investigator Daniel Sherick at the county's main barracks.

They left their weapons and phones in the car. After passing through security, they were shown to the warden's office. True to his word, Danny had paved the way for them.

"Detectives. Please, come in. Have a seat."

Warden Wells Perry had a Napoleon complex. Chelsea didn't like to judge people, but it was obvious. The chairs on the visitors' side of the desk were slightly too large, which made the people in them look and feel small. She certainly did as she sat across from him. Perry's chair, on the other hand, was on the diminutive side, so it gave him the illusion of stature — an illusion he needed, because he was a rather small man. Maybe five-eight, and that was probably with lifts in his shoes. And if he weighed more than one fifty, he had pebbles in his pockets.

She shifted in the too-large seat, crossed her ankles, and waited for Jim to take the lead on this one.

He cleared his throat. "Thanks for seeing us, Warden."

"Well, as you can imagine, I'm a busy man. There's a lot for me to do here on an average day. But this is no average day."

"No, it's not. That's why we're here."

"That's what the Investigator Sherick said. I understand he and his partner are the leads on this case. As a favor to them, I've made myself available to you. But I'm not sure why we're doing this twice."

"The State Police are handling the investigation because they can cross county lines. But my partner and I are experts in Scott Fletcher. We know how he thinks better than anyone else on the planet. So, we're consulting with Sherick and his department to bring this matter to a close as quickly and quietly as possible. I'd think that's something a man in your esteemed position could understand. And would want."

"Well, yes. Of course. How can I help?"

"We want to talk to his cellmate. His guards. The doctor, of course. And we want access to any correspondence he had. Particularly fans of his."

"The doctor is gone for the day. Fletcher's cellmate was released last week, and he hasn't gotten another yet. Obviously all the guards aren't on duty right now. I can have my secretary take you to see the guards who are here. By the time you're done interviewing them, I'll have the names you want and copies of the most flagrant correspondences made for you."

"Only the most flagrant? And who decides what 'flagrant' is? You?"

"Actually, Investigators Sherick and Stack did. I told them I'd send them the complete file as soon as Mildred could copy it all, but they selected the letters they wanted to take with them. I'll make sure you leave with the same ones."

Chelsea stood and extended her hand. "Thank you, Warden."

He rose and shook the tips of her fingers.

Jim wrinkled his nose and didn't bother extending his hand. He just walked to the door.

"If you need anything else, Detective," the warden said, "just let me know."

In the lobby, Jim was already telling the secretary what they needed. But when Warden Perry walked Chelsea to the door, he instructed Mildred to take them to a visitation room. "I'll have her send the guards up to you."

Jim tried to get the secretary to talk about Perry as she led them through the facility, but either the walls had ears or she liked the guy because she didn't say anything. Not a single word, good or bad. When they got to a visitation room, she opened the door, gestured for them to enter, then closed it, sealing them inside.

"You think she's mute?" Jim asked.

"I think she's afraid to bite the hand that feeds her."

"She didn't even say hello."

"What's the matter? Not used to your smile having no effect on a woman?"

"Maybe we should revisit the back-scratching."

Chelsea stuck her tongue out at him then looked around. She expected a glass partition and a phone to speak through the divider, but they were in a wide-open room with a series of round, scarred tables. The chairs were hard plastic and quite uncomfortable. But there was nothing to keep prisoners from touching their visitors.

If Fletcher walked through that door right now, he could step right up to her. He could wrap his fingers around her throat. Squeeze until she couldn't breathe and make her death slow and painful. Or he could snap her neck and end her life in an instant.

Jim snapped his fingers in front of her face. "Earth to Sullivan."

She blinked a few times then focused on him. "Hmm. What?"

"You zoned out."

"Sorry. I was just thinking."

"Didn't look like happy thoughts."

"We're in a prison."

"You up for this?"

"Of course. Aren't you?"

"I'm not the one—"

But the door opened, cutting him off. In came a prison guard, smaller in stature than she thought was safe for a guard, though bigger than the warden. His mustache reminded her of Yosemite Sam, and he walked with every bit as much swagger in his step. He dropped down at their table then drummed his fingers like he was already bored with their conversation even though it hadn't begun yet.

"And you are?" Jim asked.

"Ross Bradley. I'm one of the guards in Cellblock C. Where the Grimm Reaper's kept? This ringing any bells? They told me you wanted to see me, but if you don't know what I'm talking about, I can go." He pushed slowly to his feet.

"Sit down, Bradley."

He stared at Jim for a long time before plopping into his chair again.

"I asked for your name, not your attitude."

"Look, man. I've been through this already. Perry's on our asses about it, and he's making us take a shorter lunch because of these interviews. I just want to put in my time, punch the clock, then go home, you know? It's not like I'm earning extra for all this harassment."

"Harassment?" Chelsea said. "You do understand one of the most violent killers in America is now on the loose, right? A man you could possibly have heard or seen plotting his escape. We're trying to learn anything we can about his whereabouts. Who might have helped him. Where he might have gone. What his plans are now that he's out. No one's trying to harass you, Mr. Bradley. We're relying on your expertise. You could be the hero in this story."

He sat up straighter and cleared his throat. "Hero, you say? The first guys didn't tell me that."

"The first guys probably never thought about it. But I'm telling you, your information is vital."

"*If* you have anything of use to us," Jim added.

"Well, what do you want to know?"

"Did you ever accompany Fletcher to the doctor here?"

He paused for a moment, looked up as he thought. "I don't remember."

"How long has he been pretending to be sick?"

Another pause. "I don't remember."

"Did you ever overhear him talking to any prisoners about plans to break out?"

The same hesitation, then, "I don't remember."

Chelsea looked at Jim. He nodded at her. She took over the questioning. "Mr. Bradley, did you know anything about Fletcher planning to break out?"

He looked at her, then he looked up while he thought. "Nothing comes to mind."

"Did you ever stand guard while he had visitors?"

"I don't know."

"How do you not know?"

"Lady, do you know how many prisoners we have here? And how many of them get visitors? And how often I pull proctor duty? I can't tell you if I ever saw him get a visitor because I don't care if he ever had a visitor. I punch in, do my job, punch out, then do it all again the next day. As long as no one gets killed or breaks out, it's a good damn day."

"But someone did break out, and people did get killed, so I guess last night wasn't a good day, was it?"

"Well, I wasn't here, so you can't blame me for that. Are we done here?" But he stood, answering his own question.

"Send your partner down when you get back to your cellblock," Jim said.

Bradley saluted on his way out.

"Charming fellow." Chelsea shook her head. "What do you think the next one will be like?"

"Can't be worse than that one."

Chapter Five

JIM LOOKED up when the room got darker.

A man stood in the doorway, blocking the light from the hallway beyond. Backlit, all his silhouette revealed was his gargantuan size. He tapped one knuckle gently against the metal doorframe, the soft rap surprising from someone of his stature.

The timbre of his voice was not a shock. It was a deep bass, resonant and full. "Bradley said you wanted to see me."

"You're the other guard from Cellblock C?" Chelsea asked.

He stepped inside. Looked like Mr. Clean, but without the earring. Or the smile. "Yes, ma'am. Milo Hartman. Been here ten years. Started in intake. Worked there for two years. Then A for two. Been in C ever since."

"Isn't C where the roughest guys are?" Jim asked.

"Yes, sir."

"Shouldn't you have been promoted out of there by now?"

Hartman's brows furrowed and he looked down at Jim with disgust. "Is that what Bradley told you?"

"No. That's just been my experience with guards. They pull the difficult assignment, work it a few years, then flame out. It gets to you after a while. You need the cushier detail."

"I requested C. *Sir*. I consider it important work."

Chelsea took his elbow. "Why don't you sit down? I'm guessing you're on your feet all day. You could probably use a break."

He studied her for a moment, then his features relaxed. He lowered himself into a chair, but his posture remained rigid.

"Would you like a cup of coffee or something?"

Jim had no idea where she planned on getting any. And he doubted caffeine would help the guy. But she was having more luck with Hartman than he was, so if she wanted to take point, great. He'd study the man while his attention was on her.

"No, thank you."

She slipped into a chair beside him. "So, you requested Cellblock C?"

"Yes, ma'am. I was raised to strive to be the best at what I do. If I wanted to be a doctor, I would have been a brain surgeon. If I wanted to be a pilot, I'd have been an astronaut. If I wanted to be in the military, I'd have been a SEAL."

"But you wanted to be a prison guard?" Jim asked.

"Do you know any little boys who dream of growing up to be prison guards?"

Chelsea shot Jim a look.

He held up his hands.

"Not that I have to justify my career to you, but I had to quit school because of family obligations. I have no regrets. This is my vocation now, and I'm going to do it to the best of my ability. If the worst offenders are in Cellblock C, then I'm going to be in Cellblock C to make sure they're paying for their crimes."

"Do you know the prisoners well?" she asked.

"I do. And I know Fletcher very well. He's twisted."

"What can you tell us about him?"

"He's incredibly smart. I mean book smart. But he's also very clever. He somehow managed to get perks in this place that other prisoners are denied. How'd he talk the guards and warden into that? Some kind of voodoo? No, I don't think so. I don't believe in that kind of mumbo jumbo. He knows how to manipulate the mind."

"Well, he was a doctor," Jim said.

"But not a psychologist. He was a coroner."

"But he's clinically insane," Chelsea added.

"You know that's only a legal term. There's no such thing as medical insanity."

Jim scoffed. "He stripped his victims and staged the murder scenes from fairy tales. He's batshit nuts."

"You can call it whatever you like. It doesn't make it a medical diagnosis. And it doesn't change the facts. He got away with things in here that other prisoners didn't. It's a breach of protocol. And I'd like to know why. Because I filed no fewer than thirty-eight reports, and yet nothing was done about it."

"You were his guard," Jim said. "Why didn't you just stop him?"

"When I was in charge, I did. Unless I was overruled. And sometimes I was."

"Who overruled you?" Chelsea asked.

"The only people who could. If it was a medical issue, the doctor. If it was anything else, the warden."

"I'm assuming your reports will be in his file," she said.

Hartman shook his head. "I wouldn't assume anything in this place. Like I said, the rules don't seem to mean anything here. At least, they didn't where Fletcher was concerned. He did something to their minds."

"But not to yours." Jim tapped the table to get his attention.

The guard looked at him.

"Why not you?"

"What do you mean?"

"You said Fletcher corrupted the doctor, the warden, Bradley."

"Other inmates, too."

"So why not you?"

"Mental fortitude, I suppose."

"Mental fortitude?"

Hartman stood. "I don't think I like what you're implying."

"What am I implying?"

He huffed and his cheeks reddened as he stared down at him. "I … I don't know. What are you implying?"

Jim shrugged. "Nothing, actually. I'm just curious why everyone was so susceptible to mental manipulations of the Grimm Reaper except for you."

"Maybe because everyone was afraid of him except for me."

"Why weren't you afraid of him?"

"Because he was an inmate. I was his jailor. There was a clear chain of command, and he was at the bottom of it. He knew it, and I knew it. He never even tried any mind games on me."

"That you knew of," Jim said.

"What?"

"That you knew of. Maybe he was manipulating you

the whole time, too, but you just didn't know it. That's how those guys work. They work on you, but they're so sly, you never see their games until it's too late. Maybe not even then."

"I never did anything for him. Never gave him any perks. Did him any favors."

"You might have and not even known."

"I didn't!"

"You ever do *anything* for him? Bring him a magazine? Let him make a call?"

"Never. If it was against the rules, I didn't do it. Bradley broke regulation for him all the time. Check my reports. But I didn't. And I can't say what the other guards did. I can't be here on every shift."

"Any chance you have copies of your reports?" Chelsea asked.

"Of course."

"You mind emailing them to us?"

"They're on my laptop at home."

She gave him her card.

"I'll send them when I'm off duty."

"Thank you." She shook his hand.

"I need to get back. God only knows what Bradley is doing. Or not doing." He left without acknowledging Jim.

They headed back to the warden's office.

"What do you think?" she said.

"He's certainly a by-the-book kind of guy."

"We need to talk to the doctor."

"Who's gone for the day." He sighed. "Let's see what files the warden gives us. Maybe we'll have something else to go on until we can talk to the good doctor."

"Danny may have tracked him down at home. I can call him."

"Might *Danny* have talked to him? You know, I don't think you need an excuse to call the guy. He seemed happy enough to hear from you without it being a work call."

"It's not like that."

"Want to tell me the back-scratching story?"

"Oh, look. We've reached the warden's office." She smiled at Mildred, his secretary. "Is the warden in?"

She didn't smile back. Just handed over a thick file. "Warden Perry is gone for the day. He asked me to give you this."

Jim took it. "This is all?"

Her only answer was a slow, deliberate blink.

"I'm guessing if there's more, he'll send it. Or we can request something specific. Right?" Chelsea asked.

Another blink.

"Okay. Well, thanks. We'll see ourselves out. Come on, Jim." She pulled on his elbow until he turned around, then she started dragging him down the hallway.

"That woman has the personality of a clipped toenail. That you find in your salad."

"That's disgusting. And how would you ever find a toenail clipping in your salad?"

"That's my point. It's nothing that you want, and it's nothing that makes sense. Why's she so hostile? What'd we do to deserve that?"

"You're just mad because your usual smile-and-compliment routine didn't work on her."

"I didn't even try it on her. And it's not a routine. It's called manners. You smile when you meet people."

"Whatever. It's not like we have to work with her. Why do you care?"

"Because secretaries are usually the best sources of information. The warden was never going to tell us anything. It would either implicate him or reveal him as incompetent. But if she wasn't so hostile, she'd probably be our Deep Throat. I bet she knows more about what goes on in that prison than the prisoners and guards combined."

"Well, she's not going to tell us. So, we'll have to do it the hard way." Chelsea tapped the folder before climbing into the car. After Jim started driving, she started going through the papers. "It's as I feared. Not a single report filed by Milo Hartman is in Fletcher's file."

"Figures. What is in there?"

"It seems he had quite a fan club."

"All serial killers do."

"And three girlfriends."

"Ugh. I don't get that. What kind of woman is turned on by that kind of man?"

She scoffed. "You should know. You're the one obsessed by serial killers."

"I'm not obsessed. I just study them. It's part of our job."

"Yet you don't know why women seek them out."

"It's twisted. I don't get it."

"Some of them think they can rehabilitate them. Others are attracted to the power. The rest think the relationship is safe because they never have to actually see the guy, so they'll never be hurt by him."

"Like I said, twisted."

"Is anything about a serial killer *not* twisted?"

"Touché." He reached for the radio, then thought better of it and left it off. "You want to stop somewhere for food? We haven't had anything since the pastry you brought in this morning, and I'm famished."

"Let's grab takeout and eat at our desks. I want to start

running background checks on all these people. And maybe we'll have more to go through from the State Police once we get back."

"From the *State Police*. Okay."

"Yes, Jim. From the State Police."

"What do you want to eat, Sullivan? Burgers? Subs? Pizza? Chinese?"

She rolled her eyes.

"What?"

"You're grumpy when you're hungry."

"Just pick something."

She sighed. "Go to Sloppy's."

"You hate Sloppy's."

"But you love it. And you can get a lot of food for cheap. I feel like this is going to be one of those 'lot of food' orders."

"Of course it is. I just said I'm starving. But I'm not worried about the money." She probably was, though. And if she chose Sloppy's, she was hungry, too. "Call the station. Ask Davenport if the *State Police* sent us anything. And see if Charlie and Norm are still there."

She called in. Told the captain what they learned at the penitentiary. Found out Sherick and Stack had sent preliminary crime reports over. Norm and Charlie were wrapping up their work for the day and had volunteered to stick around in case they needed help.

Everyone wanted to bring in Fletcher.

Sullivan told them they'd be back in about fifteen minutes.

As she was ending her call, Jim was placing one to the precinct's favorite pizza place. He ordered five mega pizzas with various toppings, a large antipasto salad — that he knew only Chelsea would touch — six two-liter bottles of soda, and two dozen cookies. If it wasn't enough food, he'd call back. If it was too much, the uniforms downstairs would no doubt find reasons to walk through the bullpen and help themselves.

She smiled her gratitude as he ended the call. "No Sloppy's, huh?"

"I wasn't really in the mood for burgers."

Chelsea squirmed in her seat to reach for the tiny wallet that fit in her pocket. "Let me pitch in."

"Put that away. My decision, my treat."

"Then I'm paying for lunch tomorrow."

"You bought breakfast. We're even."

"I don't think that's how math works."

"What else is in the file?"

She sighed and leafed through the pages then looked up at Jim. "There are no reports from Hartman in here. But there's one from Bradley."

"Against who?"

"Against Doctor Ellerby."

"What about?"

"Favoritism and special treatment for one of the inmates, specifically Scott Fletcher, possibly putting the prison and the public at risk."

"Why's it in Fletcher's prison file instead of Ellerby's personnel file?"

"Because first Ellerby said Bradley was just trying to get him in trouble because he had filed a report against him the month before."

"Of course. What the fuck's going on over there?"

"But then," Chelsea continued, "he claimed it all started because Fletcher coerced him into giving him drugs."

"What drugs?"

"It doesn't say."

"Coerced him how?"

"It doesn't say."

"And Fletcher was still allowed to be seen in the med bay without guards present?"

"I don't know."

"We really need to talk to Ellerby."

Chapter Six

CHELSEA TOSSED her napkin into the trash then pressed her hand to her belly. She was stuffed. Sloppy's would have been a better choice. She never over-ate there because the food was so bad.

The same couldn't be said for Giannini's. There wasn't a bad item on the menu.

She drained her glass — thank God for carbonation — then looked over her laptop screen at Jim. "I'm looking through Bradley's financials. He strike you as an independently wealthy man?"

"If he came from money, he wouldn't work. And certainly not at the prison. Maybe a fake VP job at Daddy's company. Why?"

"His bank account's fat."

"Going back how far?"

"Not family-money far."

"Devil's advocate. He hit the lottery? Win at the track?"

"Right before Fletcher broke out?"

He sat back in his seat. "Slow down, Sullivan. We need to do this by the book."

She was starting to get indigestion. And it wasn't from the pizza. "Why are you fighting me on this? Connect the dots, Jim. Fletcher clearly bribed him to help him escape."

"I can see where you'd think that. And you're probably right. But an accusation like that, especially against someone in the corrections field, could ruin a career. We have to make sure we're right before we publicly accuse him."

Chelsea took a deep breath. She knew in her gut, sick as it was, that Bradley was dirty. She also knew Jim was right. Because he'd been there before. He'd been on the wrong end of a false accusation that nearly destroyed his career. And his reputation. So of course he'd be careful about doing the same thing to someone else.

Even someone clearly in the wrong.

"We need to find out where that deposit came from. In the meantime, I was doing a little digging on my own."

"On what name?"

"Actually, none of them."

"Then what were you looking into?"

"Other escapees. There's only one in recent history who hasn't been caught."

"What do you consider recent?"

"Eighteen months ago."

"That's pretty recent. Shouldn't we know about this guy?"

"I remember when he escaped. But we all get busy with our own cases. Fresh news stories take over for old ones. I totally forgot about this guy."

"Who was he? I don't remember even seeing the news coverage."

"Shane Warren. He was an armed robber. Held up

more than twenty gas stations and convenience stores in the area. Shot and killed a clerk at one of them."

"How'd he escape?"

"They never did figure it out. But would you like to guess what cellblock he was in?"

"C."

"And the guard on duty that night?"

"Bradley and Hartman."

"Actually, just Bradley. Report says Hartman was on bereavement leave and they couldn't get anyone to fill in."

"So they were short-staffed that night, and Warren took advantage of the situation."

"And the lady wins the prize."

"We need to talk to his family. Maybe they know where he is. If we can find him, he can implicate Bradley. And if we can nail Bradley, we might get him to turn on Fletcher."

"It's a long shot. No one's been able to get the parents to give up their kid in a year and a half."

"I'm sure they're protecting him. But we still have to try."

"Oh, I'm not so sure about that," Jim said. "They're the ones who turned him in to begin with."

She was not expecting that.

"But you're right. We have to try. Let's go."

So, they went.

It got dark early in the evening, and the Warrens lived in the middle of the woods, so there were no street lights to illuminate their way. Even the high beams did little to cut through the gloom of the forest. When a family of deer darted across the road in front of them, Jim slammed on the brakes. They fishtailed on the wet leaves, then almost went over the embankment. He steered into the skid and regained control perilously close to the edge of the road.

Chelsea pressed her hand to her chest. "I hate this time of night."

"Can't blame the deer. It's their home. We're the intruders out here."

"You sound like a woodsman."

He snorted. "You know better than that. But it's true. They were here long before the road was. I'll drive slower."

"As a general rule, you should always drive slower."

"Yeah, that's not going to happen."

The rest of the drive was without incident, and five minutes later, they arrived at the Warren residence. As they approached the door, a dog started barking and floodlights brightened the front of the property.

"You are trespassing on private land," came a voice from a loud speaker. "I have a gun, the dog bites, and the authorities are on speed dial. I suggest you turn around and leave. Now."

"I guess they have one of those video and audio surveillance systems," Chelsea whispered.

"We are the authorities." Jim moved his jacket aside so his shield was visible and he pitched his voice loud so the people inside could hear him. "I have to ask you to restrain your dog and stow your weapon, sir. We'd like to talk to you."

The dog got quiet. The door opened. "Sorry. We have an unlisted number, but people still manage to find our new address. Please, come in. Gun's put away."

Chelsea approached the porch, keeping her eye out for the dog or a gun or any other signs of danger. But she didn't see any. She climbed the two steps then extended her hand. "I'm Detective Sullivan. This is my partner, Detective McPherson. We'd like to talk to you about your son."

He held the door wide and gestured for them to enter.

"We figured it was only a matter of time before someone came by. Have a seat."

The house was small, but it was a lovely open-concept log cabin, with a two-story vaulted ceiling, a charming stone fireplace, and a wall of windows overlooking a spacious patio and the woods beyond.

A woman came in from the kitchen with a tray of refreshments. She set it on the coffee table. "Please. Help yourselves."

Chelsea sat beside Jim on the sofa, but neither of them took anything.

Mrs. Warren sat in an oak rocker.

Mr. Warren chose a recliner that seemed molded to his body. "We don't know where he is. Never did."

"Straight to the point. I like that in a man." Jim nodded. "If you did, you'd tell us, though. Right?"

"You know we would. Did before."

Mrs. Warren rocked a little.

Mr. Warren sighed. "Relax, Mother. They're just doing their jobs." He turned his attention back to Jim. "If you know my son's case, then you know we're the ones who turned him in. That's not an easy thing for a man to do. I wasn't even certain it was him. But when that girl got shot, I couldn't wait for proof anymore. I went to the police with my suspicions and let them do the investigating. Figured if I was right, I'd stop more bloodshed. And if I was wrong, I'd have to beg my son to forgive me and pray he would."

"Why did you suspect him?" Chelsea asked.

"Well, he was guilty. So, obviously, we were right," Mrs. Warren said. "What does it matter?"

"They clearly think it matters, Mother." He shook his head. "I'm sorry. You can't understand how difficult this is for her. Shane was a good boy. He *is* a good boy. But he fell in with the wrong crowd. Started getting in trouble at school. His grades began dropping. Then the drugs. We tried getting him clean. Thought we could help him ourselves, then when that didn't work, we took him to rehab. But that only works if the user wants it to work. And he didn't. His addiction got worse. He had no job, and we wouldn't give him money. But he was still feeding his habit. It only stood to reason he was doing something illegal to get the drugs. Then I found a gun in his room. I heard the description of the armed robber on the news. I didn't want to believe it was him, but our house was right in the center of the places that were hit. It all added up. Before I decided what to do, the clerk was shot. Then I knew I had no choice."

She believed him. If he turned his son in the first time, he'd have turned him in this time. So he really didn't know where he was. "That had to be incredibly difficult. It was very brave of you."

"It was the right thing to do. And we've been paying for it ever since. We had to move. People rioted outside our house. Vandalized it. Set our car on fire. My wife was attacked. Now we live like prisoners in our own home, practically behind bars ourselves."

"Forgive me for asking," Jim said, but why didn't you leave the state and start fresh somewhere else where no one knew you?"

"He's our son, Detective," Mrs. Warren said. "If he needs a place to go, he'll come here."

"But you're in a different house with an unlisted address. He doesn't know where you are."

"He'll know," Mr. Warren said. "This property has been in the family for generations. We used to have a hunting cabin here. Me and the boy came here every deer season for a father-and-son weekend. Mother and her sister would go Christmas shopping, and we'd come here. If he needs us, he'll know where to find us."

"And you'll turn him in?" Jim asked.

"It depends on what kind of help he needs," Mrs. Warren said. "No offense, Detective, but we tried it our way, and it didn't work. We tried it your way, and it didn't work. This far, it seems the only thing that's working is his way. So I'm going to wait and see what my boy needs before I decide what to do."

"Aiding and abetting a fugitive is a crime, ma'am."

"So is abandoning your son when he needs you."

"No, it's not."

"It's a crime against nature."

"Mother." Mr. Warren shook his head.

"Did anything unusual happen at the prison leading up to him breaking out?" Jim asked. "Did he get a new cell-mate? Did he mention getting chummy with any of the guards? Anything different at all?"

"I don't know about his relationships there," Mr. Warren said. "But I think he started using again."

"No, Pup. You can't use drugs in jail."

"What makes you say that, Mr. Warren?" Chelsea asked.

"He asked us to deposit money into his account. Not the nickel and dime stuff he'd been using in the commissary for shampoo and gum and the like. But big amounts. Told me he needed it but couldn't tell me why. Said they listen to the phone calls, which of course I knew, and it was none of their business what he was doing. But he said it was good news and would help him out. Stressed the word 'out.' I didn't think much of it at the time, but in retrospect, I noted it. And of course we gave him the money. His mood was a lot better in those last weeks. That's why I think he was using again."

"You don't know that. It's a prison, Pup. They watch those boys in there. How would he get illegal drugs in a prison? You shouldn't have said that."

"We've taken enough of your time. If you happen to think of anything, please give us a call." Chelsea stood, put her card on the coffee table, then headed toward the door.

On the porch, Mr. Warren closed the door behind them. "You have to understand, this has all been very difficult for my wife. You can't imagine the toll it takes, not knowing where your son is. Hearing the awful things people say about him. Knowing some of it is true, probably most of it is. Then being driven from your home. Attacked. Living essentially in exile."

"I'm sorry, sir. You're right. I can't imagine."

"If I hear anything that might help you find that Fletcher, I'll call you. That's what this is really about, after all. Right?"

Chelsea nodded. "It is. And we'd appreciate that."

"If you find my boy, I ask that you do all you can to bring him in alive. I don't think she could take the stress of losing him on top of everything else."

"You know we can't make any promises, sir," Jim said.

She shot him a look before turning to Mr. Warren. "But preservation of life is always our number one priority. We'll do everything we can."

"I appreciate that. Shane … he just fell in with the wrong crowd. That's all. He's a good boy. Just—" He cleared his throat. "Well, that's all in the past. When we get him back, our lawyer assures us he'll get him in a rehab center. The boy just needs help, is all. We'll get him straightened out. You'll see."

"Thank you, Mr. Warren." Chelsea shook his hand, then headed for the car.

As Jim turned the vehicle around, he shook his head. "You shouldn't have done that."

"Done what?"

"Given him false hope."

"How'd I do that?"

"You left him thinking we're going to find his kid and get him in a rehab facility. Chances are he's in Mexico. Or dead. But if we do find him, he's going back to prison. And since he broke out, he's lost his shot at parole. They're never getting their kid back."

"And you telling him you might have to shoot him was helpful?"

"I was being honest."

"You were being belligerent."

The silence stretched between them for a few miles, the tension as thick as the woods. Chelsea strained to see signs of deer or other creatures about to jump onto the road, but this time, the drive was peril-free.

When they turned onto the highway, some of the stress started to melt away with the gloom of the forest behind her. She sank back into her seat and let out a small sigh.

Jim glanced at her. "I don't know about you, but it kind of sets my teeth on edge when married people call each other 'Mother' and 'Pup' or stuff like that."

"I think it's kind of nice. Reminds me of my grandparents."

"I think that's how serial killers are born."

She sighed. "There's something wrong with you."

"You're not the first person to tell me that. For that matter, it's not the first time you've told me that."

"And yet, you don't change."

"You love me just as I am."

"Yeah."

"Call the prison. See if they can tell us what Warren spent that money on."

"You think anyone's going to talk to us at this hour?"

"It's worth a shot. Maybe we'll get a moron in the commissary or an intern in accounting who doesn't know better."

She dialed the prison but the operator wouldn't transfer her to any department since it was after five. "No luck."

"Well, it was worth a shot. Pick all this up in the morning?"

"Might as well. I'm wiped."

"Davenport has guards at both our places. You just want me to drop you off and pick you up tomorrow?"

"I need to take all that stuff to my dad's."

"Nothing's perishable. Leave it overnight. You have your keys?"

"Yeah."

"I'm dropping you off. No arguments."

It wasn't worth the wasted breath. He wouldn't listen to her and would do what he wanted. She was tired, anyway, and it would save her half an hour.

When Jim let her off in front of her apartment building, they both took note of the unmarked police car on the street.

That gave her little comfort. If they both found it so simple to spot, couldn't Fletcher find it just as easily?

Chelsea hurried up to her apartment. No need to make herself an easy target on the sidewalk.

Chapter Seven

HE TRUDGED toward Dad's shed. Exhausted. Broken. Beaten. Couldn't think of another day in his life that had lasted longer. It was three-quarters over, but it felt like it had lasted about three-quarters of a month. And the next six hours might take six years.

Dad always said when life gives you lemons, make lemonade. But life hadn't given him lemons. It had given him sour grapes. He supposed he could try to make wine, but he'd probably end up with vinegar.

Over the last few days, Dad had been hiding out here more and more. Should have been at the house, but everyone handled pain in his or her own way. So, he'd given Dad space. But now, he was starting to worry. The old man had been out there a long time.

Too long.

Nothing good came from hiding away like that. At some point, a man needed to face his problems.

Dad taught him that, too.

He almost knocked but then thought better of it. Better to ask forgiveness than permission. Another phrase he'd grown up hearing.

Damn, the old man was full of wisdom.

The day heavy on his bones and heavier on his heart, he slid open the door then slipped inside. Stopped dead in his tracks.

"Don't just stand there, boy. In or out. I want the damn door closed."

He shut them inside, then turned to face his father. "Uh … what are you doing, Dad?"

"What am I doing? What does it look like I'm doing? I'm finishing my latest taxidermy project. Gotta say, boy, I think this one is a real showstopper. What do you think, huh?" He spun it around.

Saliva pooled in his mouth. His stomach roiled. He took a deep breath, then swallowed and prayed he didn't spew the few bites of dinner he'd managed to choke down all over his father's so-called masterpiece.

The specimen was posed standing upright, legs were bent as though he was about to break into a run. His arms were outstretched as though he was clutching at something, and his mouth was open wide enough to count every tooth.

Dad looked at his work with reverence. "Don't you think he looks like he's about to chomp down on you? I was going for that wild, savage look."

"I think he looks like he's screaming in terror."

"Well, I suppose that makes sense, as that's how he died. He begged me not to shoot him, but he was trespassing. See? Here's the bullet wound. I did a pretty good job matching the paint color, but if you look closely, you can see it."

"Trespassing?"

"Yep. He was almost at our damn door. Shot him point blank. What's mine is mine, I said. He wouldn't leave. Was babbling about a hunting cabin, but there ain't no hunting cabin 'round here. It was a ruse, and I caught on to his game right away. So, I shot him. But I had things to do and couldn't deal with him then and there. By the time I got back to him, rigor mortis had set in. So, I was stuck with this expression. Damn shame, too. But I don't think you can tell if it's fear or feral. I didn't use a form, you know. That's his actual skeleton. That takes real skill. Not too many people can do that. All them taxidermy animals in the museums? Forms. Not real bones under them'uns." Dad opened a bottle of beer then took a deep pull. "Want one?"

He rubbed his temple. Felt his pulse pounding under his fingertips. "I'm sorry. Are you telling me you killed this man then stuffed him?"

"Did you not hear me? He was on my land."

"Dad, you can't kill people for trespassing!"

His father took another pull of his beer, draining it dry. He threw the empty bottle into a pile of others. A very large pile. "What are you trying to say, boy?"

"Dad, murder's against the law!"

"Ain't murder if it's self-defense. Which this was."

"You weren't defending yourself. Was he armed?"

"Are you daft? Pay attention. I was defending my land." He opened another beer. "He was on my property. I got a right to protect what's mine."

"Even if that's true, and that's a big if, you don't have the right to skin him, remove all his organs, re-stretch his flesh over his skeleton, then stuff him for your amusement."

"It's not just for my amusement. It's practical, too."

"How could that possibly be practical?"

"We ate some of him for dinner. The rest of him's in the freezer."

Now his stomach did revolt. He didn't even have time to run outside, just vomited all over the floor.

Dad grabbed his work of art and stroked its hair. "You almost got your sick all over it. Now, clean up that mess. I need to find a place to display my hard work. I was thinking about the dining room."

"The dining room?" he asked, still bent over.

"You hear me, boy? I said clean up your damn puke."

He righted himself, wiped his mouth with the back of his hand, then grabbed a shovel to scoop up his mess.

His father picked up the taxidermied man. "That's okay," he crooned. "The clumsy fool didn't get any on you. We'll take you in the house and find you some of the boy's clothes." He started for the door.

"Dad, you can't take that into the house. You can't take that out of the shed! We need to destroy it."

Dad put his handiwork down then drew his gun. "Like hell I will. I told you, this is my masterpiece. My *legacy*."

Funny. He thought he'd be his father's legacy.

"The world will remember me by this work."

"Yeah, Dad. That's what I'm afraid of."

"Don't sass me, boy. I've had about enough of your mouth. What have you contributed to this family these last three days? Just moping about, tears rolling down your face like a sissy."

"People cry at funerals, Dad."

"Not men! Not in this family. While you were wetting your hankies, I was putting meat in your belly and culture in our home. Not to mention protecting our land. You're soft. Weak! You should be ashamed."

"Ashamed? Dad, I'm not the one—"

He pulled back the hammer. "Ah, ah, ah. You better think about your next words very carefully."

"You're drunk."

"You're an ingrate. And I've had enough." Dad squeezed the trigger, but the shot went well wide of its mark. The recoil of the gun's discharge knocked him further off balance, and he almost fell.

He couldn't believe his father shot at him. Still, his first reaction was to help steady him. He reached for his dad's elbow.

But Dad shrugged him off. "I don't need you. I don't need anybody." Then he cocked the hammer again. "Fuck you, boy. Get out of my house. Get out of my life!"

This time, he was much closer to his father. And the bullet was much closer to him. So when he reacted, it wasn't to steady his father's balance. It was to lash out in self-defense. He swung the shovel, thinking he'd hit the gun out of his father's hand. Somewhere along the way, his plan changed.

He hit his father in the head.

A second time.

And again. And again. And again.

He did it so many times, he lost count. Did it until his father's face was unrecognizable and his blood pooled at his feet. It ran across the floor then mingled with the vomited remains of the human flesh he'd eaten for dinner.

His breath came in labored huffs. Sweat dripped off his forehead to plop in the puddle of bodily fluids beneath him.

Dad had taught him taxidermy, and he was every bit as good at it as his father. Maybe better. But there was no amount of skill or even magic that could help him preserve his father. His face was damaged beyond repair.

Sour fucking grapes.

At least it was dark out. He had six more hours before this incredibly long day was over. Six hours that were going to feel like six years. And while the sky was still black and he was still hidden from the world, he had to bury what was left of his father.

Chapter Eight

CASES DIDN'T USUALLY GET to Jim, but this one was under his skin. Something about a patrol car outside his apartment kept him on edge.

Or maybe it was the fact that a serial killer was on the loose. Again. One that he and his partner had already put away once.

One who'd abducted Sullivan the first time and planned on making her his final masterpiece.

The thought had made his skin crawl and had kept him up all night.

Somehow, 5:00 a.m. finally came. He punished himself with an hour on the home gym followed by a cold shower then a hot K-Cup, but it all did little to make him less tired. Or less grouchy. When he picked up Sullivan at 7:00, he was ready to sleep at the wheel.

She yawned as she slipped into the passenger's seat.

"What's the matter?" he growled at her. "Didn't you sleep?"

"I slept fine. What's it to you? It was just a yawn. People yawn in the morning."

"Yawns are contagious." His eyes watered as he failed to stifle one. "Now you have me yawning. We're supposed to be alert. Focused. We have a lot to do today."

"You get up on the wrong side of the bed this morning? Or is the problem that you were alone in bed?"

"I thought you were done criticizing my love life."

She shrugged.

"And all this time, I thought you had the moral high-ground, Miss Back-Scratcher."

"Oh, would you just let it go, already? I'm allowed to have a history, too. Just because my little black book is smaller than yours doesn't mean my pages are bare."

"No one has a little black book anymore, Sullivan."

"You know what I mean."

"Oh, my God! Why do you even care about Danny?"

"Why do you care who I date at all?"

"I don't."

"Then why'd you bring it up?"

"Because you're being such a jerk this morning, and I knew it would make you mad."

"I'm in a bad mood, so you wanted to make it worse?"

"I'm not in a great mood, either, you know. I lashed out, okay?" She took a deep breath then exhaled slowly. "I didn't sleep."

"Yeah. I guess you noticed I didn't, either."

"Maybe it wasn't a good idea for us to force our way onto this case."

"Would you have slept well if you weren't looking for Fletcher?"

"No." She shook her head. "It would drive me nuts not knowing what's going on and what's being done and where the heck he might be."

He nodded. "Me, too."

"But it's driving us nuts, anyway."

"Perks of the job."

"Wonderful."

He turned into the Hill of Beans drive-thru, then ordered them both large coffees with two shots of espresso, hers with a splash of cream. "Now we're ready to start the day."

"Or will be soon." She sipped hers as he made the short drive to the station. "So, we start by tracking the money in Shane Warren's prison account?"

"Yeah. Then I'd like to follow up with some of the other names the warden gave us."

"The girlfriends and the fans."

"Especially the girlfriends."

"Why them first?"

"I don't know. Just a hunch. But we'll run them all down." He pulled into the lot and parked beside her car.

She peeked through her window to make sure all her purchases for her dad were still in there — which they were. It was unlikely anyone would mess with a car in a secure police lot. Then they went upstairs and got to work.

While Jim was tracking down addresses for all the girl-friends, Chelsea called the prison for information about Shane Warren's account. He was just getting the third address when she hung up the phone.

"You're not going to believe this."

"What?"

"He has no money in his account."

"So, what did he spend it on?"

"The accountant said the Warrens never wired any in."

"He's claiming they lied? Why would they lie? It's easy enough for us to verify."

"I know, right? Someone's cooking the books over there."

"Call the Warrens and ask them to send us records of

their deposits. I think we need to get a forensic accountant involved in this."

She shook her head. "We can, but it's not going to help. If the money isn't showing as deposited to begin with, but the bank wired it in, that to me says hacker. I don't think we need an accountant. I think we need—"

"A white-hat," he finished for her.

Chelsea nodded. "Yeah. We need someone who can trace where the money went. Either the accountant at the prison has no idea someone stole the money, or he stole it. But he's a roadblock regardless."

Jim stood and grabbed his jacket. "Call Devani in the crime lab. Tell her what we need. If she can't do it, she might know who can."

"Where are we going?" She put on her own coat then grabbed her phone.

"The first girlfriend on the list."

"I can't believe he has three girlfriends. I spend most weekends home alone."

He held the door for her. "I'm choosing not to bring up a certain State Police investigator."

"Good."

"I could bring up Kingston Kane."

Chelsea scowled as she passed him and started dialing.

He smirked.

On the way down the stairs, she told Devani what they needed. By the time they were on the road, the conversation was over. "She said she'd check it out and see what she could do. If it was beyond her scope, she'd talk to Davenport about who to pass it along to. So, who are we talking to first?"

"Ainsley Edwards."

"What do we know about her?"

"Other than she's got a thing for a serial killer? Nothing."

"Great."

"Driver's license says she's twenty-five."

"You're super helpful today."

"I aim to please."

A short while later, they pulled up to a tiny cape cod in the middle of a block of nearly identical row houses. The only thing distinguishing this one from the others on the street was the color of the siding and trim. The rest of the homes had chosen neutral colors of siding — white, ivory, beige, or gray — and dark though traditional trim colors of charcoal, brown, navy, or black. The Edwards house, however, had lavender siding with fuchsia trim and cornflower blue shingles and shutters.

"I didn't know you could get a roof in that color," Chelsea said.

"I didn't know anyone would want to." He shook his head. "Come on."

No fewer than thirty jack-o'-lanterns decorated the small porch, each smile more disturbingly happy than the last. Jim couldn't imagine any parent letting a child trick-or-treat at this house. As they got closer to the porch, he noticed little lawn ornaments in the shape of woodland creatures nestled into the landscaping, all facing the home. A chill skittered up his back.

Chelsea rang the doorbell.

A woman answered the door in a blue pinafore dress over a white blouse with puffy sleeves. Her long blonde hair was tied with matching ribbons into two low ponytails, the ends of which hung in soft curls. She carried a teddy bear in the crook of her arm. The wide smile on her face faded when she saw them. "Oh. Hello. May I help you?"

"Were you expecting someone else?" Jim asked.

"As a matter of fact, yes."

"Might we ask who?" Chelsea said.

"No." Her brow furrowed. "Who are you and what do you want?"

"Detectives McPherson and Sullivan." Jim flashed his badge. "Could we come in?"

She bit her lip for a second, then opened the door wide and gestured for them to enter.

Inside, he glanced at Chelsea. Her face had paled. They'd gone to Fletcher's apartment after he'd been arrested, so they knew what his style was and what he owned. They also knew his furniture had been sold at auction after his incarceration.

And now they knew who bought it.

He cleared his throat. "Why are you dressed like Alice in Wonderland?"

She huffed and flicked one of her ponytails. "I'm not Alice. I'm Goldilocks."

"Why Goldilocks?"

"You know. Because she wants everything to be 'just right' for her Prince Charming."

Chelsea gave a sad chuckle. "Hate to tell you, Miss Edwards, but you're mixing stories. There's no Prince Charming in 'Goldilocks and the Three Bears.' Furthermore, in most versions of the story, Goldilocks doesn't get away. Best case scenario, she's never heard from again. Worst case, the bears eat her."

"No." But her voice began to falter. "Fairy tales have happily ever afters."

"Not the originals."

Ainsley turned toward the kitchen. The teddy bear hung at her side for a few seconds, then it fell from her fingers and landed silently on the floor.

"You mind if we look around, Miss Edwards?" Jim asked.

"Whatever." She waved them on as she mumbled to herself.

Chelsea looked at him, eyes wide, as they walked down the hallway toward where the bedrooms and bathroom should be.

Once they were out of Ainsley's line of sight, Jim spun his finger beside his head.

She slapped his hand down and whispered, "That's not nice."

"I'm not wrong."

"There's no such thing as crazy." She stepped into one of the bedrooms, shook her head, then reached into her pocket for a pair of gloves. "There is, however, such a thing as an unhealthy obsession."

Jim followed her gaze. A giant map was tacked to the wall with a route traced from the prison to the middle of nowhere.

Ainsley appeared at the door. "I want you to leave. Now!"

"Sorry, miss," Jim said. "You invited us in and gave us permission to look around."

"Well, I take it back."

"That's not the way it works."

"Get out! Get out now!"

Chelsea took a picture of the map.

Ainsley lunged for her.

Jim caught her around the waist.

She started punching and kicking and thrashing. Spunky little thing got a few shots in before he had her wrangled. His shin would definitely have a bruise, and he might even end up with a shiner. "Sullivan? You mind cuffing her while I have her arms pinned?"

"I figured her for a fighter when I saw all the jack-o'-lanterns." She slapped the restraints on her wrists.

"I called it when I saw the purple siding."

"It's lavender."

"Don't start, Sullivan."

"The color's actually iced lilac," Ainsley said.

"I hate days like this." Chelsea bagged the map.

"Let's go." Jim started walking her to the car. "You have the right to remain silent."

"Good, because I'm not telling you anything."

"And yet you're talking right now."

"Jim …"

He finished Mirandizing her before they got to the SUV. After she was in the back seat, he held out his hand. "Let me see that map."

Chelsea took it back out of the bag then passed it over.

"It's in the middle of nowhere."

"I know."

"There's not even a road going past it."

"I know."

He pulled up a map on his phone so he could zoom in on the coordinates. "There's really nothing there."

She sighed.

Then he hit the satellite imaging option. "Son of a bitch."

Ainsley started kicking the back of the passenger seat, shaking the whole vehicle.

"Hey!" He knocked on the window.

She kept kicking.

"She's not going to stop."

"I'm going to have to detail the whole car."

"That's why you should drive a department vehicle. Or call a uniform to transport suspects."

"Get her out of there." He called for a patrol unit as well as crime scene investigators while Chelsea hauled her out of the backseat. "You better not have scratched the leather."

She spat at him.

"Nice."

"What did you see on the satellite?" Chelsea asked.

"There's an abandoned barn at the end of the route."

"She helped Fletcher plan his escape, and that's where he's hiding."

"That's my guess."

Sirens sounded in the distance.

Jim looked at the damage she did inside — probably nothing permanent — then smiled at her. "Looks like your ride's almost here, Alice."

She howled and lunged at him, but Chelsea held her tight. After they passed her off to the uniforms, she took out her phone.

"Who you calling?"

"Sherick."

"Why?"

"To tell him about the barn."

"What if he beats us there?"

"What if he does?"

"Don't you want to be there when Fletcher goes down again?"

"Jim, at this point, every second counts. He could be leaving as we speak or could already have moved on. We shouldn't have waited to call Danny, but I was afraid if I let go of Edwards she'd physically assault you, and that was more paperwork than I cared to deal with. And asking you to call would have led to having this argument with you in front of her, which would undoubtedly have led to an IA nightmare. So, I'm calling him now. I don't care if we get there first or if he does or if by some miracle the Australian Coast Guard shows up and beats us both. The important thing is to find Fletcher and stop him."

Then she made the call.

Chapter Nine

CHELSEA SENSED Jim's caffeine was wearing off. Or he didn't like that she'd called Danny.

Or both.

In either case, calling him 'testy' was an understatement. So she kept her comments to a minimum.

His mood improved slightly when they got to the barn and found they were the first responders. She briefly considered saying they should wait for backup, but she had just given him a speech about not wanting Fletcher to have a chance to get away. Suggesting they wait now would go over about as well as a gambling ban in Vegas.

They approached the barn with caution. Chelsea scanned the ground for signs of recent activity. The tall grass was trampled, but there was no muddy path to find a clear footprint. Best she could tell, someone had been there recently. But it could just as easily have been an animal as a person.

Or a killer.

She didn't notice a surveillance system, but that didn't mean there wasn't a hidden camera or two announcing their presence. And while it wasn't Fletcher's MO, she couldn't help worrying about boobytraps. Fear of *going* to prison was one thing. Fear of *returning* was another. That changed things. Upped the stakes. She and Jim knew Fletcher better than anyone else, but they knew the *old* Grimm Reaper. Prison changed people. Who he was now was really anyone's guess.

But she saw no trip wires. No signs of turned earth that would indicate pressure plates.

The barn really did look abandoned.

The windows were too high to peer in, so they had to enter blind. Her gun felt heavy in her sweat-slicked hand. Her pulse pounded, her roaring blood too loud in her ears.

Jim grabbed the handle of the door and met her gaze. His lips formed words, but she couldn't hear them. She wasn't sure if he was just mouthing them or if she couldn't make them out over the cacophony in her head.

He flung open the door, then they rushed inside. Cobwebs clouded most of the corners. A few rays of sunlight cut at a sharp angle through one of the windows, catching the dust motes they kicked up as they stormed through. The space was wide open, with only a few stalls to the side and a loft above.

A chill skittered up her spine. Anyone in the loft had the high ground. They were in a kill box.

"Cover me," Jim said.

She planted her feet and kept a laser focus on the loft. Didn't see so much as a flicker of movement up there. Her shoulders started to ache, but she didn't relax for a second.

He quickly checked the stalls before climbing the ladder. "Clear."

Chelsea holstered her weapon, shook out her arms.

"We need to check that first stall," Jim said.

"Why? What's in it?" She was really thinking *who* but couldn't bring herself to say the word.

"Come here." He led her over to the pen in the corner. It looked like a child's clubhouse. Though this barn had clearly not been used in a long time, several bales of fresh hay had been spread, and more had been stacked in the corner to make a seating area. On top of all of it, someone had spread blankets to cushion the prickle of the straw. A few folded blankets were also left for warmth, as well as a couple of pillows.

Chelsea took several pictures of the scene, then she pulled on a pair of gloves before stepping into the stall. It was disturbing on so many levels, thinking she was standing in what was essentially Fletcher's bedroom. The last time she was in a room where he slept—

Nope. Not taking that trip down memory lane.

She picked up one of the pillows. An envelope fell to the floor. "Hey. Jim. Check this out."

He looked over her shoulder as she pulled out the card along with a shower of glitter. The cover showed a unicorn dancing over a rainbow in a field of wildflowers with the word "congratulations" in gold block letters.

"Was this for a child?" Jim asked.

"Or made by one?"

"Let's see. Open it." He nudged her.

Chelsea unfolded the card.

I'M SO *happy for you! Congratulations on your freedom! I can't wait until we're together, and by the time you read this, we will be! Love you bunches and bunches! xoxoxo ~Your Gwenivere*

"I THINK I got a cavity reading that," she said.

"I've known a lot of clingy women in my time, but this is a whole new level. I'm telling you, there's something wrong with the women who fall for serial killers. First Edwards thought she was Goldilocks. Now she thinks she's King Arthur's wife?"

"Did you see the spelling? It's wrong."

"Huh?"

"Her name should be G-U-I-N-E-V-E-R-E. Not G-W-E-N."

"So, she made a mistake."

"I think it's a play on words. Isn't one of the girlfriends named Gwen?"

"Yeah." He took out his phone to look at the list of names. "Gwendolyn Cole. We're supposed to see her next."

"I bet she left this card. It's probably a private joke between them."

"But Guinevere, however you spell it, isn't one of Grimm's fairy tales."

"You're splitting hairs, Jim. Besides, she was a princess."

"You think they were working together."

Chelsea shrugged. "It's possible. Actually, it's kind of genius. If Fletcher gave everyone just one piece of the puzzle to do, they all had plausible deniability about the whole plan."

"But it would also be harder to pull off. If even one person dropped the ball, the whole thing would fall apart."

"I don't think that matters. Whether one person has five parts or five people have one part each, there are still five parts that have to be done, right? Either a ball is dropped or it isn't."

"But the coordination would be more difficult."

"You said yourself, these people are acolytes. Devotees. They're committed. They aren't going to let him down."

"I hate this shit." He ran his hand through his hair and stormed out of the stall. "It's bad enough when we have to catch a run of the mill murderer or a spree killer. But serial killers and their followers are a special kind of twisted."

"We'll catch him, Jim." But Fletcher wasn't there. This is where the map said he'd be, but he wasn't. Furthermore, there was no sign he'd been there at all. So, not only did they not have him, they had precious few leads. And fewer by the minute. She was starting to wonder if they would catch him.

"We need to get this card to the lab." He took a bag from his pocket.

She shook her head. "This isn't really our crime scene. We need to leave it for Danny and his partner. They should be here soon."

"Shit," Jim said. "They should have been here already."

"You don't know where they were coming from. Or what they were doing."

"This should have been a priority."

"Maybe they're coordinating a response."

"Which is a waste of resources. No one's here."

"They didn't know that."

"They knew time was of the essence."

"If Scott was here, it was the right move."

"Back to Scott now? First name basis with him? Don't get emotionally invested, Chels."

She flinched.

Jim sighed. "Just leave the card and send him a text. We actually have leads to run down."

"If we don't keep Danny in the loop, he'll shut us out."

"We *are* keeping him in the loop."

Chelsea put down the envelope and began a text to Danny. Just before she hit send, Jim called out. She joined him in the next stall.

He'd found a bunch of MREs and water in two military-grade knapsacks.

"Kind of puts my big box store provisions to shame, huh?"

"You can ask Thompson all about it when we get back to the station. I took pictures. Now let's get out of here."

She added the knapsacks to the text to Danny, sent it, then followed Jim to the car. He hadn't even started the engine when her phone was ringing.

"Don't answer that." Jim turned the key.

"It's Danny."

"I know."

"He's going to know I'm available. I just texted him."

"Had you sent him straight to voicemail, he'd have thought you'd turned off your phone." Jim pulled onto the road — in the opposite direction of how they'd come.

"Well, it's too late for that." Chelsea glanced behind them. She could just make out clouds of dust and flashing lights. The calvary was almost at the barn. "I have to answer it now."

"You let it ring too long. He already knows you don't want to talk."

She turned to face forward again. "But I can still grab it."

"He'll know you were stalling, though."

"Stalling isn't as bad as—now it's too late."

Jim shrugged.

"You did that on purpose."

"I told you to send it to voicemail."

"I didn't want to send it to voicemail."

"Well, you obviously didn't want to talk to him, either, or you would have answered it no matter what I said."

"You're infuriating."

"We need to split up."

"What?" She wheeled toward him.

"I don't mean our partnership. I mean in this investigation. Your boy Danny is probably going to shut us out now that you're dodging his calls."

"I'm not—"

"We've got Edwards on ice at the station and evidence that Cole was involved in preparing a place for Fletcher to stay. And there's still the third girlfriend to talk to. That's a lot of ground to cover in a short while. We don't have the manpower as it is, especially if we stay together. How about I drop you at the station to talk to Edwards while I go and check out Cole?"

"I'm fine with talking to Edwards on my own. Do you think you should talk to Cole by yourself?"

"I can take a uniform with me."

"Take Giadone. Rafferty tells me she's showing real promise. And you should have a woman with you if you need to take her into custody, anyway."

"She the new cadet?"

"She's not a cadet anymore. She graduated in May. And she's only a year younger than I am."

"Why'd she start so late?"

"How is that relevant?"

"It's not. Just curious."

"You have a problem with her?"

"Nope. If you say she's good, I trust you."

"I say she's nice. Neil says she's good."

"Works for me. Send her out. If she isn't in there, send out anybody. We're on the clock."

"Even Thompson?"

"God, no."

She laughed. "I'll call ahead and see if Sophia's available." Chelsea dialed the station and talked to Davenport. After filling him in, she made arrangements to have Giadone ride along with Jim to see Gwen Cole while she talked to Ainsley Edwards.

After a quick run through a drive-thru, Jim dropped her off at the precinct. Chelsea was heading toward the interrogation room when Thompson barreled around the corner and plowed into her. If she didn't smack into the wall, she would have toppled to the floor. As it was, she banged her funny bone and saw stars. While she rubbed her elbow, she looked up at him. "Where in the world are you running to?"

"I … family emergency."

"Sorry. Is everything all right?"

He shrugged.

"You know, if you need time off, Davenport will—"

"It's fine."

"Okay." She glanced at her elbow. His brusque demeanor reminded her of their argument about her purchases at the big box store, and that reminded her of him bragging about his knowledge of MREs. "Hey, Oliver. You said you know a lot about freeze-dried food and the survivalist lifestyle. Do you think I could pick your brain later? If you're not taking any time off, that is?"

"For your dad?"

"About a case, actually."

"Come find me." He ran around her then down the stairs.

"He is so weird." She started again toward the interrogation room then stopped mid-stride, turned around, and headed for Davenport's office.

"Come in."

Chelsea closed the door behind her. "Captain, I have a favor to ask, and I'm not trying to cause problems. In fact, I hope I'm wrong. But there's something I need to check, and I can't do it because I don't have clearance, and if I could do it without involving you, I would, because it's not fair to make you think of one of your subordinates a certain way if there's no reason to, and to make you think *I* think—"

"Holy shit, Sullivan. You're giving me a headache. I won't think less of you or anyone else if you're trying to solve a problem. What do you need?"

"Access to a personnel file."

"Whose? And why?"

"Officer Oliver Thompson."

He scowled. "Again, why?"

"It might be related to a case."

"What case?"

"Fletcher."

"Fuck."

His fingers clacked on his keyboard. She started to round his desk, but he waved her off. "No. You don't need to see his file. Tell me what you're looking for, and I'll tell you if it's there."

"Any family members by the name of Nell, Nellie. Any variation of the name."

"Mom and sister, both named Eleanor. Mom's deceased. Why?"

She dropped into the seat across from him, rested her elbows on her knees, and held her head in her hands. "I'm afraid he's helping his sister."

"That's usually a good thing when family helps each other."

Chelsea looked up at him. "Not when your sister is dating a serial killer."

Chapter Ten

Jim glanced at Giadone. "You ever accompany a detective on an interrogation before?"

"No, sir."

"I appreciate the respect, Giadone, but we're not in front of a camera or the brass. McPherson or Jim is fine. Detective if it makes you twitchy."

"Okay."

He'd just become her father-in-law, forever relegated to namelessness. She'd only speak to him if he made eye contact first.

"This visit is simple enough. I'll do the talking. You're here because it's a good idea to have a woman on hand for female interrogations in case we need to make an arrest."

"Sad times we live in, huh?"

"You got that right."

"What's this one's story?"

"Sorry?"

"Rumor is she has something to do with the Grimm Reaper. She really his girlfriend?"

"One of them, yeah."

Giadone shook her head. "One of them? My brother's a nice guy. Smart. Good looking. Gainfully employed. But he's still single. It's breaking my mother's heart. And he hears about it every Sunday at the family dinner. Meanwhile, this yutz is in prison for killing women all over the city, yet he manages to have multiple girlfriends. It makes no sense."

"Your mom sounds like my mom."

"Yeah?"

"Yeah. I try to avoid family functions because I don't want the guilt trip."

"Italians specialize in guilt trips. My brother calls me every Sunday evening to tell me how brutal the meal was."

"Wait, you don't go?"

"God, no. Then she'd be all over me because I don't have a boyfriend. I tell them I have to work."

"But you don't?"

Giadone shook her head.

Jim laughed, and she joined him. He was still chuckling when his phone rang. It was Chelsea. She couldn't have been talking to Edwards for more than five minutes, so she must have something important. That sobered him right up. "Hey, Sullivan. What's going on?"

"Where are you?"

"I'm actually just pulling up to Gwendolyn Cole's place. Did Edwards give you something useful?"

"I haven't even talked to her yet."

"Then why are you calling?"

"Because something happened."

His blood ran cold. "What?"

"I'll connect the dots for you later. The important thing is, we have a mole. Or we might have a mole."

"You might want to connect a few dots."

"Girlfriend number three."

"Yeah. Nell Thompson. What about her?"

"It just hit me. So I had Davenport check the personnel files. Her real name is Eleanor Thompson, but Nell is a nickname. She's—"

"Oliver Thompson's sister. Shit. Why didn't I think of it?"

"Thompson's a common name."

"Still, it's our job to make these connections."

"And we did," she said.

"*You* did."

"It doesn't matter who did. What matters is we figured it out."

"Does Thompson know you suspect him?"

"I don't know. He got all squirrelly and ran away. I went straight to Davenport's office."

"We're definitely on borrowed time. He could be on to us. Might be warning his sister now."

"If he is helping Fletcher," Giadone said, "he could be helping him this very second."

"Damn it." Jim pounded the steering wheel.

"Oh. Hi, Sophia."

"Hey, Chels."

"Jim, I should call Danny."

"Why are you always trying to call him? Has he called us once?"

"Yes. And you wouldn't let me answer the call."

"He was calling to yell at you. That's different. Other than sending over the preliminary report, he hasn't given us anything. We've done more legwork than they have. And Fletcher was our collar, not his."

"This case isn't personal, Jim."

"Like hell, it's not! He almost killed you."

"That's why I don't care who puts him away. Just as long as someone does."

"And that's why it should be us. Poetic justice."

"Any justice works for me."

He sighed. "Check the duty logs. See how often Thompson gets the prison transport assignment."

The sound of clacking keys came through the car speakers.

"We're all assigned the transport in rotation," Giadone said.

"Yeah," Chelsea's voice came through the speakers. "But Thompson has switched with a lot of you. It looks like he makes that run three times more than anyone else."

Jim scowled. "Then he probably knows the doctor and the guards—"

"And the warden," she interrupted.

"Maybe even the prisoners," he said. "Possibly one in particular. One he already knew who used to be our ME."

"Wait a minute," Giadone said. "I know you guys have a lot of years and experience on me, but I think you're making a huge leap. Just because a guy takes a bunch of extra shifts at work doesn't mean he's up to no good. He might just be looking to make some extra money. And even if he did intend to help the Grimm Reaper, do you have any idea how many stars would have to align for a prisoner transporter to not only meet an inmate in the maximum-security wing but get to help him plan his breakout? I mean, it's not like they send gen pop out as a welcoming committee when the newbies show up."

"You might have a point," Chelsea said.

"Can you at least look up who drove Fletcher to Black Meadow?" Jim asked.

"Let me see if I can access those logs. They might be archived." More clacking came through the speakers, followed by a soft gasp. "Thompson did."

"That's one hell of a coincidence," Jim said.

"It doesn't mean anything," Giadone said.

"She's right. We need tangible proof, not circumstantial evidence."

"Criminals have been convicted on less."

"So have innocent people."

He scowled at his car mate.

"I'm going to talk to Edwards," Sullivan said. "You go interview Cole. We'll reconvene when we're done and figure out what to do about both Thompsons." She ended the call before he could argue.

Giadone scratched her nose to hide a smile. It didn't work.

"I was ready to hang up, anyway."

"I know."

"Let's go."

But either Gwendolyn Cole wasn't home or she didn't answer the door. As long as they'd sat in front of her house, he'd given her plenty of time to hide or sneak out. They tried to look through windows, but all the blinds were drawn. And they checked the back yard, but the fence was locked.

"Back to the precinct?" Giadone said.

"How do you feel about cruising past Nell Thompson's place?"

"Chelsea will kill you."

"I didn't say we were going in. I just want to get the lay of the land."

"And if you tip your hand?"

"How? We won't even slow down. Sullivan's going to be tied up for a while. If we go back now, I could join her in interrogation and you'll be back on patrol. Or I could keep you with me a few minutes longer. Which sounds better?"

"That's not fair."

"So you want to go back?"

"Of course not."

"Then, let's go."

"I don't think it's a good idea."

"Good thing you're not driving." Jim folded himself into the driver's seat. Even at that angle, he could see her roll her eyes. He grinned at her and gunned the engine when she climbed into the passenger's side. "Buckle up."

She strapped in.

"Mind if I put on music?"

"No."

"Have a preference?"

"What are my choices?"

He opened his music app then handed her his phone. "Pick a playlist."

"You've got an eclectic mix."

"My moods change."

"What are you in the mood for now?"

"Nothing slow."

"You have Shakira on here."

"Her hips don't lie."

"That was at least ten years ago."

"Probably more. But are you saying her hips are dishonest now?"

She laughed and put on J.Lo. "I'm surprised you have a Latina playlist."

"You'll really be surprised when I tell you why."

"Why?"

"For my mom."

"Really?"

"She's part Peruvian and totally in touch with that side of her heritage. When she visits, that's what I play."

"And you hate it."

"I used to. It's grown on me, actually."

"You have a favorite? Don't say Bad Bunny."

"That's blasphemy. You won't find that shit on my phone."

"Just checking to see if you really liked the music or simply downloaded what was trending."

"I asked Mom what she liked, listened to it, then downloaded what I could tolerate until I developed a taste for it. If I had to pick a favorite now, I guess I'd probably go with Luis Fonzi."

"You do listen to this stuff."

"I'm like Shakira's hips. I don't lie."

Giadone groaned again.

"Look up Nell Thompson on LiveLyfe. See if you can find anything on her."

"There are three."

"Cross reference with Oliver. When you find the profile that lists him as her brother, you found the right one."

She was quiet for a few seconds. "I got her. Very few friends on there. She doesn't use it as a personal profile. It's more like a business page. She's an artist."

"Yeah? What kind? Paint? Sculpture? Jewelry?"

"Lots of different media, actually. She's really into digital. Looks like she does a lot of stuff for graphic novels. But some commercial art. A few paintings that are pretty cool. And apparently some sculpture, too, but she seems to just do that for fun, not her career."

He slowed down as he turned onto Nell Thompson's street.

Giadone looked up as they rounded the bend. "Two more blocks, up on the left. Two-one-seven. Should be almost at the end.

Jim went a little faster until he reached the correct block. Then he coasted.

When they approached the house, she said, "Speed up."

"Fuck." He gently hit the gas, but he already knew they were screwed. His engine was loud even when the motor was idling, and his vehicle stood out in a crowd.

Oliver Thompson was on his sister's porch, and he turned to see who was driving down the street. When he saw Jim, he burst into his sister's house then slammed the door closed.

Chapter Eleven

When Chelsea entered the interrogation room, Ainsley Edwards flipped her off. Talk about starting off on a high note. She bit back a sigh, took a seat across from her, opened the case file, then began looking through it. They didn't have much on her — that was the point of the questioning — nothing more than her name, address, and the map, really. But Chelsea suspected not many flowers managed to bloom in Ainsley's brain, so she decided to let the woman stew and hang herself. She nodded here, shook her head there, and gave the occasional non-committal grunt.

Ainsley stared at her intently. The first time Chelsea made a noise, the girl said, "What?"

But Chelsea just kept studying the file.

And Ainsley kept studying her.

By the time she'd read her address for the fifth time, Ainsley was visibly vibrating.

On her sixth pass, the girl cracked. "What're you reading about me?"

She closed the folder. "This is your file."

"I figured that. What's in it?"

"All the information we have on you."

"I figured that, too, genius."

Chelsea smiled and clasped her hands over the manila packet, a subtle hint that Ainsley wasn't going to get access to it.

"I mean, what details are in there?"

"You know what you did. You know what's in here."

Ainsley opened her mouth, then she closed it. She sprawled in the chair and grinned. "You ain't got nothin'. You're fishin'."

"Fishing?"

"Alls you got is a map, which don't mean shit. And you know it."

"What's the map for, Ainsley?"

"Why, I believe it's a map of Western PA, Detective. You're the one who took it off my wall. You should know."

"But you mapped out a route. Why?"

She crossed one leg over the other and started bouncing it. But she didn't say a word.

"Why were you interested in Scott Fletcher?"

"Are you kidding me? That's like asking why someone's interested in Jack the Ripper or the Zodiac Killer."

"Those men are curiosities because they haven't yet been identified."

"What about Charles Manson? Son of Sam? Ted Bundy? Richard Ramirez? Jeffrey Dahmer? People are interested in them, and we know who they are. People are interested because they're compelling figures. Everyone's interested in them. Just like everyone's interested in the Grimm Reaper."

"I don't think that's true. And of the people who are interested in serial killers, particularly in Scott Fletcher, most aren't as interested as you are."

"What can I say? When I find something that strikes my fancy, I go all in."

"Are you all in, Miss Edwards?"

"What do you mean?"

"We know you corresponded with Fletcher. We know you were granted visitation rights. We found the map on your wall plotting the route the EMTs would take from the prison, and it continued to an abandoned barn that was stocked with provisions for a fugitive."

"How do you know it wasn't stocked with provisions for some high school kid to have a picnic with his girl and maybe get lucky on a blanket in a horse stall?"

"How do you know there was a makeshift bed in a horse stall?"

"I'm just throwing out a 'what-if' scenario. My first time wasn't in a car. Neither of us had our licenses yet. It was on a ratty old quilt in the woods with my junior high school boyfriend."

"Charming."

"Point is, kids get busy in all kinds of places."

"Places the deranged fans of serial killers map out that happen to coincide with their successful escape attempt?"

"I take exception to that."

Chelsea started to choke out an apology for calling her deranged.

But Ainsley didn't give her a chance. "I'm more than Scott's fan. We're gonna be married."

Her eyebrows arched. "Excuse me?"

"We're engaged. I guess that's not in your precious file."

"No." She closed her eyes and squeezed the bridge of her nose. "No, it's not."

"Cram that up your … pipe and smoke it."

"Ainsley," Chelsea lowered her hand and met the girl's gaze, "does the warden know about your plans?"

She shrugged. "I dunno. What does it matter?"

"Where do you plan on having these nuptials?"

"I thought we could do it at Disney World, at the castle. A real fairy tale ceremony, you know?"

"You think the warden would give Fletcher a pass for that? And even if he did, you think the park would want a serial killer on their grounds?"

She opened her mouth, closed it again, then scowled. "You asked where I wanted my wedding. It's my dream. Obviously, we're going to have it at the prison. As soon as you incompetents find my man. Unless he's granted parole, of course."

"He's not eligible for parole. Especially not now that he's escaped. Even if he was, no board in their right minds would grant it. But Ainsley, I didn't ask where you wanted your dream wedding. I asked where you planned on having your actual wedding. So, you clearly expected Fletcher to be free from prison and living under an assumed identity. A public, Disney World ceremony is pretty bold, even for him. But honestly, I'd be surprised if he planned on going through with it. I think he was just using you to get free. I think that's why he never went to the barn."

"Scott wouldn't use me."

"Don't kid yourself. Scott would absolutely use you and anyone else if it got him what he wanted."

"You're just jealous because he didn't want you."

"Oh, he wanted me, all right. Consider yourself lucky he didn't want you as much." Chelsea stood and left the room to Ainsley screaming insults after her.

In the hall, she bumped into Oliver Thompson's perpetual sidekicks, Ethan Miller and Jeremy Berger. They'd been watching through the observation window, and she'd stormed out so abruptly, they hadn't had time to retreat without her noticing. "What are you two doing here?"

They exchanged guilty glances. Miller cleared his throat. "We were on break."

"Yeah. And?"

Berger shrugged. "We often spend our breaks watching interrogations. No better way to learn what detectives do than to watch them, you know? Besides, you guys have better coffee."

"I know that's a lie."

"Well, it's not worse than ours," Miller said. "And you sometimes have donuts. We come up here, grab whatever's left after you guys have picked through the good stuff, then watch you work over whatever poor schlub was caught doing something stupid."

"We don't 'work over' our suspects, Miller."

"You know what I mean."

"Didn't you ever spend time at the window watching the guys question someone?"

Chelsea had never spent her breaks at the window. She'd worked through every one of them. But she had to admit, she'd spent many off-hours watching Charlie and Norm interrogating suspects, learning when to lean on them and when to be friendly, when to let them stew and when to make them sweat. It was through the guys and not books or instructors that she learned what to say and what not to say as well as when and how.

Still, she'd never seen any of the three stooges at the window before today and suspected this was not the inno-cent lesson they professed it was.

"Yeah, I've done my time at the window. What did you guys take from this session?"

Another guilty exchange of looks.

Miller shook his head. "Sorry. By the time we got our coffee and donuts, you were walking out the door."

She tipped her head toward their hands. "You don't have mugs or napkins or anything."

"We ate at the table," Scott said.

"And drained scalding cups of joe?"

"Probably should have brought it with us. Burned my damn tongue."

Miller nodded, then he glanced at his watch. "We need to get back. Detective."

"Detective." Berger doffed an imaginary cap then followed his buddy toward the stairs. He reached in his pocket, removed his phone, then started texting.

Chelsea was pretty sure she knew who he was texting, and she was pretty sure she knew what he was texting about. The coffee-and-donut story was quite possibly the weakest lie she'd heard since … well, since Ainsley had tried to act like she wasn't part of Fletcher's escape plan. There had been no donuts at the break table before she'd gone into the interrogation room, so the boys hadn't eaten anything. As for piping hot coffee? Another lie. She'd poured herself a cup before going in and it had been hours old and room temperature. Unless the caffeine fairy had paid the station a visit, no one had made a fresh pot.

Berger and Miller were either keeping tabs on Ainsley on their own or Thompson had told them to. In any case, she'd bet good money Berger was texting his buddy right now everything he'd learned during the interrogation.

And that meant that Thompson was helping his sister. Which meant his sister was definitely involved. And three cops were now, too.

She needed to tell Jim.

She needed to tell Davenport.

Chelsea walked to the captain's office, raised her hand

to knock, but paused. This could ruin the careers — and lives — of three officers if she was wrong. But there was a serial killer on the loose. If she was right, she couldn't afford to keep this information to herself.

"You going to stand there all day, Sullivan?" Davenport called from inside.

How did he do that?

She let herself into his office. "Sir, I have a … situation."

"Spill it."

After closing the door, she started to pace.

"Sullivan, my budget doesn't have a line item to replace the floor because you wear a rut in it."

"What? Oh." She stopped walking behind a chair and gripped the back of it. Her knuckles whitened.

"I don't have the money to replace the chair, either."

Chelsea sighed.

"Spit it out. You'll feel better."

"I doubt it."

"At least we can both get back to work."

"I have reason to believe we have three corrupt officers in the department. But I don't have proof. Just suspicion. And I don't know what to do. If I tell you and I'm wrong, I ruin their reputation. If I don't tell you and I'm right, Fletcher might … you know. Do what Fletcher does best. For longer than he should. Or maybe we never catch him."

"Sullivan, if you have suspicions, you come to me. No one's lives or careers get ruined until we have proof. And that's on me to find. You did the right thing coming to me. Now, out with it. What's going on?"

Chelsea told him everything she knew. Or rather, everything she thought. As she was finishing, her phone buzzed with a text from Jim. She glanced at the screen, shook her head, and scowled. "I guess I can add a little more to it."

"Oh? What's that?"

"Jim did a drive-by of Nell Thompson's place. He saw Oliver Thompson on the porch. Unfortunately, Officer Thompson saw him, too."

"And?"

"And instead of a friendly wave or simply ignoring Jim, he freaked out, bolted inside his sister's house, then slammed the door shut."

"Damn it." Davenport threw a pen across his desk. "Take a uniform with you and get over there."

"I'll take Rafferty."

"I'll call downstairs for you. And don't—"

"Let Miller or Berger know. Do I look stupid?"

"Just go."

On her way through the bullpen, she stopped to talk to Charlie and Norm. "Hey, guys. Can you do me a small favor?"

They both looked up and smiled.

"If we can," Norm said.

"I have a witness in Interrogation One. If you see anyone sniffing around her, especially Miller and Berger from downstairs, will you shoot me a text? I have to go rescue Jim."

"Maverick's in trouble again, huh?" Charlie asked.

"Isn't he always?"

Norm nodded. "If we see anything, we'll let you know."

"Thanks." She jogged down the stairs in search of Neil Rafferty. As he was currently partnered with Thompson and Thompson wasn't in the station, there was a good chance he wasn't out on a call. And luck was on her side. She found him writing reports. "Neil!"

He glanced up, a look of boredom melting away at the sight of her. A broad smile spread across his face. "Chels! What are you doing down in the slums?"

She sidled up to his desk then pitched her voice low. "Where are Miller and Berger?"

"They just left? Why?"

"You're with me. Let's go."

"I need to tell my CO."

"Davenport's calling him. Come on."

He popped up from his desk and joined her. "Where are we going? And what are we doing?"

"I'll fill you in on the way. You're driving."

Chapter Twelve

Private Prison Cell, Undisclosed Location
3:18 a.m.

THE WOMAN HAD BEEN CRYING for an hour. She'd vacillated between hysterical wails and soft snuffles but hadn't stopped for even a second since coming to.

Why did they always cry? Like it would change their situation.

It was grating on his nerves. Had been for fifty-nine and three-quarters of the last sixty minutes.

He'd considered knocking her out again a few times, but that wasn't a solution so much as a stop-gap measure. Better to let her get the tears out then be done with it.

Besides, once her lover came to, they could get down to business. Then he wouldn't have to listen to her any longer. Chances were largely in his favor that she'd be shocked into silence.

Maybe he could nudge her in that direction now.

His approach was slow, deliberate, his hiking boots echoing on the concrete floor with each methodical step. He stopped in front of her chair. Bent down to meet her gaze at her level.

Her eyes opened wide when his nose brushed hers.

He backed off a few inches, not out of respect for her personal space — prisoners had no such rights — but because if she blubbered again, she'd blow snot on his face, and he had no interest in receiving a sinus shower from her.

The tears continued to flow. Actually, they fell more freely now. But her sobbing abated, replaced by rapid breathing. Hyperventilating, really, that through the gag sounded almost like slurping.

"Tsk, tsk, tsk." He shook his head. "If you start drooling, I won't clean you up. Good hygiene is your responsibility. And I should warn you, slovenliness is against the rules in my ward. Disobedience won't be tolerated. Violators will be punished. Ask prisoner 04091970 what happens to those who don't follow the rules." He gestured to his first prisoner, standing still against the wall, though he looked poised to run.

She turned her head and followed his gaze to a corner that had escaped her notice thus far. Then she screamed. Thrashed in her chair. Yanked on her restraints. Howled at the hopelessness of her situation as the cuffs dug into her flesh but didn't give under her efforts.

"Hmm. I thought you'd appreciate having such a model example in your midst. He hasn't put a toe out of line in months."

Her shrieks must have been enough to bring her partner to, because he finally began to stir.

About time. "Now, we can begin."

The man's lids fluttered then snapped open. His eyes

showed remarkable clarity for someone coming out of unconsciousness to find himself bound and gagged in strange surroundings.

"I'd apologize for the taser. And the drugs. But I'm sure you can understand my position."

He didn't try to talk. Merely glanced down at his gag.

"You want me to take that off?"

His response felt sarcastic — an arch of the eyebrows and a tip of his head.

"You know no one will hear you if you call out."

Nothing but a deliberate blink.

The woman's cries subsided. Foolish. She thought her man had things under control now, but there was nothing he could do. He, like her, was restrained. They were several feet below the earth where no one would ever think to look for them. And even if they would get free and somehow overpower him — which was not possible — they'd never get past his failsafes.

"Very well." He lowered the man's gag.

"I assume you know who I am."

The woman looked adoringly at her mate.

"Do you not know who *I* am?"

He blinked at him. Recognition flickered in his eyes. "Oh. Now I understand."

"Then you know why you're here."

"I suppose I do. And you know what I'm capable of."

"I know what crimes you committed. I know you're now in my custody. And I'm not a tolerant warden."

"Warden?" He scoffed. "You're no warden. You're a kidnapper."

His lover screamed in her gag. Her head bobbed and snapped toward the corner of the room, and she thrashed in her chair.

He turned to look in the direction she seemed to be

indicating. Then he looked at his captor, his face contorted in a sneer of derision. "You're joking."

"I see you've met Prisoner 04091970."

"*Met* him? Hate to break it to you, pal, but you can't 'meet' a dead man."

"Prisoner 04091970 isn't dead."

"He's not alive. Correct me if I'm wrong, but he's stuffed."

His lover moaned. Her face turned green.

"I wouldn't suggest vomiting. If you do and the gag makes you choke, I will not save you."

She turned her head toward the other side of the room. Labored breaths, fast and heavy, huffed through the material stretched across her mouth.

"You do understand the human body wasn't designed for taxidermy, right?" the prisoner continued. "Look at that specimen."

"He's not a specimen." He strode across the room until he reached the man in the corner, then he straightened the uniform he'd carefully dressed him in. "This is Prisoner 04091970."

"It's not a man or a prisoner or anything other than a macabre experiment gone tragically wrong. Taxidermists don't like to work on pets because getting the exact shape right is next to impossible. They never look like themselves. And those are animals that are covered with fur or feathers or scales. But this? You're talking about a human being here. Not only is there nothing to help fudge the shape if you get the form wrong, there's nothing to cover the desiccation of the skin! My God, man. I've seen some horrific things in my time—"

He glanced over his shoulder. "You've *done* some horrific things in your time."

"That … poor soul you have posed like a mannequin

over there is a freak show. A Hollywood makeup artist couldn't conceal the discoloration to his flesh, not to mention—"

"I have an artist coming. Or I did."

"Ah." A knowing smile crossed the prisoner's face. "So that's what this is really about."

"No!" He wheeled around. Stormed across the room. Bent so he was face to face with his newest inmate. "This is about justice. You committed crimes, so you must pay. And as your warden, I'm going to make sure that happens."

"Warden? We've covered this. You're no warden."

He spread his arms wide. "Look around you. This is your prison, and I am in charge. If not your warden, than what am I?"

"Insane? Jealous? Out of your depth?"

Maniacal laughter, muffled though it was, came from behind him. He turned to find his other inmate with tears still falling down her face. But this time, they were tears of mirth instead of tears of fright.

Rage roiled through him. He clenched his fists to keep his hands from trembling. To keep his fingers from wrapping around her throat. "Your allegiance is misplaced. He cannot help you. He has no power here."

"I think you'll find you're mistaken, buddy. I'm always the smartest guy in every room."

"And yet you're the man strapped to the chair. In my prison. With no hope of escape."

"The prison where you appointed yourself warden because you have no authority outside these walls? Okay. I'll give you that one. But we won't be stuck down here forever. It won't take me long to get free. Then we'll see who really has all the power."

"Well, I'm nothing if not humble. I'm willing to admit when I'm wrong."

The man grinned.

The woman let loose another jubilant cackle.

"You were right to say I'm not currently the warden here."

"Now that's more like it. If you just uncuff me and the lady, I might be persuaded to forget this whole ugly incident even happened."

"I am, however," he continued as though his prisoner had never spoken, "your judge, jury, and executioner."

The woman fell silent.

The man's eyebrows arched. "I'm sorry?"

"You will be." He unsheathed his bowie. "I find you guilty of crimes against humanity. And against me. Your sentence is death. And it's to be carried out immediately."

"Wait!"

But he didn't. He stabbed the male inmate in the gut. Twisted the blade. Pulled up on the knife. Yanked it free.

The woman screamed as blood and entrails pooled on the floor.

He figured the hysterics wouldn't stop again for a long while, and he'd already had more than enough of that, so he left the room. Her shrieks followed him down the hall until he closed the steel door behind him and welcomed the sweet sound of silence.

Chapter Thirteen

Jim TURNED TO Sophia. "Text Sullivan. Tell her what's going on. Stay with the car. If Thompson runs this way, you're my backup. With any luck, I'll catch him myself. If not, I might flush him your way."

She nodded and started texting.

He approached the house. Before he reached the porch, he caught a flash of movement in the back yard.

Thompson.

Damn it.

Praying there were no man-hungry dogs poised to strike, Jim broke into a run, darting between Nell Thompson's house and her neighbor's. He only hesitated a second before bursting around the corner, but there were no animals in sight. Then he kicked it into high gear before losing sight of Oliver in the alley behind the neighbor's garage.

He pumped his arms, willing his legs to go faster. Sucked in deep breaths, expanding his lungs and sending oxygen to muscles he'd apparently been neglecting. The cobblestone pavers made every step perilous, and he slowed a little.

Luckily, the treacherous passage did Thompson no favors, either, but he didn't reduce his speed. Taking such a risk was a gamble, and it didn't pay off. He rolled his ankle, slammed his knee on the ground, somersaulted into someone's driveway, then popped awkwardly to his feet again. When he started running, his pace was much slower and he was limping.

Bonus? Jim had closed the distance considerably. And was gaining.

Thompson turned down a tree-lined street. When he came to a T, he went right.

He was headed for Willow Park. It was a damp, chilly day. Probably wouldn't be a lot of Mommy-and-Me visitors. School was in session, so the older kids wouldn't be there until after three. Except for diehard walkers or joggers, the place should be pretty well deserted. So, unless Thompson planned on swimming across the river or having one of his friends pick him up, he'd penned himself in.

Jim slowed to catch his breath. Didn't want to sound like he had emphysema while he talked to the guy. He reached for his phone to call Sullivan, but then remembered he'd left it with Giadone and swore under his breath. This was what happens when he let people pick music in his car.

Thompson dropped onto a bench then started rubbing his ankle. He looked up when Jim approached. "Hey, Detective. What are you doing here?"

"Chasing your sorry ass through town."

His eyebrows arched. "Come again?"

"Don't play dumb with me, Thompson. Even if you don't have to fake it."

His face darkened, but he didn't say anything.

"You know damn well I've been running after you since you saw me outside your sister's house."

"You were at my sister's?"

Jim sighed. "That really how you want to play this?"

"I'm not playing at anything."

"Well, I suppose you're right about that. This is some pretty serious shit you're mixed up in."

"I don't know what you're talking about."

"I'm talking about aiding and abetting, for starters."

"Aiding and abetting who?"

"Definitely your sister."

"My sister isn't a criminal."

"She helped a convicted serial killer escape prison."

"You don't know what you're talking about."

"Then again, my money's on you helping him directly."

Thompson put his foot down then slowly rose from the bench. "There's only one person here who's guilty of being a dirty cop, and it's not me. You don't see IA in my business. You don't see me using my family connections to get out of trouble. You don't see me transferring because no one wanted me in my own zone."

"There's rumor and innuendo, and then there's fact. You can believe what you hear, Thompson, but that doesn't make it true. On the other hand, I'm looking at the facts. And you and your sister are in this mess up to your corrupt eyeballs."

"Well, I guess you'd know what corrupt eyeballs look like."

"Is that a confession?"

"More like an accusation."

"Let's go."

"Where?"

"Back to the station. Your break's long over."

"I'm not on break. I took the afternoon off. And as this is my personal time, I don't have to answer to you. So I'm well within my rights to say leave me the fuck alone."

"Ah, well, I'm not on personal time. This is business, and I need you to come with me."

"On what grounds?"

On the grounds that he was a total douchebag probably weren't going to cut it. "On the grounds that you're a person of interest. You fled the scene of a crime."

"What scene of a crime?"

"Your sister's house."

"What crime was committed there?"

"I don't answer to you, Thompson. I'm extending you a professional courtesy by letting you walk back with me. Would you prefer I cuff you and haul your ass through town like the criminal we both know you are?"

"If you were so certain I'm a piece of shit, you would cuff me. You're treading lightly because you've got nothing."

Jim grabbed his cuffs.

"Fine. I'm coming." Thompson started walking. "But you and I both know this is bullshit."

"You and I both know that's not true."

"So, jogging's a crime now?"

They left the park and headed back up the street. "Jogging? You looked like you were trying out for the Olympics."

"I'm fast, old man. You're just jealous."

"And yet I ran you down."

"Only because I got hurt."

"Why are you 'jogging' at your sister's? Why not at your own place?"

"Because I like to run at Willow, not that it's any of your business."

"You've got an answer for everything, don't you?"

"I've got nothing to hide."

"Good. Then you won't mind us going into your sister's house and looking around."

"It's not my house. I can't give you permission to do that."

"But you can tell her to let us."

"And why would I do that? You're on a witch hunt."

"But you're so innocent."

"Doesn't mean you won't twist things. Or plant something. I know how dirty cops work."

Jim bristled. "Because you are one?"

They turned down the alley. Thompson glared at the rut he'd tripped in, but he didn't say anything more.

There was a lot more Jim wanted to say, but he kept his mouth shut, too. He was afraid Thompson was going to push him too far and they'd end up brawling again. Between Norm, Charlie, and Davenport, his part in their last altercation got swept under the rug. He wasn't too sure that would happen again and didn't want to put his captain in the position of having to get him out of trouble.

As for Thompson, a family friendship with the mayor got him out of trouble. But Jim doubted he could play that card when the Grimm Reaper was involved. Hopefully not, anyway.

He led Thompson to his car. Giadone wasn't in the passenger seat. She was standing in the street, talking to Chelsea, who had arrived with Neil Rafferty.

Thompson sneered at him. "What are you doing here? Davenport calling me back to work?"

"No. Detective Sullivan needed a uniform, so she asked me to come with her."

"Fuck." He shook his head. "You think you're going to arrest me? I'm your *partner*, dickhead."

"I'm just doing my job, Oliver."

"Well, do it better."

"That's enough." Chelsea sighed. "Rafferty, keep an eye on Thompson while I talk to my partner." She pulled Jim aside. "When I got here, I approached the house with Giadone and Rafferty. The front door was open, so we went in."

"That can't be right. Thompson slammed the door when he ran inside."

"Is it possible he slammed it hard enough that it bounced back open?"

"I don't know. I guess anything's possible."

Chelsea rubbed her temples. "Or maybe his sister opened the door to peek out and see if the coast was clear?"

"That makes more sense. Wait. You're saying this like she wasn't in there."

"She wasn't in there."

Jim flung both hands in the air, then he clapped them behind his neck. "He was drawing me away from the house. He didn't care if I caught him or not. He was just buying his sister time. He was bait, and I fell for it. Fuck, he even mentioned *fishing*, and I didn't catch on. I hate that the little shit manipulated me like that, and I didn't even *see* it. He's probably over there right now, smiling like a fucking Cheshire cat."

"Stop worrying about him for a minute, would you?"

"Wait a second." He dropped his arms to his side. "How'd his sister get away? Giadone was sitting on the house."

"My guess is Nell looked out front, saw Sophia, then went out the back and took a route that would guarantee she wouldn't be spotted. She could be anywhere by now."

"And you're sure she was at the house when I got here?"

"Positive. Come inside. I'll prove it to you."

∽

CHELSEA LED Jim to the front door.

"Hey!" Thompson called. "You don't have permission to go in there. Anything you find is inadmissible in court."

"Nice try," she said. "We had probable cause when we entered."

"Did you really?" Jim asked quietly.

"We actually did," she whispered back. "She has a cat."

"That explains it."

She chuckled. "I told you the door had been left ajar, which, in this weather, was odd enough. But when we reached the porch, we heard a crash inside. We announced our presence, but no one answered. Concerned someone was in distress, we entered. Turned out, her cat had knocked over a vase. But we found so much more."

They walked inside.

"I'll take you through the things I found as I noticed them, once we'd determined there was no one here. First, you can see there's ice in her drink. A little less now than there was, but it's still there. I took pictures. So we knew she'd been here recently. Also, her laptop and phone are gone but her desktop unit is on, and the screensaver hadn't kicked on."

"No offense, Chels, but the screensaver still hasn't kicked on."

She rolled her eyes at him. "That's because I disabled

it, I didn't want us to lose access to it. I turned off the password option, too, so we'll be able to get back into it even after it's turned off for transport."

"Good thinking."

"Anyway, I started looking through some of the files, and you won't believe what's in here." Chelsea clicked open a file folder.

Jim leaned over her shoulder. "Holy shit."

"You can't tell the difference from the real thing, can you?"

"Blow it up."

She zoomed in on the file.

He shook his head, blown away. They were looking at a replica of a Canadian Passport for Scott Fletcher, but the name on it was Florian Ulysses Aeris. "That's some alter ego."

"I'm sure he got quite a kick out of it."

"What do you mean?"

"Aeris is the Latin word for copper."

"Cuprum is the Latin word for copper."

"Only after aeris became a common word for several alloys."

"Why do you know this?"

"Because I paid attention in school."

Jim rolled his eyes.

"Regardless, Aeris. Copper … a nickname for cops? The initials are F. U. plus copper? He's flipping us off. It's his last insult to us before he disappears."

He looked at the screen again. "She really does remarkable work. But what about the biometric chip?"

"This passport is dated before one was necessary. It'll work for a few more years. But I also found files with a lot of research on them. I'm guessing she's going to try to master that, too. And if she does, she'll be one of the hottest forgers on the planet. Seems like she's already well on her way. Look at this place." She gestured around the room. "I admit, she's a talented artist. But my guess is she's not affording a house like this and the high-end furnishings on an artist's salary. Not even a well-compensated, highly-sought-after artist would be living like this."

Chelsea hated the style, but she could appreciate the cost and the quality. While the house itself was in a traditional upper-middle class suburban neighborhood, the decor was all either right out of a gallery or done by Nell Thompson or her extremely talented — and terrifyingly edgy — friends. The living room walls were painted stark white and held giant black-and-white photographs of industrial settings. The kitchen had polished concrete waterfall countertops that bled onto the polished concrete floors. Black appliances blended into black cabinets along two of the walls, and the third wall was painted blood red. White sculptures of lovers in compromising poses were recessed into black niches in that wall all the way down the hallway. *Architectural Digest* would kill to do a feature in the place, but Nell would surely consider it beneath her.

"Okay. I see what you're saying. Sure seems like she might be doing some work under the table. And if her brother is constantly surrounded by the dregs of society, he'd probably be in the perfect position to feed her clients."

"Ah, the family business. How lovely."

"I assume the rest of the house looks like this?"

"All but one room."

"Her brother's, I'm guessing."

Chelsea shook her head. "If Oliver has a room here, it's just a random guest room with the same kind of bold art that you see out here. It's her room that doesn't fit the mold."

"Scarier than this?"

She nodded.

"I can't imagine."

"You got that right."

"Show me."

As much as she hated to, she let him down the crimson corridor to the bedroom at the end of the hall. Before she opened the door, she paused.

"Come on, Sullivan."

Instead of grabbing the knob, she stepped aside and let him do it himself.

He slipped on gloves, shot her a frustrated look, then flung open the door.

She started to follow him in, but his feet faltered at the threshold, and she bumped into his back. That got him moving, then they both entered.

The bold, edgy artist with the affinity for neutral design accented with a single pop of color was nowhere to be found in this room. This room looked like it had been decorated by Mother Goose. The carpet — the only room so far that had been carpeted — was a soft sage frieze reminiscent of grass. The walls were painted a warm apricot ombre that ended in a pale peach. Collections of potted plants in various shapes and shades and sizes clustered in all the corners and under the windows, which were draped with gossamer fabric that fluttered as the furnace kicked on, almost like clouds drifting on a summer breeze in front of a fiery sunset. The room had a distinct woodland feel.

More specifically, it had a "Snow White in the woods" feel. Probably because her bed was in the center of the room, encased in a plexiglass box.

And if that wasn't disturbing enough, Nell Thompson had made sure to get the "woodland creatures in mourning" effect by having dozens of taxidermied animals surrounding the clear coffin, many of which were posed on two feet, holding bouquets of flowers or heart-shaped boxes.

Jim turned around and looked at Chelsea. His eyes were wide, his mouth agape.

She shrugged.

He spun around and walked farther into the room to peer into the glass box. "I thought I'd seen everything on this job. I mean, I really thought I'd seen everything there was to see."

"It kind of steals your breath, doesn't it?"

"I don't want to look at it, but I can't look away."

"Takes all kinds."

Jim tore his gaze from the bed. "We need to get a BOLO out on Nell Thompson."

"And all her aliases."

"Her aliases?"

"That passport we found for Fletcher? She has a bunch for her, too. She planned to go with him. For whatever reason, she was still here. But we scared her away. If she'd printed any of those documents yet, she can be on the run under one of seven different identities."

Chapter Fourteen

Jim told Rafferty and Giadone to take Thompson in for questioning. And he made sure they knew not to let his buddies have a chance to talk to him. He didn't want the dickhead to give his lackeys instructions about how to contact his sister. There would be no warnings or messages passed to her on his watch.

While he talked to the uniforms, Chelsea called for crime scene processing. They'd have a field day with this place. Some psychiatrist could get famous off this girl alone.

But he was less interested in why women fell in love — or thought they did — with imprisoned serial killers and more interested in the contents of the desktop system Nell Thompson had left behind. They'd only scratched the surface of what was on there. There was no telling how many criminals she'd done work for. She could have half the city's underworld on there.

Chelsea approached him as she ended her call.

"You let MCU know what to expect?"

"I did. I also filled in Danny."

He turned around and reached behind him.

"Jim? What are you doing?"

"I was hoping you could take the knife out of my back. I can't grab it myself."

She sighed.

He stood facing away from her while his emotions ran the gamut from betrayal to frustration to anger.

"Would you please look at me?"

It was his turn to sigh, but he did turn around. "I've already had one disloyal partner, Sullivan. I know how that ends. I don't care to repeat that."

"Don't you dare put me in the same company as Dom."

His eyebrows shot up. "You're indignant with me? Don't you think it's kind of late for you to take the moral high ground on this one?"

"No, I do not. These two situations are completely different, and you know it. Dom was your best friend, and he betrayed you and the entire force. He made a mockery of the shield and all it stands for. I would never do that. We made a deal with Danny. Grimm Reaper was our case. *Was*. We put him away. Now that he's out, it's his case. His and *his* partner's. And they're letting us in on things because we understand how Fletcher thinks and because it's a professional courtesy to let the original cops have peace of mind to work the case. And, in case you've forgotten, because we — he and I — have history. He's doing me a favor. If I keep cutting him out because you have a bug up your butt about something that I can't even figure out, then he's going to cut both of us out. Then where will we be? That's not something I can abide by. Because as much as I don't want to have to find Fletcher again, I don't want to be kept from finding him more. So either you tell me why you're so proprietary over this or you get over it. Now."

Jim scuffed his toe in a clump of wet grass on the ground. "I'm not being proprietary."

"And now you're being obstinate."

"Would you stop using your three-dollar words?"

"Stop stalling and tell me what's going on."

He started walking toward his car.

She followed.

When he got in, he didn't unlock her door. She stood there and waited. He started the engine and considered just leaving her there to get a ride with the crime techs, but he knew that would be childish. So he flipped the lock.

Chelsea opened the door, climbed into the passenger seat, then glared at him. "You are so lucky you made the right choice."

"Strap in." He started driving without waiting for her to fasten her belt.

"Would you please tell me what your problem is?"

"I'm scared for you, all right?"

"Jim, I—"

"Don't." He took the corner far faster than was safe in a residential zone. Realizing how out of control he was, he drove the few short blocks to Willow Park then got out of the car. His long legs made short work of the distance between the road and the bench. He didn't want her to follow him, but he heard the car door shut. Soon he saw her shadow stretch in front of him. He felt more than saw her sit beside him. His head was turned toward the trees. A bracing wind had picked up, and the willow branches whipped nearly perpendicular to the ground. Many of their leaves, yellowed for fall, couldn't stand the onslaught and danced in the air across the field like giant golden snowflakes. Jim watched one of them flutter away until he was facing her.

"Can we please talk about this?" Chelsea's hair also lashed in the wind. She peeled the tresses out of her eyes, but they just ended up there again. She blinked against the stinging assault but didn't leave him or even suggest that they seek shelter.

"What do you want from me?"

"I want you to understand that what happened wasn't your fault!"

He shook his head. "All the clues were there. If I'd spent less time teasing you about him and more time analyzing the signs, I'd have seen it sooner. Then he never would have gotten so close. He never would have grabbed you at the hospital. He never would have—"

"Stop!" She placed her hand on his arm and shook her head. "Has this been weighing on you all this time?"

Jim shrugged. "What kind of partner am I — what kind of cop am I — if I missed something so obvious? It nearly got you killed."

"In case you didn't notice, you're the one who found me. No one else put those pieces of the puzzle together. That's what kind of cop you are. A damn good one."

"Chelsea, I—"

"No." She shook her head. "You know me, Jim. I'm by the book, all the way. And I expect that of the people I work with, too. I told you today that you were wrong, didn't I?"

"Well, yeah."

"Then trust me when I say that I'd tell you if you were wrong then. You weren't. But it is wrong to try to leave out Danny and his partner now. That's why I called them and told them what we found at Nell Thompson's."

"Fine."

"He said their lab has processed the barn and we're welcome to go back and look for anything. Despite not being thrilled with us barging in there first, he's not kicking us off. Yet. And he's going to tell us what his lab comes up with."

"Okay."

"Want to go to the barn?"

"Sure. But let's swing by Gwendolyn Cole's first. She wasn't home earlier when I checked."

"Sounds like a plan." She squeezed his arm, then headed back to the car.

Jim was happy to notice his phone in the cupholder. The only reason he even realized it was there — and not in his pocket — was because Chelsea raised her eyebrow when Shakira came on.

"Is this the radio?"

"Playlist."

"You have 'Hips Don't Lie' on a playlist?"

"I do. Let me guess, you don't like this, either."

"No, I like it. I'm just surprised you do."

"I'm a man of mystery."

"It's your mom's list, isn't it?"

He chuckled. "Damn, Sullivan. You won't let me get away with anything. It's not her list, but it's a list I made for her."

"So you don't like it?"

"I've grown to like some Latin music. This song's catchy. How can anyone not like Shakira?"

"Why do I think that has more to do with her hips than her singing?"

"Oh, look, we're at Gwendolyn Cole's house."

But like last time, she wasn't home.

"Do you think she was Lucky Bachelorette Number Two?" he asked on the way to the barn.

"What?"

"You know, like the Dating Game? Fletcher seemed to be toying with three different women. Maybe she's the one who won, and now the two of them are off somewhere."

"Without Nell Thompson's fake IDs? Without any of the provisions at the barn? I don't know, Jim. I think there's more going on here than meets the eye."

"Why three women? What did they all bring to the table?"

"Well, we know what Thompson was giving him."

He turned onto the road to the barn. "And Edwards mapped out the route. She was probably picking him up and driving him to his hideout."

"So, maybe Cole stocked the barn. We found the card there from the misspelled Gwenivere. We guessed she'd been there. It's not a leap to think she was the one who put all the stuff there."

Jim shook his head. "Why not just use Nell for all of it? She could easily have stocked the barn and picked him up at the designated spot. Why all three?"

"Divide and conquer? If they split the chores, they couldn't all be responsible for helping him because they didn't all help him with the whole thing."

"Maybe they didn't all know the whole thing. It wouldn't surprise me if he tried to keep them in the dark about each other's parts so if one of them got caught, the whole thing didn't crumble."

"But he didn't count on Nell Thompson being so darn smart."

"Or you."

"Us." She smiled. "I wonder if Fletcher knew Nell and Oliver are related."

"I'm sure he does. He always knows everything. He probably considers it an asset."

"But is it? Having a cop for a relative could be a liability."

"Not a dirty cop."

She shrugged. "We don't know that he's dirty."

"Seriously? Look at the evidence, Chels."

"You, of all people, should know that how things look and how things aren't necessarily the same thing."

"Oliver Thompson has been helping set this up for months. I wouldn't be surprised if he knew Fletcher was the Grimm Reaper when he worked here. He could be an acolyte."

"Now you're really off the deep end. You just don't like the guy and want him to be guilty."

"I don't like the guy, and I do want him to be guilty. But that doesn't mean I'm wrong."

"That doesn't mean you're right, either."

They pulled up to the barn. This time, they didn't have to stop a million miles away and hike in stealth-mode to the building. Instead, they rolled right up to the door. "Nice. Makes a difference, doesn't it?"

"I think you're getting lazy."

"I ran half a marathon today."

"If you're talking about the run from Thompson's to the park, it was a few blocks. And you walked back." She got out of the car.

Jim followed her around the perimeter of the barn, which they had not had time to analyze earlier. They found a flag in a patch of grassless soft earth where a pristine print — probably made by a man's boot — had been catalogued. He held his foot in the air near it. "What do you think that is? Thirteen?"

"What size do you wear?"

"Twelve."

"Yeah, that's probably a thirteen. Geez, that's a big foot."

"Don't go talking about Bigfoot out here. We have enough wild theories without adding him to the mix."

She giggled.

"You have any idea what size Fletcher wore?"

"This again?"

"People are usually proportional."

"You're getting dangerously close to crossing an inappropriate line, McPherson."

"What I mean is, your height is usually the same as your wingspan, fingertip to fingertip. Your foot is usually the size of the crook of your arm to your wrist."

"And what corresponds to distance between your tip of your pointer and the tip of your thumb?"

He shoved his hands in his pockets. "Now who's crossing a line?"

"So you understand why I don't like you asking those questions?"

"I wasn't asking about you."

"You were asking about my sex life."

"I'm asking how big his damn arm is. Or his foot!"

She sighed. "Sorry. I'm … wound up. He wasn't even as tall as you. I'm guessing his feet were smaller, assuming his feet were proportional."

"Thompson's around my height."

"So, his feet are probably a size twelve?"

"It's not an exact formula, Sullivan. Your feet are big for your height. His feet could be a little bigger, too. When we get back, maybe I can sneak a peek in his locker."

Her phone buzzed. She took it from her pocket while Jim used his to snap a photo of the print.

"It's a text from Danny. His lab techs have the size and make of this print. You were right. It is a size thirteen. And he says it's a brand popular with preppers and survivalists. NaturAll XLT. They're pretty expensive, so it's not likely that it was just some random high schoolers partying out here."

"We need to finish looking around inside, then we need to get back to the station. I want a look at Thompson's feet."

Chapter Fifteen

JIM LOOKED through the window of Interrogation Room Two. It was empty. He elbowed Chelsea. "Thompson's not in there."

"Maybe he's not through processing yet."

"We didn't arrest him. He shouldn't be in processing at all."

"I can call Rafferty …"

He brushed past her as he barged past the room, hurrying down the hall toward the observation closet for Interrogation Room One. After he entered, relief sluiced through him at the sight of Thompson through the one-way mirror. Through the open doorway, Jim called, "He's in here."

Chelsea ran in after him. She shook her head. "No. This can't be right. I left Ainsley Edwards in here."

"Don't know what to tell you, Sullivan. You're looking at him, so he's clearly here. And she clearly isn't."

"Then where is she?"

"I don't know."

She turned and stormed out of the closet.

He followed her to Charlie's and Norm's desks.

"Hey!"

They both turned and looked at her. Norm arched his eyebrows. "You yelling at us?"

"Yeah. What'd you do with Ainsley Edwards?"

"We didn't do anything with her."

"You were supposed to be watching her for me."

He crossed his arms.

Charlie stood. "You better dial back the attitude, little girl."

"Little—"

"Easy, folks." Jim stepped between them. "I think this conversation got off on the wrong foot."

"He called me—"

"I heard, Chels."

"When you charge over here acting like a petulant child, what do you expect?"

"Charlie." Norm shot him a pointed stare.

"I'm not wrong," he muttered.

"I don't know what happened to Edwards," Norm said. "Yes, you asked us to keep tabs on her. And yes, we agreed to."

"And yes, we fucking did," Charlie growled.

Norm rolled his eyes before meeting Chelsea's gaze. "No one got near her while we were here. But we also had our own work to do, and we were on a call for about an hour. Since we've been back, no one's even approached Interrogation One. But if she's not in there, I'd check with Davenport."

"Thanks, guys," Jim said.

Norm nodded.

Charlie grunted.

"Chelsea?" Jim prompted.

"Thanks," she muttered.

He nudged her.

She sighed. "And I'm sorry I lost my temper. But she's—"

Jim cleared his throat.

"I'm sorry." This time, she sounded more contrite.

Norm shrugged. "I was starting to wonder if anything fazed you."

Charlie clapped her on her back. "About damn time you unloaded on someone. Wish it wasn't us. Should'a been your good-for-nothin' partner. But still. About damn time." He winked then took his seat.

She gaped at them.

Jim grabbed her by the shoulders and turned her around. Then he shoved her toward Davenport's office until she started walking on her own.

"I don't understand them."

"That's obvious."

"They're happy I yelled at them?"

"No. But they're happy you're finally comfortable enough with them to be that relaxed. Until now, you've treated them like superiors instead of colleagues. You could hear the unspoken 'sir' in every exchange. This was another wall hurdled. Or crumbled. It's a relief."

"I hate boys' clubs."

"Being this isn't one, I guess you don't have to worry about that." He knocked on Davenport's door.

"Come in!"

Jim turned to Chelsea. "Don't yell at him like you did the boys, okay? The 'sir' to him shouldn't be unspoken."

She rolled her eyes as she brushed past him and entered the captain's office.

He followed her in. Much as he'd prefer to pace — much as he'd prefer to get in the ring with Thompson and box fifteen rounds or as many as the chump would last —

he took the seat beside her and resisted the urge to bounce his knee, drum his fingers, or beat his head off the desk. Somehow he didn't think that would go over too well.

"You have news on the Fletcher case?" Davenport asked.

"Sherick and Stack sent us preliminary findings from the abandoned barn," Jim said. "They grabbed a footprint from outside. Definitely a man's print, but it's bigger than Fletcher's foot. And it's a specialty boot, so it's not a random kid partying out there."

"You think it's an accomplice?"

"Well, sir, one of the three women Fletcher was seeing is the sister of one of our officers. He happens to be a survivalist, and the boot that made that print is a size thirteen NaturAll boot, which is a very expensive brand of footwear popular with the prepper community. We were hoping you'd let us look through his locker to see if he's a size thirteen. Even better, to see if we could find that exact boot."

"You're talking about Thompson."

He nodded.

"Those are some serious allegations."

Chelsea leaned forward. "Sir, I've already discussed some of this with you. You know what we think is going on. But it's worse than what we thought. His sister is a master artist. Worse, she's a forger. We found evidence of several fake IDs for her and for Fletcher, and now she's in the wind. The two of them could be anywhere under any number of aliases by now. At best, Thompson knew, which means he turned a blind eye to the crimes. At worst, he helped commit them."

"So, go interrogate him and find out how complicit he is. And yes, you have permission to search his locker. It's police property, not private property. You don't need a warrant for that." He opened his top drawer, rooted through some junk, fished out a key, then slid it across the desk.

"Thank you, sir," Jim said.

"Why are you still here?"

Chelsea glanced at Jim, then she looked at the captain. "Well, sir, it's about Ainsley Edwards."

"What about her?"

"I wasn't done interrogating her when I went to Nell Thompson's house."

"And?"

"And now she's missing."

"Did she leave town? She was told not to leave town."

"You mean you let her leave the station?"

"I didn't have a choice. Her lawyer showed up."

"How? She never asked me for one. She never made a call."

Davenport shrugged. "Don't know what to tell you, Sullivan, but someone knew she was here and made damn sure she didn't stay a second longer than she had to. He got her arraigned practically immediately and she's out on bail."

"Bail?" Chelsea's voice went up an octave. "She's being accused of helping a serial killer escape prison!"

"Apparently she has a good lawyer. And her arresting officers weren't available to give testimony arguing to the contrary. The DA's office is none too pleased."

"Are you fucking kidding me?" Now Jim did get up to pace. "This whole thing feels like a setup."

"From who?" Davenport asked. "If it's a setup, it's personal. Who would be out to get you?"

"Fletcher."

"He has his own problems. The entire state is looking

for him. I don't think he's trying to drive you to drink right now."

"Yeah, well, trying or not, he's succeeding."

"Don't you have a locker to search? And a cop to question?"

Chelsea rose. "Thank you, sir."

Jim touched two fingers to his forehead in a half-hearted salute. Then he led his partner out of the room. In the bullpen, he turned to her. "Want to come with me to the men's locker room?"

"Gee. When have I ever had such a romantic invitation?"

"You know what I mean."

"I was going to start questioning Oliver."

"I want to be there for that. Come with me. It'll beat standing around waiting for me."

"Going to a smelly locker room and rooting through a pile of sweaty jock straps beats standing here with a cup of coffee and a donut?"

"You honestly think Thompson's locker is filled with three dozen dirty jocks?"

"I don't know. Unlike men, who fantasize about what goes on in women's locker rooms, I don't spend my days thinking about men's locker rooms."

"That's slumber parties and showers, not locker rooms. And you're stereotyping again."

"If I'm stereotyping, why did you know how to correct me?"

"Just because I know what the stereotype is doesn't mean I — or anyone else — lives up to it."

"It wouldn't be a stereotype if it wasn't a popular thing to do."

"Are you coming with me or not?"

"Not. I'm getting coffee."

"Fine. I'll be back in a little bit. Don't go to see Thompson without me."

Chelsea headed for the snack bar.

Jim walked down the hall. She was in a mood today. Maybe he deserved it. He'd been kind of a dick about Sherick and sharing information with him and his partner. But Charlie and Norm hadn't done anything to deserve her attitude.

It was Fletcher.

Fucking Fletcher. Bastard was getting to her, too.

In the locker room, since Chelsea wasn't with him, Jim took a minute to freshen up. He splashed water on his face then peered closely at his reflection. Damn eyes were bloodshot. No wonder. Hadn't slept more than an hour the night before. He took a deep breath then vented it slowly. Wrinkled his nose.

He smelled like that barn.

Jim whipped off his shirt then sniffed under his arms. Recoiled.

Whew! He was ripe. No time for a shower, but hell if he was going to walk around smelling like a pig's sty. He scrubbed up with sink soap and dried with the sandpaper the department called paper towels. Then he went to his own locker.

Jim kept his things tidy. Top shelf held a toiletry kit, a clean towel, three tees, and some ammo. The right hook held a complete change of clothes still in the dry cleaner's plastic and a few shirts, the left hook held a spare jacket. On the bottom were a pair of shoes and a pair of boots, each with socks tucked inside and a couple of plastic bags. He opened the leather case, retrieved his antiperspirant, then applied it generously. Dabbed on some cologne much less liberally. He balled up his dirty shirt, shoved it in a bag that he kept in the bottom of his locker, then he added his muddy shoes to it.

Felt better already.

Pulled a henley over his head and the boots on his feet. After tying them, he straightened his things then locked up.

Time for what he actually came for.

He went to Thompson's locker. It was around the corner, in the officers' section of the locker room. Because there were more unis than there were detectives, but the square footage of the rooms were the same, the lockers were — of necessity — smaller. To Jim's way of thinking, that meant neatness was even more imperative. Apparently to Thompson, that meant cram a bunch of shit inside, slam the door shut, then hope nothing fell out when he opened it.

Which it absolutely would.

Because it did when Jim opened the door.

An avalanche of detritus hit his feet. No sweaty jocks — that he noticed, anyway — but no shoes or boots, either. Something sweaty, though, because the odor was rank. Part of him wanted to organize the mess, the other part wanted to run from it. He started flinging stuff back into the locker, hoping he'd come across any footwear at all to determine Thompson's size. The survivalist boots were looking like a pipe dream at this point.

"What the fuck do you think you're doing?"

Perfect.

Jim turned around.

Miller was standing there, glaring at him.

"What the fuck does it look like I'm doing?"

"You planting fake evidence, dirty cop?" He turned his head and yelled into the back of the room, "Hey, Berger!"

"Little busy here!"

"We got trouble!"

A toilet flushed. Jeremy Berger came out, zipping his fly. His face darkened when he took in the situation.

"Aren't you at least going to wash your hands?" Jim asked.

"You planting something on our boy?" Berger asked.

Jim rolled his eyes and sighed. "You know, I'm getting pretty damn tired of this shit. I expect it from short-sighted Neanderthals like Thompson, but I really thought you two knew better."

"What I know is you've been accused of planting evidence before," Berger said.

"And you're in Thompson's things now," Miller added.

"I'm in Thompson's things because I'm looking for his shoes."

Berger started shoving stuff back into the locker. "What do you need his shoes for?"

"That information's on a need-to-know basis. And you don't need to know." Jim thought he saw the sole of sneaker and tried to snatch it from the heap of locker litter. Turned out it was only a soda bottle.

But Miller started wrestling him for it, anyway.

Berger joined in.

The three of them rolled around on the floor.

He caught a fist to the lip and tasted blood.

Jim punched someone in the gut. Heard an *oof* as hot breath whooshed past his ear.

He took an elbow just below the eye.

The bottle was ripped from his grip. "Damn it!" Might have made a decent weapon. He gave someone a knee to the groin as he rolled away from the melee. When gained his feet, he squared off, prepared for them to tag-team him. But they were so busy fighting, they didn't notice he'd broken away.

"Hey."

Jim turned.

Chelsea nodded at the door. "You took too long."

"We need to find his shoe size."

Tweedles Dumb and Dumber broke apart and started to clamber to their feet.

"Not right now." She shook her head and pushed him out the door before round two could start. "We have something more pressing to deal with."

"What could be more pressing?"

"Fletcher's first victim's been found. The Grimm Reaper is active again."

Chapter Sixteen

CHELSEA SCANNED the group of onlookers, searching for anyone who looked like Fletcher in disguise. She and Jim used to look at the crowd for anyone who seemed interested beyond that initial bout of morbid curiosity or horrified realization. It wasn't until after he was caught that she had to come to terms with the fact that their serial killer had been at the scene of the crimes all along, reliving the brutality of the kills and the so-called artistry of his poses. They'd *invited* him there, for Pete's sake.

This time, however, he wouldn't be given a front-row seat. But would he be able to avoid the temptation of returning to the scene? Fletcher considered himself a kind of maestro. A virtuoso. The DaVinci of murderers. He wouldn't be able to withstand the draw. There was an energy to a newly-discovered crime scene. The detectives, the crime scene investigators, the officers, media, and local spectators. So many people with so many agendas made for an amalgam of high-pressure, high-tempered activity. You never knew what might happen. Accidents. Arguments. Insights. Chases. Arrests. The potential was too great to avoid.

And that was on top of his chance at a last look at his handiwork.

So she scanned the crowd again.

"See anything?"

"No."

He opened his phone, held it so she could see it, then scrolled through the fake ID photos Nell Thompson had on her desktop. Thanks to his mastery at makeup, some of them hardly looked like Fletcher at all.

Then they both scanned the crowd again.

Nothing.

Chelsea sighed. "He might not look like any of these renderings. With his cosmetic artistry, he could literally look like anyone."

"I'm going to tell Rafferty and Giadone to make sure they take pictures of all the people loitering here. I want names and contact info, too."

She scoffed. They both knew what a waste of time that was. "You should tell them to send everyone away."

He headed down the hill toward the officers.

Chelsea turned back toward the victim. For a moment, all she saw was the room Fletcher had held her in — stone walls, gilded picture frames, four poster bed, ornate fabrics. He'd gone out of his way to recreate the Sleeping Beauty fairy tale to the nth degree. Her blood chilled, and her skin pebbled with gooseflesh as the hair rose on the back of her neck. She blinked a few times to clear the picture from her vision and see what was really in front of her.

A recreation of Ariel, the Little Mermaid.

More accurately, a poor recreation of the tale.

This girl was a red-head, but not a true ginger. She had brown roots — about three-quarters of an inch showing.

All of her clothes had been cut off of her and left in a pile a few feet from her — miniskirt, thong, bra, and sweater. A mermaid's tail had been tugged hastily over her legs, not quite coming up high enough to cover all it should, possibly to expose an intricate tattoo of roses and barbed wire that wound over both hip bones then disappeared into all that was left after her Brazilian wax. A navel ring sparkled in the portable spotlights, the sun having set at least an hour earlier. Two plastic seashells had been glued to her breasts and were barely big enough to do their job. Stuffed Sebastian and Flounder toys were placed in her right and left hands. A shell pendant necklace had been fastened around her, but the charm had fallen to the side and tangled in her hair. Her tongue had been cut out, and blood had dripped down her cheek and into her ear.

Jim stepped up beside her. "So, tell me what you know about *The Little Mermaid*? Because I know it's more than I know. I only know what I've seen in Disney commercials."

She looked up at him. "That's the thing, Jim. It seems like that's all this killer knew, too."

"I don't follow."

"What do we know about Fletcher? More specifically, about the Grimm Reaper? He's meticulous, right? He knows his stories very well, and he follows them to the letter. Particularly old versions of Brothers Grimm stories. He was working out of a second edition that his mother used to read to him."

"Yeah, I remember."

"And he chose his vics very carefully. Girls he felt had a reputation for being wholesome but had failed at that in some way, right?"

"Yeah."

"No offense to the dead, but does she strike you as someone with a wholesome reputation? Thong and miniskirt? That sweater looks like it was pretty tight. And that's a demi-bra, not a sensible bra."

"You're being judgmental."

"What about the tattoo? The naval ring?"

"Still judgy."

"She was barely out of high school, Jim."

"That means she was an adult and could make decisions for herself."

"Even bad ones?"

"That's how you learn."

"Fine. Wholesomeness — or lack thereof — notwithstanding, the details are wrong. Look at her hair. She's not a real ginger. The Grimm Reaper wouldn't have chosen a fake redhead."

"Still reaching."

"What about the fact that this isn't even a Brothers Grimm story?"

"That I find mildly interesting. Who wrote it?"

"Hans Christian Andersen."

He frowned. Then he sighed. "So, it's still a fairy tale. Just not a Grimm fairy tale. And if we search hard enough through your book, we'll probably find one that approximates this one, right? Didn't your dad once say there are a lot of crossovers?"

"I gave that book to the library. We'd have to go there and look. But yeah, there are a lot of crossovers."

"So, this could still be Fletcher."

"It doesn't feel like his work."

"He's been locked up. He's desperate for a fix. He doesn't have time to be picky."

"He also is a perfectionist. He wouldn't want to settle for some cheap Disney knockoff. This costume was bought at a Halloween store. These are stuffed animals from the cartoon. They aren't characters from the real story."

"Are you sure? Did your dad read you the real tale when you were a kid? You said this one wasn't in your book."

"He didn't. But I looked it up on my phone. It's ridiculous. She gives up her tongue and her voice to try to win a prince's love and a soul. But the sea witch kind of tricks her. And of course, she fails. Just before turning to sea foam forever, her sea sisters give her a dagger to kill the prince so she can return to the sea and live with them again. But she can't kill him. She ends up being granted three hundred years to serve mankind and earn a soul."

"It sounds kind of nice."

"It sounds like the man got everything he wanted and the woman got indentured servitude with no guarantee of salvation at the end. But whatever. You're missing my point. This murder was staged to look like the Disney version, with Sebastian and Flounder and the shell around Ariel's neck holding her voice."

"But what about the cut-out tongue? That's from the original version, right?"

"I think it's a trophy. We didn't find it here."

"Fletcher didn't take trophies. In fact, he usually left items behind."

"That's my point!"

"I'll give you that."

"What about the most obvious clue, then?"

"Which is?"

"Fletcher posed his vics naked, he didn't dress them in a costume. The fairy tale clues were around the bodies, not on them."

"Yeah, you got me there."

"This isn't Fletcher. This is a copycat. Or a poor imitation thereof. Other than these stupid stuffed animals, there are no clues here. There's nothing about this scene that says careful planning or wholesome-girl-gone-bad. This isn't a Grimm Reaper kill, Jim. This is a misdirect."

"Why?"

"I don't know. Either he asked an acolyte to do this to keep us busy and off his trail, or one of his fans did this as a tribute to him. Maybe as a way to get his attention."

"If that's true, it'll piss him off."

"You and I know that. His whacko wannabes obviously don't."

Jim sighed. "If you're right, that means we not only have a serial killer to find, and all his helpers, but we now have an active copycat, too."

She rubbed her head. "Yeah. I know."

"We need to go through the list of all his fans again. Probably talk to the warden again."

"And maybe the guards."

He nodded.

"Sounds like fun."

"You need sleep."

Chelsea scoffed. "You need it more. Your eyes are more bloodshot than a drunk in a field of ragweed."

He looked at her and his eyebrows arched. "What?"

"Sorry. My mom used to say that to my dad when he'd been on a stakeout. He'd tell her some eyedrops and a steak dinner and he'd be fine."

"And did that work?"

"I don't know. He usually fell asleep while she was cooking the steak."

Jim chuckled. "Let's get out of here. We can start going through that list tomorrow."

"What about Thompson? We left him in Interrogation."

"He can sleep on the table if he gets tired. I'm ready for bed."

Chelsea was, too. She hadn't slept well the night before, knowing Fletcher was out there somewhere and Davenport was so concerned, he'd put a unit on her apartment. Tonight, she was so exhausted, she didn't think any of that would keep her awake.

But when Jim dropped her off and she saw that unmarked car pull into a spot in front of her building, she had a feeling she was in for another restless night. Chelsea exchanged a look with her partner before heading inside.

She suspected he wasn't going to get much rest, either.

Chapter Seventeen

Two Years Ago
   Around Mom's Sick Bed
   7:13 a.m.

HE KEPT his gaze locked on his mother's sleeping form while his father prattled on. It could go one of two ways — Dad would get tired and the rant would fizzle out, or he'd bluster and billow into a full-blown rage until his anger ended in blows.

Well, just one. Dad would hit him across the face. It would sting — more than he'd care to admit but nothing insufferable — then he'd take a dive. Dad, satisfied he had taught his "stupid, lazy, good for nothin', ingrate" son whatever lesson he'd been trying to impart, would step over him, maybe kicking him once for good measure, then stomp off to settle down. Once he lumbered away — which coincided with the alcohol wearing off — he'd come back with a muttered apology and a face red with shame.

Most people wouldn't be able to tell the difference between a flush of embarrassment and a flush of drunkenness, but he and Mom had become experts since she'd taken ill.

At seven in the morning, most people would think a ruddy complexion was from a freshly scrubbed face. Maybe a brisk walk in the cold air. Any neighbors, with a quick glance, would assume so as they passed by.

If they had any neighbors. Which they didn't.

Not that it mattered. Because this morning, there was no one to see Dad's red cheeks but him. No one was around for miles, and Mom was asleep.

Even if he couldn't see the difference, he could deduce the cause.

Dad hadn't showered. Hadn't been out in the cold.

Smelled like a fucking distillery.

His father had gotten hammered. Had already tied one on at the crack of dawn. Or maybe he was still going from the night before.

That's why, as the old man ranted and raved and wove on his feet, it was best not to make eye contact or acknowledge anything he said.

So, he stared at Mom. At the too-slow rise and fall of her chest as her lungs sucked in rattling breaths of air. At the atlas of veins and tendons standing out in stark relief underneath the crepe paper skin of her once-soft hands. At the sharp, gray edges of her too-prominent cheekbones that used to be round and rosy with smiles for her only child. At her eyeballs moving rapidly under her tissue-thin lids.

Did she dream of the days when she danced through the kitchen? Walked down the hall? Even sat in this godforsaken bed and spoke his name or lifted the corners of her lips in a half-hearted smile?

He ran his finger gently over hers, struck by how different they looked next to one another. His firm and full, hers withered and wrinkled. His warm and lifelike, hers cold and—

The blow took him by surprise, coming from his blindside and covering half his face. As he didn't see it coming, he reacted on instinct, and instead of taking a dive, he took exception to the attack and came up swinging, catching his dad under the chin and sending him half-sailing, half-stumbling backward into the dresser.

The few items on the dusty surface — brush, comb, perfume bottle — scattered then clattered to the floor. The crystal bottle, along with the mirror above the massive, handmade piece of furniture, shattered into countless shards.

Dad huffed. Crouched. Snarled. His bloodshot eyes no longer rolled beneath barely open lids. Now his gaze seemed predator-sharp, and it was focused on his son. He tensed then pounced, fingers bent into makeshift talons intent to claw any soft tissue he could find on his prey's face.

Mom's soft moan did more to stop Dad than any attack could. He slowly lowered his hands, stood upright, then stumbled to his wife's bedside. Sitting on the edge of her sagging mattress, he gently took her frail hand with his trembling fingers. "I'm sorry the boy woke you, sweetheart. Now, don't you worry. I'll have him clean this mess right away."

She tried to swallow, coughed with the effort.

Dad swatted his leg. "What's the matter with you, boy? Can't you see she's suffering? Get her some water!"

He hurried to the other side of the bed then poured her a glass from the old porcelain pitcher sitting on her nightstand. When he tried to hold it to her lips, Dad slapped his hand then snatched the drink from him. But when he assisted his wife, he was tender.

Mom managed a sip or two, though more of the water dribbled down her chin than anything else. As Dad turned to set the cup on the other bedside table, she turned her face and rubbed it dry on the pillow.

His heart ached to see Mom like that, but what could he do? His father wouldn't let him touch her.

Dad turned around after putting the glass on the tray. "I told you to clean up that glass, boy. It's upsetting your mother."

She shook her head. "No. Wait." Her voice was raspy. Her forehead wrinkled. She coughed again.

He could tell it pained her to speak, but Dad had a rapturous smile on his face with every word she uttered.

Denial. It was half of their problems. And impossible to overcome.

"I'm always so tired."

"So, sleep, sweetheart." Dad glared at him as he pushed the hair from her face.

"While I'm up, I want both of my boys with me. Don't make him work right now."

"I don't want him keeping you up with all the noise while he cleans."

"Don't worry. I sleep like the dead."

Her words hit him harder than any blow his dad could deliver. "Mom—"

She chuckled until it turned into a cough.

"See what you went and did, boy?" Dad grabbed her water glass then held it to her lips. It sloshed all over her sheets and nightgown and face before she finally got a sip or two to settle the rasp in her throat.

He dabbed at her face with a dry corner of the quilt

until his father slapped his hand away and grabbed the blanket.

"That's enough," Mom snapped. Her voice sounded as strong as it ever had. Like it used to … before.

Dad lowered the bedspread.

She raised her hand to lay it on his cheek. There was barely a tremor in her fingers. "My darling. I know my illness is hurting you more than it's hurting me."

"Shhh." His father shook his head and placed his hand over hers to hold it in place. "I don't want to talk about this."

"We need to talk about this. It's almost time."

"No."

"Yes."

"NO."

"I'm dying. You know it, I know it. We need to make peace with it. We need to make plans for after."

"Stop."

"And if you love me—"

"What do you mean, if?"

"If you love me, you'll stop acting like a horse's ass and make my last days better, not worse. You'll stop trying to drink yourself into a grave before me. And you'll stop taking out your misery on our son."

"Never doubt my love for you."

"Then never give me reason to. Honor my wishes."

He squeezed her hand, pressed his lips to her palm, then lay it on the bed beside her.

"I love you, you big galoot."

"I love you more." Then Dad left the room.

Mom sighed and seemed to sink into her pillow. "Didn't I tell him I wanted to spend my awake time with both of you?"

"Maybe he went to make coffee and try to sober up."

"I think we both know he went to sulk because he's not getting his way."

"He loves you, Ma."

"He loves both of us."

Taking her hand, he held it gently, then kissed her fingers.

"He loves both of us," she repeated. "You remember how he was. Before I got sick. You two were thick as thieves."

It seemed like forever ago. Maybe a fairy tale about two different men. He didn't recognize those people anymore.

"He just needs to come to terms with this," she yawned. "You'll see." Her eyelids fluttered closed.

"I love you, Mom."

"I lo …" But she was asleep again.

He sat with her a while, again watching her chest rise and fall too slowly, her eyes racing as she lived a life in a dreamworld that her emaciated body could no longer keep up with.

When bearing it became impossible, he got up to clean the floor. It was hard to say how long Mom would be asleep, but he didn't want her to wake to a mess. He was surprised to find the house silent as he walked down the hallway. No sounds of Dad cooking or eating or watching TV. He might have gone to his workshop, which meant he was a danger to himself. Or hunting, which made him a danger to others. Maybe he'd just passed out and was sleeping off his latest bender.

That was the best-case scenario for everybody.

He walked into the kitchen to fetch the broom and dustpan and was surprised to find his father standing at the sink, staring out the window. "I didn't know you were here."

"Where the hell else would I be? It's my home, isn't it?"

"I meant, I thought you'd left."

"You'd like that, wouldn't you?"

"That's not what I said."

"But that's what you meant."

Maybe. Sometimes. Yes. "No."

Dad turned around, his hands behind his back while he leaned against the sink. "You think I don't know what's going on here?"

He scratched his head. "Well, I don't know what's going on, so I guess you're going to have to tell me."

"You're jealous."

"Of what?"

"Not of what, moron. Of who."

"Okay. Of who?"

"Me, asshole."

His eyebrows arched. "I'm jealous of you?"

"'Course you are. It all makes sense now."

"It does?"

Dad went on, gaining speed. "Your girlfriend coming around more and more often, asking for more and more presents, right?"

"They're not *presents*. She just got a new house. I'm helping her decorate it."

"She's *using* you. That's why you're jealous of me. In my relationship, I was the care-*receiver*. But in your relationship, you're the care-*giver*. You're nothing to her. Why, I bet she's not even giving it to you, is she?"

His face flamed. His vision tinged red at the edges. "I'm not going to talk about my sex life with you."

Dad laughed, the sound biting and bitter. "She's not!

You're not her boyfriend. You're her errand boy. A lackey. If she needs to have work done, she calls you. But if she needs to have *work done*" — he winked — "she calls someone who can get the *job done*, if you know what I mean."

"I'm warning you."

"Or are you her cuckold?"

His fists clenched.

"Does she make you watch while she fucks other guys?"

He launched across the room, arms out, head to the side. Perfect form to jam his shoulder into his father's midsection and drive him into next week. If he'd done that drill in football practice once, he'd done it ten thousand times.

Never did it when the opposing team came up with a butcher's knife, though.

If Dad hadn't been drunk, it would have embedded in his liver. Because he was three sheets to the wind, his aim was off and his reflexes were slow. Same couldn't be said for his son's reflexes.

He feinted, dodged. Spun.

The blade sliced through his side, went in about an inch deep. Hurt like hell and caused quite a bit of blood to spill.

But it wasn't fatal.

Continuing his spin until he was out of his dad's reach, he finished the move with the grace of a dancer, then grabbed a dish towel. He pressed it to his side to staunch the bleeding.

His father met his gaze from across the room, murder, hate, jealousy, and spite still flashing in his eyes.

"This isn't what Mom wants."

"Then you shouldn't be trying to take her from me."

"I didn't make her sick. And I'm not trying to take her from you. I don't want to lose her, either."

"I won't lose her. And God help you if I do." Then Dad stormed out of the room.

Chapter Eighteen

CHELSEA, unfortunately, was right. She couldn't sleep. Couldn't rest. Couldn't even sit down. She paced her apartment for about half an hour before finally giving up, getting dressed, then going downstairs to talk to the cops parked outside.

"Detective, you're giving up our position."

"Hate to break it to you, but you're pretty noticeable. Fletcher used to work for the department. He'll be able to spot you a mile away."

"Well, you've blown our cover now, for sure."

"Doesn't matter. You're not staying."

"We have orders—"

"Your orders are to watch me, right?"

They nodded.

"Well, I'm down here talking to you because I'm not staying, either. I need you to drive me to the station. My car's not here."

"Detective—"

"Look, it's not your call. I'm a grown woman who can

make her own decisions. So, either you drive me or I call FASTr."

The officer behind the wheel scowled. "Get in. We'll take you."

"Glad to see you're being agreeable." She walked around to the passenger side then opened the front door. "Get in the back."

He looked up at her. "What?"

"Sorry. One, I have seniority. Two, I don't trust you guys to let me out when we get to the station. Get in the back."

The two officers exchanged looks before the one in the passenger seat climbed out.

"Don't worry," she said. "I'll actually let you out when we get there."

He grimaced but climbed into the back seat. "It's sticky back here. And it smells bad."

"Those were my third and fourth reasons."

It was a short ride to the station, and she was too tense to force small talk. They didn't seem to mind, so she didn't let it bother her. She was barely out of the car when the uni was knocking on his window. Chelsea liberated him with a sigh. "I didn't forget you."

"You going inside now?"

"No. Like I said, I just needed my car."

"You said you needed a ride here because you didn't have a car. Not that you needed to come here because you wanted to take a ride. That's a big difference."

"Semantics."

"We're going to have to call this in."

"Rookie mistake." She shook her head.

"We're not rookies."

"And you took advantage of us."

"I'm just going to my dad's. Relax." She left them

arguing about what to do and crossed the parking lot. It had only been a couple of days since she'd been in her car, but it felt like an eternity. After turning on the engine, she engaged the heated seat, cranked up the temperature, and waited a few seconds for the chill to dissipate.

It was fast to leave the air. She suspected it would take a while before it left her body. Probably because it was soul-deep.

Chelsea pulled out of the parking lot then headed for her dad's apartment. It was also a short drive, so she left the music off to gather her thoughts. Which, she came to realize, was not only pointless but was a horrible idea because it let her thoughts run wild. Every headlight behind her was Fletcher's acolyte running her down. Every shadow along or between the buildings was the Grimm Reaper himself.

By the time she reached her father's place, she had almost talked herself into turning around and going back to the station. It was only stubborn pride that had her getting out of the car. She waved at her protection detail and beckoned them over to her.

It was obvious they weren't thrilled to get out of the car, but she felt better having them physically near.

"Help me out." She started shoving bulk items into their arms. "This way, I only have to make one trip up the stairs."

"He doesn't have an elevator?" the heavier one asked.

"Just come on."

"Yeah. I noticed you took toilet paper and paper towels. You gave me the water."

"She gave me pickles and beans. Who eats this many pickles and beans?"

"I hope they don't plan on eating them together."

"You mean as a couple? Or as a meal?"

"What the hell are you talking about?" he was starting to huff.

"Do you mean you hope the detective doesn't eat the food with her dad? Or do you mean you hope they don't plan on eating pickles and beans together as a meal?"

"Why … would I … hope … the old man … would eat … alone … in an … apocalypse?" He wheezed between words.

"But you don't care if the detective does?"

"Timmons," he growled, "right now … I wouldn't care … if the … fucking apocalypse … happened this instant … and blew us all … to hell … in the process."

"You don't mean that."

"At least … I'd have … water with me … down there."

"We're here," Chelsea said in a chipper voice and knocked softly on the door.

"Whoop-de … fucking … do." He started to cough.

"Dad'll be happy to give you a glass of water in a sec."

"Bottles … right here."

"Those are for an emergency."

He kept coughing.

She rapped softly a second time.

"Maybe you should knock louder."

"I don't want to wake the neighbors."

"As loud as Leith is hacking, you're probably too late."

The door flew open. The room was dark, but there was no mistaking the hall light glinting off the cold steel of a handgun, the barrel aimed at her chest.

The shrink-wrapped packages of veggies and water hit the floor with echoing thuds as the officers drew their own weapons.

Chelsea dropped her own bundles as rushed to push their hands aside. She screamed, "Hold your fire! Hold your fire!"

Dad stepped into the light of the hallway and lowered his firearm. One by one, his neighbors' doors cracked open.

Why people gravitated toward the notification of a potential shooting, Chelsea would never understand, but they always did. She shook her head and started waving people back into their units. "Police. There's no danger here. Nothing to see. Go back into your apartments, folks."

Mutters and murmurs sounded then faded as the doors closed.

"Chelsea, what in the name of God are you doing here at this hour?"

"I couldn't sleep, so I brought you the stuff I bought at the big box store the other day."

He stared at her. Blinked. Rubbed the sleep from the corner of his eye.

When Leith coughed, Chelsea said, "Dad, these officers helped me carry all this stuff upstairs. How about you give them a drink before we send them on their way?"

He pushed open the door as he stepped inside. Didn't say a word, but lights came on.

She was relieved to find the tiny place tidy. It wasn't too long ago that his apartment was a disaster. That *he* was a disaster. But he pulled himself together after the Grimm Reaper case nearly cost him everything. Now, he kept his home as orderly as she kept hers.

Chelsea offered the officers seats, but they declined, Timmons standing in the foyer and Leith leaning against the threshold. She headed to the kitchen, but her father came out, robe billowing behind him, a glass of water in each hand. They each took the beverage with a nod of thanks, but Leith downed his with noticeable desperation, then gasped when he'd drained it dry. At least the coughing, panting, and wheezing had stopped.

"We through here, Detective?" Timmons asked.

"I'm going to visit for a while."

"We'll be in the car, then." He nodded and handed her his half-full glass.

Leith passed her his empty one. "Thanks."

She smiled.

They left, closing the door behind them.

Dad grabbed the pickles and beans, still without uttering a word. She followed him with the water. He carried them into the kitchen and piled them against the far wall behind the table. The cheerful burble of percolating coffee started to rise from the corner of the room. The rich aroma wafted toward her, smoothing some of the tension in the air.

By the time she added the water to the stack and had it tucked neatly out of the way, he'd returned with the paper towels and toilet paper. Somehow he managed to place them on top of the tower without the whole thing tumbling down on him.

"Dad …"

He went to the cupboard for two mugs. Filled them both, then added a splash of cream to hers.

"Dad …"

Still didn't answer her. Just walked into the living room.

She followed, meekly. He was already in his recliner when she took her usual spot on the sofa.

"Dad? I'm not sure why—"

"Of all the stupid, risky, hare-brained, nonsensical, ludicrous, rash, reckless, dangerous—"

"You're just saying the same thing."

"I could have killed you!"

She sunk into her seat. At least she knew why he was angry. As he unloaded, she felt loved. Safe. And for the first time in days, at ease. Her lids drooped a little, and all the stress she'd been holding in her neck and shoulders started to melt away.

"Are you listening to me?"

"Dad, home invaders seldom knock."

"Sometimes they do."

"Hardly ever."

"What's going on, Chels?"

"Just dropping off your stuff while I had the chance." She yawned, and her lids fluttered.

"Why wouldn't you have a chance in the daylight like a normal person?"

Her eyes snapped open. "Dad, when was the last time you watched the news?"

"I don't know. It's been a few days. I had the survivalist meeting. Then we watched the football game. Hockey's been on back-to-back. Had a doctor's appointment this afternoon. Why?"

She propped her elbows on her knees and rested her head in her hands. "Dad, I keep telling you, you have to watch something other than sports. Put the news on for at least the first five minutes so you catch the important stuff."

"What did I miss?"

Chelsea looked up at him. "Fletcher broke out."

The blood drained from his face so what little was left of his golf tan became a faded memory. He slammed the footrest of his recliner down then joined her on the sofa. The cushion sagged under his weight, and she toppled into him. His arm snaked around her shoulder.

She hadn't known she needed her father's embrace, but at that moment, the realization hit her like a wrecking ball. Chelsea nestled into him and started to sob.

He hugged her, rocked her, crooned in her ear.

At some point, it occurred to her he wasn't just humming nonsensical soothing sounds. It was a lullaby.

She pushed away from him then dried her eyes. "What is that?"

"I used to sing that to you when you were young."

"I thought I recognized it. What is it?"

"It's not really anything. I just made it up when you were little."

"It's beautiful."

"It's nonsense."

Chelsea shook her head. "No, Dad. It's beautiful."

"Well, my baby girl was beautiful. Still is. But right now, she's looking a little ragged and needs some sleep. Why don't you go home and get some?"

"It's still early."

He glanced at his wrist where a watch would be if he hadn't already taken it off when he went to bed.

"Let's catch up, Dad. Tell me what you've been up to."

After a deep breath, he said, "I'll make you a deal. You lie here — pillow and blanket — and we'll talk."

"I don't need to lie down."

"Those are my terms. Take off your shoes. Get comfortable. I'll get you a pillow. Grab the throw off the back of the sofa."

Chelsea knew he was manipulating her into staying the night. And she appreciated it. She kicked off her shoes then whipped the afghan off the back of the couch. She was nestled under it before Dad returned and barely had the strength to lift her head for the pillow. But boy, was she glad she did. It was the perfect height so her neck didn't bend in a weird angle, and it wasn't too hard or too soft. It was just right.

The Goldilocks Zone.

Her eyelids snapped open and she started to sit up.

"Lie down, Chelsea."

"Tell me about what you and your prepper buddies talked about at your meeting."

"This week, we covered how to hide the entrances to our bunkers."

"Why would you want to do that? How are you going to find them in an emergency if you're freaking out? How will your family and friends find you?"

"Your bunker needs to be a secret, Chels. That's how you keep people from descending on you. If everyone knows where you are, you can be overrun. And without enough provisions, everyone starves. You don't want that."

"No," she murmured.

"That's why you stock enough for your family. Why you lay boobytraps. Set up your defenses."

"Defenses."

"I'll keep you safe, my beautiful girl." He started singing her lullaby.

"Safe." She drifted to sleep to his soft, baritone voice wrapping her in a blanket of security as warm as the one she'd nestled under.

Chapter Nineteen

Jim GLARED at Chelsea across their desks. "I still can't believe you went out last night."

"Would you get off it? I didn't go out. I went to my dad's."

"In the middle of the night."

"It was barely midnight."

"Timmons and Leith said it was close to one."

"It was the only way I was going to get any sleep. I was worried about his stuff in my car. I didn't even have my car. I was tired of needing rides everywhere. There were a million odds and ends that were driving me nuts. I needed to handle this to check a few things off my list."

"I think you weren't sleeping because this case is getting to you."

Chelsea grabbed her sheaf of papers, then wheeled her chair around their desks until she was beside him. When they were next to each other, she rolled up her pages and smacked him with the makeshift baton.

"Hey! What was that for?'

"For being an A-double-S-hole."

Jim splayed his fingers wide across his chest and gaped at her in mock indignation. "Your father know you use that language?"

She bopped him over the head.

He laughed and raised his arm to fend off further attacks. "Okay. Cut it out."

"I'm serious, McPherson."

"Oooh. Last-naming me. You do mean business."

Chelsea sighed. But she didn't hit him again.

"I'm serious, too, you know."

She put down the pages and looked up at him.

"When I got to your apartment and your detail wasn't there and you weren't there, I freaked. Until I found out where you were and what happened? Until I saw for myself that you were okay? I kind of lost my shit a little. We just talked yesterday about this case eating at our rational selves a bit, then you pulled the rug out from under me."

"I'm sorry. You're right. I shouldn't have disappeared on you like that. I should have at least texted you so you didn't worry."

"You shouldn't have left at all."

"I needed to not be alone at my place last night."

"I'm starting to think you shouldn't be there at all. Maybe you should be in a safe house."

"Don't start with this again."

"Chelsea—"

"No."

"Think about how much better you felt once you were out of there last night."

"I'm not discussing this right again."

"We'll table the discussion. For now. But think about it."

"If I have to, I can stay at my dad's."

"And put him at risk?"

"Fletcher knows who he is and where he lives. He's at risk, anyway."

"Yet you got rest there? Come to think of it, maybe he should be in a safe house, too."

"And what about you? What about your parents? What about Davenport? Where does it end?"

Jim rolled his eyes. "Let's get back to this list of fans. We need to start narrowing down our suspect pool to people who might be the acolyte."

They scanned the list of Grimm Reaper fans the warden provided them, separating them into two groups — the ones Fletcher directly corresponded with and the ones deemed too dangerous to allow them to communicate.

"I don't know which ones to question first," she said. "The ones the warden flagged are scarier, so I could see them being capable of this kind of thing."

"Obviously. He didn't let them through for a reason. But it's hard to be an acolyte if you aren't in touch with the object of your obsession."

She dropped her pages then rubbed her forehead. "Is there any kind of secret communication channel they could use?"

"There's always a way. Spies used to use crossword clues in the newspapers."

Chelsea lowered her hands and stared at him. "You're kidding?"

"Nope." He shook his head. "I saw it on a documentary once."

"Well, that's just wonderful. If you can use something as innocent as a puzzle in a newspaper, you could use anything. I know prisoners aren't allowed on many websites, but they could have messages imbedded on the ones they can go on."

"We can have Devani look through Fletcher's search history."

"Does the prison even track which inmate looks at which site? It's not like they have their own laptops."

"I'm sure they have their own logins to keep track of who visits which sites."

"We need to talk to the guards again. They might be able to share some insights on who Fletcher corresponded with." She stood then started wheeling her chair back to her desk. "Maybe he talked about one of them more than the others. Maybe one of them visited."

"We have the visitor logs."

"I'll cross-reference them as we drive out there. Besides, we only talked to one shift of guards so far. We have two more shifts to meet with."

"Yeah, but the same guards are on duty now as the last time we were there." He stood, anyway.

"Come on. I'll buy you breakfast on the way."

"You brought in pastries the other day."

"You always buy. I'm sure I owe you dozens of times over."

Jim was sure she was keeping an exact count and decided not to push her on it. Unlike her, he hadn't slept well again last night and needed a stronger cup of coffee than the station offered. So, he took her up on her offer. The guards and warden were unlikely to shed any new light on the situation, but he and Chelsea were out of leads.

Other than Oliver Thompson, who Jim was perfectly happy to let sit on ice for a few more hours while they rode up to the state penitentiary. He needed to get his partner out of there before she remembered him, so he grabbed his jacket. "Let's go."

The coffee and breakfast sandwiches were just what he needed to perk him up. Made the ride pass a lot faster, too. They reached Black Meadow in record time. Warden Perry, supposedly tied up in a meeting, sent his regards with a not-so-subtle admonishment that more notice is necessary if they planned on making any future visits. He did, however, instruct his charming secretary to allow them to speak to the guards again.

She showed them to the same visiting room as before.

Jim smiled at her. "You think you can—"

But Mildred was already in the hall. She closed the door on him.

"What is her problem?"

"She really doesn't like you."

"She doesn't seem too fond of you, either."

Chelsea slipped into one of the chairs at a round table. "I assume she's sending the guards down to us. Or does she expect us to call them?" She glanced at the phone on the wall by the door on the other side of the room. The guards had used it the last time they were there.

Before he had to guess whether the warden's assistant was playing control freak or tormentor, the big, hyper-vigilant guard they'd spoken to the first time they'd conducted interviews knocked on the door then stepped inside. "I was told you wanted to see me."

"Yes." Chelsea smiled at him. "Milo, right?"

"Yes, ma'am. Milo Hartman."

"Please, have a seat."

He sat across from her.

Jim pulled out the chair beside her then folded himself into it. "And you regularly work with Ross Bradley?"

Hartman scowled. "Regularly. Yes, sir. But he hasn't been in for the last two days."

"Come again?" Jim said.

"Right after the two of you left, he came down with a sudden stomach bug. Hasn't been back. I've been breaking in a new guy the last two days. Probably shouldn't leave him alone too long, truth be told." He glanced over his shoulder.

"You're telling me that right after a serial killer engineered a breakout, one of your guards has been absent?" Chelsea asked.

"Doesn't sit right with you, either, huh? Funny, it doesn't seem to bother Warden Perry."

She leaned forward. "Do you have proof that Bradley had anything to do with Fletcher escaping? Or that the warden knew anything about it?"

"All I know is what I see and hear. I can put the pieces of the puzzle together in my head and in my gut, but I don't have any tangible proof."

"Well, what are your head and gut telling you?" Chelsea asked.

Jim kicked her under the table. "What have you seen and heard?"

Hartman stared hard at him for a pregnant moment. "I checked up on you two after you left the last time. You put Fletcher away. But there's a cloud over your head. A stain on your record."

"He's innocent," Chelsea said. "IA didn't—"

Jim held up his hand. "I can speak for myself, Sullivan."

"Then why don't you?" Hartman asked.

"Because I don't owe you an explanation. I'm a detective looking for an escaped felon. You're a guard who works at the super-max he escaped from. If you're an honest man who's good at his job, I'd think you'd want to help me do mine. And that's all that should matter."

"Mr. Hartman—"

"It's all right, Detective," Hartman said to Chelsea, though his gaze was still locked on Jim's. "I'll tell you what I've seen. What I suspect."

"I … okay." She sighed. "Go ahead."

"Two years ago, Warden Perry cut our wages. Again. Said all the money in the budget had to go toward facility improvements and there was no money left for manpower. But he implied — though I'm sure if he were asked about it, he'd insist anyone who got this message merely wrongfully inferred it — we had other means available to us to make money."

Jim sat back and let his partner take the lead. Hartman clearly didn't trust him, so this would have to be Chelsea's rodeo.

"Such as?" she prompted.

"Warden Perry told us a story about a prison he'd read about where guards told inmates to have their families deposit money into their accounts. Then, when they went to the commissary, instead of buying gum or deodorant or whatnot, they bought special favors from the guards."

"How would that even work? Walk into the store and spend a hundred bucks on protection from a beating in the yard?"

"No. The commissary isn't even involved. It funnels through the accountant because he has to fix the books. My guess is money never even shows up in the inmates' accounts. Probably goes straight to the guards who took the warden's incentive plan."

"He couldn't possibly have been serious."

"Linderman got a new Tesla a month after that budget speech. Carmichael paid cash for his daughter's wedding in Hawaii. Flew his whole family there, the groom's whole family, and the bridal party. Bradley's been talking about a beach house. When you put a little heat on us the other day, he disappeared. Why? If the man wasn't guilty, he wouldn't have to run. And if he didn't have a beach house in St. Croix to run to, you'd probably be able to track him down pretty easily and ask him about it. But I'm willing to bet he's not recovering from this horrible stomach bug at his apartment down the highway."

"You really think Warden Perry started all this?"

"Detective, it wouldn't surprise me if the warden insisted on taking a cut of every transaction that went through here. I'm sure he and the bookkeeper make more money than the guards do."

"What makes you think that?"

"Because what incentive would they have to run the scheme otherwise?"

"Oh." She sat back in her seat.

Jim had to admit, that's exactly what he was thinking.

Hartman stood. "I really need to get back to the new guy. There's no telling what the weeds will do to him if he's on his own for too long."

"Weeds?"

"Trouble makers. The ones who keep coming back. Or the ones we kill."

"Charming," Jim muttered.

"Wait." It was Chelsea's turn to kick him under the table. "We actually came here to ask you about Fletcher's fans." She offered Hartman the list names they'd brought with them.

"What about them?" He didn't take the pages.

"We need a jumping off point. I don't know if you've seen the news, but there's been a murder. The victim was staged to look like a Grimm Reaper victim, but we think it was a copycat killing. We're looking for an acolyte. The odds are in our favor that it's someone on this list."

"I don't need your list for that. I'd look at three people. Phillip Boundy. Warden granted him visitor's rights within the first month of Fletcher's incarceration."

"Why?"

"I can only think of one reason." He rubbed his fingers together to indicate money had been exchanged. "Carl Jenkins. His first letter arrived before Fletcher did. They kept up a constant stream of communication, and the warden never censored a single word of either of their letters. Before you ask why, again, I'm assuming because he was paid not to. And the third guy would be Michael Dupree."

"Why him?" she asked.

"Just a gut feeling. And I always trust my gut. Now, if you'll excuse me, I have a job to do."

"Mind looking at the list, anyway?" Jim asked.

Hartman's face darkened, but he took the papers. After giving them a cursory glance, he handed them back to Chelsea. "My opinion hasn't changed."

"Thank you, Mr. Hartman." She shook his hand.

Jim let him leave without extending him the same courtesy. He scanned the list of fans the warden had provided them. "None of these people are names Perry highlighted as a high threat."

"It's not really Warden Perry's job to make that assessment, though, is it?"

"He's in a position to know."

"I think the guards are in a better position to know." She stepped closer and dropped her voice. "Particularly if the warden was facilitating visitations between convicted serial killers and mentally compromised acolytes for money."

"We have the visitor logs back at the station. We can see how often those men met with Fletcher."

"Unless that's been tampered with, too."

"The accountant doesn't have access to the visitor logs. That would bring a bigger ring of people into the circle. All security personnel would be involved. They'd have to wipe recordings. I think that's too big a thing to fudge."

"I'm not so sure."

"We have to at least look."

"What about the letters Jenkins wrote?"

"We'll have to see if any of those are in the stuff your boy Danny sent us. As for the gut feeling about Dupree, we'll just have to investigate him old school." He walked to the door. "Let's get out of here."

"Aren't we going to interview anyone else?"

"Who? Hartman's partner is new. The doctor's still MIA. The warden won't see us. His secretary's not talking. I want to get back and go through the logs. And we still need to talk to Thompson."

"Oh! I forgot all about him."

"Wish I could."

Chapter Twenty

BACK AT THE STATION, Chelsea cringed in the corner of the captain's office while Jim paced back and forth, swearing a blue streak.

"I understand how you feel," Davenport said. "Now put yourself in my position. He didn't technically break any laws. We held him for twenty-four hours on suspicion of nothing. His union rep wanted you suspended. Your union rep wanted him suspended."

"*My* union rep? Was there a hearing I wasn't aware of? And what were the charges? I'll kill that son of a bitch."

Davenport shoved a sheet of blank paper through a shredder beside his desk before Jim finished his sentence. "Sorry. Didn't hear that last part. No need to repeat yourself. Listen, this is a tricky situation. You more than anyone under this roof should know that."

"The difference is, I was innocent."

"And Thompson claims he is, too."

"Key word there being *claims*."

"Jim." Davenport rested his elbows on his desk and rubbed the bridge of his nose. "If Thompson is guilty—"

"If?"

"If he's guilty, you'll find the evidence. If he's not, we can't tank his reputation. You know how difficult it is to move on from a false accusation like that."

"But this isn't false!"

"Damn it, Jim. Stop. Prove it or drop it. What you *think* isn't enough."

"He ran from his sister's house."

"To give her time to get away."

"That's obstruction of justice, sir," Chelsea spoke up. She couldn't let him argue the point alone any longer. Maybe she didn't believe as ardently as he did, but in this one point, the fact was the fact.

"Thank you." Jim's look and tone suggested he was glad she'd finally spoken but he'd wished it was more. And sooner.

The captain picked up a pen. "Something he'd probably only get a fine for. If his attorney didn't get it thrown out."

"A good attorney would make sure he got jail time for it," Jim grumbled.

He threw the pen onto his blotter. "The kid was protecting his sister."

"Are you seriously defending him? He's a *cop*. He should have arrested her."

"He's also a brother. He's between a rock and a hard place on this one."

"There's no gray here, sir. There's black or white. He chose black."

Davenport leaned so far back in his seat, it squeaked. Chelsea feared the hinges were going to give. He sighed and shook his head. "Jim, you're a brilliant detective who can see connections in cases that Sherlock himself would miss. But sometimes, you're as blind as my Aunt Tilly."

"She visually impaired, sir?" Chelsea asked.

"Couldn't see a klieg light at midnight."

"Sullivan saw it, too. He broke the law."

"I'm not saying he didn't. But you're not seeing how similar the boy is to you."

Jim sputtered.

"Remember, you cut Dom more slack than you should have because you loved him like a brother."

"Well …"

"Yeah. *Well*. Nell is his sister. That's not *like* family. That *is* family. He's trying to help her and still do what's right."

"There's a serial killer out there. And now a copycat, too."

"Thompson's on leave," Davenport said. "And he'll eventually answer for what he's done. In the meantime, maybe he'll actually be more use to you out there. Maybe he can lead you to his sister. Maybe he can help set all this to rest and some good can come out of all this."

"Where'd you get your rose-colored glasses? I could use a pair." Jim stormed out of his office.

"Sorry, sir. He's just on edge."

"Aren't we all? What about you, Sullivan? How are you holding up?"

She shrugged. "Better than Jim, at the moment."

"You need anything?"

"I need Fletcher behind bars. And the copycat, too."

"Then go get 'em."

"Yes, sir." She walked out to the bullpen, where she found Jim behind his chair, pacing. Again. "You're going to wear a hole in the floor."

"I thought I'd be interviewing Thompson right now, so I'm trying to regroup."

"Well, we have three suspects on our potential acolyte

list to run down. We still haven't found Gwendolyn Cole. We have more information about finances at Black Meadow to give the techs. Maybe they'll be able to figure out where the money Shane Warren's family deposited went now that we suspect the warden and the accountant are keeping a second set of books."

"It doesn't feel like much."

"It's better than the nothing we had earlier. Which name do you want?"

"I'll take Boundy."

"I'll start looking through the letters Danny sent over. Maybe there's something there from Carl Jenkins that will spark a lead."

Danny had sent them what the warden had given him and his partner, which included some of Fletcher's correspondences. She suspected this wasn't nearly all of it, and for that, she was glad. What little she read from Jenkins was more than enough.

DEAREST DOCTOR GRIMM,

I have been a fan of yours since the very first picture was published. Your artistry is unrivaled, perhaps better than the work of even your namesakes themselves.

No, not perhaps. Of course it's better. Forgive me, Pater.

PATER? Seriously?

DEAREST DOCTOR GRIMM,

I've scoured every news source I can find, printed every picture in the highest resolution. Your forethought, your planning, your creative genius ... it's sheer poetry. My favorite prints I've hung in gilded frames, but the rest I've turned into a giant collage so that one entire wall of my bedroom is papered with your brilliance.

HE WALLPAPERED his bedroom with crime scene photos?

DEAREST GRIMMPATER,

GRIMMPATER?

I JUST RECEIVED *your last letter, and I can't stop crying. I've read it at least fifty times. Thank you. I can't wait.*

"HEY, Jim? I might have something here."

"What's that?"

"Fletcher wrote this weirdo back."

"What'd he say?"

"Perry didn't send outgoing copies. If he if even made any. But Jenkins referenced the letter."

"Okay. What did he say?"

She read him the last letter.

"GrimmPater?"

"I'm guessing it's a riff on 'grandfather.' Let's skip past that disturbing reference and look at the last sentence. He said he can't wait."

"Wait for what?"

"That's what I'd like to know. What if they were planning on meeting?"

"I don't know, Chels. It could be anything."

"You don't think that's odd?"

"I think it's all odd. Let me see his letters."

She passed the pages over. While he read them, she started scanning a few other letters from other correspondents.

"I agree with you that this guy's mind is a few eggs short of a dozen."

"Are you talking about the 'this is your brain on drugs' commercials? Because those are the only eggs I think are in his head."

"The point is, while this is a special brand of disturbing, I don't think this is our guy. You said yourself, Fletcher was meticulous. This guy appreciates that about him, right?"

"Yeah. He practically worships him for it."

"The crime scene is too sloppy. This guy would know better. If it makes you feel better, we can keep him in the running, but my gut tells me he's not our guy."

"Milo Hartman did tell us to trust our guts."

He scoffed.

"Speaking of Hartman's gut, did you happen to look at anything about the third guy? Michael Dupree?"

"Not intentionally. I've been running down everything I could find on Phillip Boundy."

"What's that mean?"

"There's some overlap. Dupree visited Fletcher in Black Meadow once. Once that I saw, anyway. Same day and time as Boundy's first visit."

"Warden Perry let Fletcher have two visitors at the same time? Strangers, no less?"

Jim rubbed his fingers and thumb together like Milo Hartman did to signify money had been exchanged.

"But Dupree never came back?"

"Not that I've seen. Yet."

"Well, what's that about?"

"I don't have 'proof'" — he made air quotes — "but I can tell you what my gut says."

"That seems to be the order of the day."

"Jenkins isn't our guy. Boundy is. More to the point, Fletcher tested him, and he had him use Dupree somehow."

"Dupree isn't his type."

"Then why'd he disappear?"

"We don't know he disappeared. He just didn't return to Black Meadow. And we don't even know that. Maybe he did and we just haven't found record of it yet. Let's pay him a visit."

"If we can find him." Jim stood and stretched. "But I really want to talk to Boundy."

"I know. Your gut's telling you it's him."

"Isn't yours?"

She sighed. "Honestly? Yes. But I don't want to admit it."

"Why not? It's good that we're on the same page."

"Because we don't have any *evidence*."

"We'll get it. Let's go." She stood and grabbed her jacket.

Davenport exited his office. "Hang on, you two."

"Holy crap on a cracker," Chelsea mumbled. "Now what?"

The captain shook his head. "Hate to do it to you, but I've got more bad news. Another body's been found."

"Another staged body?" Jim asked.

He nodded. "Looks like it's your guy. I'll text you the address. Scuttlebutt is it's an ugly one."

"No." Chelsea shook her head. "This is too fast. There's no cooling off period. It's more like a spree killing than a serial killer."

"Press is going to pin this on Fletcher," Davenport said. "They'll say he's making up for lost time."

"But it's not him." She pulled on her jacket.

"And when you find the real killer, you can tell them the real story."

"I had enough press with Fletcher the last time. You can do it."

"We'll worry about the semantics later," the captain said. "You need to get this guy first."

"We're on our way." Jim tugged her arm until she started walking.

Out in the car, he didn't even suggest one of his many playlists. Instead, he put on a local AM station. She wasn't sure what the regularly scheduled programming was, but it wasn't on. A special news broadcast was airing, talking about the return of the Grimm Reaper.

"In the two days since Scott Fletcher engineered his escape from Black Meadow, the state police have been spearheading efforts to locate him. Local police forces and county sheriffs' departments across the state as well as in the tri-state area have been mobilized. The FBI is consulting. Still, it seems authorities are no closer to finding the Grimm Reaper. Yesterday, the body of a young lady dressed like Ariel, the Little Mermaid, was found in a drainage culvert on the side of a road near Twisted Rill. Authorities have not yet released the identity of his first victim. And he's already struck again. Today, the body of a young woman dressed like Cinderella has been found at the entrance to Spruce Bluffs Park. Police are just now arriving at the scene, so no further details are available at this time. If you have any information—"

He turned off the radio. "That's just great. Traffic will be terrible. Gawkers will be all over the place, probably trampling evidence."

"Sounds like officers are already there, cordoning off the area."

"Not the point."

"I know."

"We could have done without the press."

"I know."

"Well, at least we know what we're walking into," he said.

"We do?"

"Davenport told us it's a real mess. The news told us the girl is dressed like Cinderella. That's more than we usually know."

"Yeah. You're right. We don't usually this much info upfront. Lucky us."

Chapter Twenty-One

"Okay." Jim stared down at their latest victim. "I feel like I was lied to."

"How's that?" Chelsea asked.

"The captain and the news reporter lulled me into a false sense of preparedness. I thought I knew what to expect. I thought I was ready for this shit."

"So did I." Her voice was tinny.

"I wasn't prepared for this."

She sighed. "Yeah. I wasn't, either."

Davenport wasn't wrong — "gruesome" was the kindest way to describe it. And the news had some of the details right. The girl was, in fact, dressed the way most people pictured the Cinderella story. So, in that loosest of definitions, Jim had been prepared for the scene he'd come to.

But only in that loosest of definitions.

The hikers' entrance to Spruce Bluffs Park was marked by three stone slabs forming a natural staircase about a yard wide. Rangers had framed them with sturdy wooden railings, the top support posts stretching about twelve feet high so a sign could span between them with the nature reserve's name engraved on it. A tall spruce tree stood on either side like stately, organic columns.

That's where the serenity ended.

The victim had been dressed in a Cinderella costume — it was a popular seller at any number of Halloween costume stores. One foot wore the "glass" slipper, as expected. But instead of the other foot being bare, it had been severed above the ankle. The shoe was found in a small puddle of blood on the bottom step, but the appendage was missing.

A streak of red led up the stone stairs to a pool of crimson. Above it, Cinderella hung from the sign, bolted into the wood by her remaining ankle on the side post and two wrists in the cross-support. Only the limb with the severed foot dangled so the blood was free to fall, but trickles from her other wounds added to the carnage below her.

None so much as from her neck wound, though, as she'd been decapitated. Her head had replaced with a pumpkin — no, a jack-o'-lantern, carved with the most hideous grin Jim had ever seen. The light flickering inside its macabre smile brought the laughter to life, and he swore he could hear it cackling.

Fuck. He actually could hear maniacal glee coming from somewhere.

Jim looked around for the source of the noise. "You hear that?"

"The sound of my last nerve fraying? I thought only I could hear it."

"No. Listen. You hear someone laughing?"

"How could anyone laugh at something this vile?"

"Someone did something this vile. There's always someone who gets their kicks from this shit. Listen."

Chelsea cocked her head to the side. A moment later, her eyes widened and she gasped. "You're right!"

"Where's it coming from?"

"I don't know."

They started walking the scene, being careful of where they stepped.

Her phone dinged. She looked at the screen.

"Well?" Jim asked.

"Danny. They're two hours away, at least. They got a lead on Fletcher's whereabouts and ran it down, but it turned out to be a dead end."

"Funny he didn't call us to be part of the takedown, if it had been credible."

"Don't start." She texted him back.

"But you're telling him what's going on here."

"I'm not revealing state secrets."

"This isn't his case, you know."

"I know." She hit send, then pocketed her phone.

Jim tried to put it out of his mind and focused on the laughing. He could hear it louder now. One mobile crime unit tech kept batting him away every time he walked closer to the body because he was in her way. But he was certain that was where it was coming from. So he walked around the other side, into the woods to come around behind her.

It was still early in the evidence-gathering process, and despite a perimeter having been set up all around the body, no one had actually looked behind her other than the initial cursory sweep for the perpetrator. Lights hadn't even been hauled back there yet, so Jim took a flashlight from his pocket of his jacket then shone the beam on the ground around him. As soon as he illuminated the path, he swore.

The victim's head was back there, hitched to a litter of

mice that didn't have a prayer in the world of dragging it anywhere.

So, they'd begun eating it where it lay.

"Hey!" he yelled. "I need techs back here. The ones that work with animals. NOW!" He took a few pictures with his cellphone then turned his flashlight back on the victim's head.

Chelsea was the first person who joined him. "What's going on?"

"Look." He pointed at where his flashlight was shining.

"Oh, God." She covered her mouth with the back of her hand.

Two more MCU techs came around the corner. One carried a cage. The other carried a large kit of some kind.

Jim didn't ask what was in it. He didn't want to know.

The one with the kit said, "What'd you find?"

"Mice. They might be eating evidence."

"Thanks," the one with the cage said. "We'll take it from here if you want to go."

"Oh, I very much do." Chelsea headed toward the front of the crime scene.

"Hargrove!" the tech yelled. "We could use some light back here!"

Jim followed her, passing who he assumed was Hargrove on the way.

The late hour had made the temperature drop considerably, so he pulled a ski cap from his pocket then tugged it down over his ears. Back in the chaos of the primary crime scene, he asked his partner, "You really find this preferable to what was back there?"

She shrugged and wrapped the scarf that had been a fashion accessory around her neck. "It's the eyes. It's always the eyes. This" — she gestured to the macabre crucifixion — "is horrific and grisly and sickening. But I can also detach from it because there's no face to associate with it. When I try to sleep at night, this isn't what will keep me awake. But that back there? That will. Those lifeless eyes will haunt me."

It all haunted him. At least until he put away the sadists responsible.

And sometimes even after.

"Let's find that laugh."

The tech who had been shooing him away was one of the ones who had gone to deal with the head and the mice, so the space under the body was clear. He climbed the stairs, careful to avoid the blood collecting beneath her, and looked up. "Are you thinking what I'm thinking?"

"I hope not."

"You know that's where it is."

She blanched and turned away.

Jim jogged down the steps then over to the nearest MCU tech. "Excuse me."

"Yeah?" But she didn't stand up or even turn around. She just continued working on the severed foot and shoe.

"Who's in charge here?"

"Why?"

"I need a ladder."

"What for?"

"I need to take down the pumpkin."

That got her attention. She stopped what she was doing, stood, then turned to face him. "Detective McPherson, right?"

"Yeah. You are?"

"Too busy to take down the pumpkin right now. It'll probably be another hour."

"Look, I don't want to tell you how to do your job, but …"

"Then don't."

"There's a phone or recording device in that jack-o'-lantern. My partner and I need it as soon as possible. If the killer's trying to communicate with us—"

"Why didn't you just say so? You don't have to bark orders at me. A simple dialogue is all that's necessary. Now that I understand what's at stake, I can shift priorities."

"*You* can?"

"Yes. To answer your earlier question, I'm the forensic investigator in charge here. Fiona Abbott." She started to hold out her hand, noted the blood on her glove, then lowered her arm and shrugged. "So, I'll retrieve the pumpkin. And whatever's inside it for you. But we need to catalogue everything."

"We're in a hurry."

"I'm trying to collect evidence so you can solve this murder."

"And we're trying to catch the killer."

"Without this evidence, even if you catch him, he'll go free. So, let's do this right. I'll be as quick as I can."

Fiona was fast but methodical, issuing orders to the techs on the scene. Someone brought her a ladder while she took a bag and a camera from her kit. Then she lithely began her climb until she was within easy reach of the pumpkin. As she began taking pictures, she called down, "You were right. This is where the device is. I can hear it."

After she'd completed her photo documentary, she passed the camera down to one of the technicians. Then she reached for the jack-o'-lantern. But it didn't move. She leaned over to peer through its grotesque smile.

"What?" Jim called up to her.

She shook her head. "The killer made sure it wouldn't fall off."

"How?" Chelsea asked.

"By impaling it on a stake."

"But that means …" He didn't finish the thought.

"That's right." Fiona tugged until it finally came off the body with a squelching sound. The ladder rocked, and she lost her balance.

A tech steadied the ladder, but too late. Her grip gave out, and she fell.

Jim rushed forward, arms extended. He caught her before she hit the ground.

The pumpkin wasn't as lucky. It landed on the stone slab with a hollow-sounding thud before shattering into chunks of orange gourd and stringy guts.

The laughter stopped.

"I'm so sorry," Fiona whispered. "It was stuck on the stake, and I couldn't get it off without yanking on it."

"It's okay," Jim said, mostly meaning it. "Are you hurt?"

"Just my pride. Are you all right?"

"Me? I'm fine. Why?"

"Because you just caught dead weight hurtling from twelve feet in the air."

"You weren't hurtling. And you were only about ten feet up."

"Maybe you should put me down now."

"Oh." He set her down and gave a soft chuckle. "See? You're so light, I hardly noticed I was holding you."

Chelsea rolled her eyes. "Are you sure you're okay?"

"I'm fine. Embarrassed. I've never ruined evidence before."

"We still have the phone," Jim said.

"But it stopped laughing."

"True," Chelsea said, "but at least now we know it wasn't a recording. It was a live connection. We can try to call back."

"If it even works," Fiona said.

"If it doesn't, we can have someone trace the call," Jim said. "The big takeaway is the number. It's a lead."

Chelsea glanced up at their Cinderella. "That poor girl. How far down do you think that stake goes?"

"Don't think about it." Fiona held her hand up to block Chelsea's vision. "Worry about the phone. That's a better lead. When my techs have something, we'll send you a report."

"Maybe you're right."

The phone rang, making them all jump.

"I guess it still works," Jim said.

"You think he's watching us?" Chelsea scanned the crowd.

They looked right back. More than one recognized her and Jim. People started pointing, and a buzz rolled through them. Camera started flashing like fireflies, and news reporters had their mics out, their professional camera operators zeroing in on the two detectives.

Jim tried to shield his partner, recognizing the early signs of panic — rapid breaths, wide eyes, trembling fingers — and hoped she'd keep focused on the case just a little while longer.

"Or he just noticed the line went dead and tried calling back," Fiona answered.

"Could have done with a better choice of words," Jim said.

Chelsea pushed him. "Answer it before he hangs up!"

She was losing it. But one problem at a time. He took another step, retrieved the phone from the detritus of jack-o'-lantern remnants, then pressed the green button to answer the call. He used the speakerphone so Chelsea and Fiona could hear. "Yeah."

More deranged laughter sounded through the speaker.

Jim was just about to end the call when the cackling abruptly stopped.

"Ah ah ah. You don't want to do that, Detective."

Chelsea looked at him, wide-eyed, and whispered, "He's watching us."

"Where are you?" He looked at all of the onlookers behind the police tape. There were dozens. Maybe hundreds. Jim turned his back to them and mouthed to Fiona, "Take pictures of the crowd. Be discreet. And fast." Then he started to walk toward them.

"No, Jim. Stay right there."

He paused. "First name basis, huh? Maybe you should introduce yourself."

The man laughed again, the same maniacal glee tinny and harsh coming through the phone's speaker.

Jim headed for the crowd again, his partner at his side.

The laughter stopped. "No. You and Chelsea need to stay where you are."

He didn't stop. Didn't even slow down. "And why is that?"

"So no one else dies tonight."

Chelsea quit walking. She grabbed his arm to stop him, then snatched the phone from his hand. "What do you mean?"

"I have a little insurance policy inside Ella."

Jim's blood ran cold. "What do you want?"

"I want you to tell the press that I'm to go free. Have them run the story so everyone stops looking for me. Then have the DA draw up the paperwork."

"I don't understand," Jim said. "Why would you go to all this trouble for someone else's benefit?"

"What do you mean?"

"If you're going to stage such elaborate crimes, why not take credit for them yourself? Phil."

There was silence on the other end of the line for a pregnant moment. Then he said, "I thought you wanted an introduction."

"I feel like we've already met. And I don't really like what I've seen so far."

"You're going to regret this."

The line went dead.

"You shouldn't have antagonized him."

He glanced at the phone then up at Cinderella. "Inside … Take out the battery. Now!"

Chelsea started fumbling with the phone.

Jim started running toward the steps. "Get away from the body! Get away from—"

Then it exploded.

Chapter Twenty-Two

CHELSEA WAS DIMLY aware of activity all around her, but she was in a tunnel. A vacuum. A nightmare she'd do anything to wake from. Her hearing was nothing but a faint ringing tinged with a distant hum. Her vision was dimming, nearly black, with auroras and halos winking in her periphery.

"Chels."

Someone called her name. Who? Why?

The voice was familiar. Male. One she wanted to gravitate toward. One she trusted.

But she heard tension in his tone. Stress. Maybe even fear.

She didn't want to gravitate toward that.

"Chelsea."

She reached out, past it, toward the warm glow of flashing lights and the welcoming hum of conversation.

But the glow wasn't warm. It was harsh. And the conversational hum wasn't welcoming but accusing.

Chelsea recoiled from it.

"Sullivan."

Jim.

She went toward his voice, toward him. Rubbed her ears until she could hear properly, then the sound was too loud. Blinked a few times until her vision cleared.

It all came rushing back. The copycat. The crucifixion. The explosion.

Chelsea covered her mouth and surveyed the scene with wide eyes. Though her instincts told her to get moving, her feet seemed fused to the ground. She wasn't sure how long she'd been stunned — it had felt like minutes had passed, but as she took a quick assessment, she thought it was probably only a second or two. Some of the crime scene technicians were still on the ground, though everyone seemed to be moving, so that was a good sign.

But their victim? She'd been destroyed. All that remained of her after the bomb were the three appendages that had been nailed to the park sign. It had been bad enough when they had to tell someone's parents their daughter had been killed and her head and foot had been severed. Chelsea couldn't even imagine the conversation this time. Let alone the pain they would endure when all they'd have left to bury would be a head, two hands, and a foot. To her knowledge, the original severed foot hadn't been found yet. This would certainly make everything more difficult.

She covered her mouth, sickened at the thought, and was surprised to find the phone still in her hand. Her fingers trembled, and she nearly dropped it.

Thank God she'd been looking down when the bomb went off. She couldn't imagine the horror of watching it detonate, watching the body …

It was bad enough thinking this might be her fault.

Could Boundy have triggered the bomb so quickly on that device after they'd ended the call? She didn't know if he'd had enough time. She'd immediately turned the phone over to try to remove the battery, so she didn't see if the screen had lit up or anything. She only knew she hadn't succeeded in getting the cover off the back, let alone taking the battery out.

But maybe it wasn't her fault. He probably had another triggering mechanism, anyway. She didn't think this phone had received a call before the explosion. While he hadn't staged the scene well enough to convince them he was the Grimm Reaper, he'd certainly made careful plans of his own. He'd planted the cellphone in the jack-o'-lantern with the open connection and stayed within viewing distance so he knew when to get their attention. When the phone fell and the call disconnected, he was prepared to call back. And when he didn't like the direction the discussion took, he had a contingency in place.

So, maybe her slow reaction wasn't to blame.

Like it mattered at this point.

She swallowed the saliva pooling in her mouth, took a deep breath, and prayed she didn't embarrass herself by vomiting or collapsing or descending into shrieking madness in the middle of the crime scene.

"Sullivan? Sullivan!" Jim waved at her from the clearing. His feet, too, seemed rooted to the spot.

Then she realized why.

He couldn't move because he was covered in evidence.

Oh, my God. Oh, my God. Oh, my—

Her brain finally managed to click her body into gear, and she burst into a run. She got to Jim in ten strides then reached toward him.

He cried, "No!"

She snatched her hand back.

Jim's jacket, pants, face, and hat were splattered with bits of blood and bone.

"Oh, my God." This time she turned and gagged.

"Don't!" he said. "You'll contaminate the scene!"

"Jim, you're—"

"I know. Trust me, I *know*. I need you to reach in my front right pocket for my car keys."

"It's your pocket. You get them."

"My hand is covered in … it's covered. I don't want to make Fiona's job harder. I need you to get my keys, go to my car, and get the spare set of clothes from the bag in my trunk."

"Can't Fiona get them?"

"She's over there checking on all her people."

Chelsea sighed. Swallowed. Breathed. Again. "Fine. Just … wait a second." She took a plastic bag from her pocket, put the cellphone in it, then placed it on the ground by Jim's feet.

As she was about to reach into his pocket, he said, "You better get another evidence bag ready."

"What for?"

"Your gloves."

"Mine? Why?"

"You're going to end up with … material on your gloves after you touch my clothes that Fiona will need to collect."

She took another bag from her pocket then opened it, ready to collect her tainted gloves. Touching as little of Jim's clothing as she could, she lifted his shirt with one hand. Two fingers, actually.

It's just paint. Just paint. Nothing but paint.

It's not paint. Not paint. That's blood. This is blood. This was a girl not long ago. A flesh-and-blood girl that isn't a flesh-and-blood anything anymore. She's barely blood anymore.

Chelsea tried to suppress a squeamish whine, but an unrecognizable noise escaped her.

"You're doing great, Chels."

"How are you doing it?" she whispered.

"I don't really have a choice, do I?"

She didn't, either. It was her job. Even if it wasn't, Jim needed help, and she couldn't leave him like this. Chelsea took a deep breath, fished in his front pocket, and retrieved his keys.

Then she was stymied. She didn't have enough hands to hold his keys and remove her dirty gloves to the evidence bag.

"Abbott!" Jim called.

Fiona looked up from the technician she was attending, frowned, said something to another technician assisting her, then hurried over. "You can't move."

"I'm not."

"I need all your clothes."

"I know."

She looked at Chelsea. "Do you have any on you?"

"Clothes?"

"Any of the victim's DNA?"

"Oh. Just on my gloves."

"Are you sure?"

"Yeah. I was down there." She pointed.

"How'd you get it on your gloves, then?"

"I reached into his pocket for his keys."

"Why on earth would—"

"I told her to. She has an evidence bag ready for her gloves but doesn't want to contaminate anything. Take the keys. She'll put the gloves in the bag. Then she can go to my car for my change of clothes. I'll give you all this stuff so you can process it, but it's freezing out, so I don't want to strip to my boxers until I have something to change into.

Don't suppose you have a privacy curtain you can put up? There's a hell of a lot of press here."

Fiona already had the keys. Chelsea was carefully putting the gloves into the evidence bag while the crime scene investigator micromanaged her actions. "Sorry, Jim. We had been putting one up because of the media, but the explosion destroyed it. I don't have another."

"Perfect. Can't wait to see this all over the evening news."

Chelsea hurried down to his vehicle. His trunk didn't have much in it. Just an emergency kit, a duffel bag, and a snow scraper. After grabbing the bag, she started to close the trunk but an idea made her stop. She opened the emergency case and quickly rooted around in it until she found what she was looking for.

Honestly, the man might be a police detective, but his life's motto was straight from the Boy Scouts' handbook because he was always prepared for everything. She grabbed the tarp from the kit, closed the trunk, then hurried back up the gentle slope. Holding up the bag, she asked, "Where can I put this?"

Fiona pointed behind Jim. "Here. The ground is clear in back of him."

He turned around as she set down the bag.

Chelsea showed them the tarp. "I found this in the emergency kit. It's not as big as the curtains you erect for privacy, but we could hold it up for him. It might help protect his modesty."

"I'm not modest."

"You want to be an underwear model now?"

"No. But I'm not *modest*."

"Are we seriously going to argue over word choice right now?"

"I'm not arguing. I'm just saying it implies embarrassment or shyness. I'm neither."

"You look like the sequel to *Carrie* right now. I can't even take you seriously."

Fiona was ignoring them. She called two of her assistants over to hold the tarp up for them. "Chelsea, I need you to help me bag his things as he disrobes. Jim, the less you disturb your clothes as you undress, the better. Try to avoid friction."

"Avoid friction?"

"Don't fold the clothes over on themselves or scrape them off the ground. In fact, Chelsea, put on fresh gloves. We're going to help him."

She firmly believed it was inappropriate to fantasize about coworkers, but if she was the type to engage in such behavior, taking Jim's clothes off like this would have been the last way she'd have dreamed of doing it — outside, freezing, with a helper and an audience. And, oh yeah, with him covered in bits of their exploded victim.

"Let's get this over with."

"Why don't we start with your face?"

"Fine."

"Guys," she said to the techs. "Rest your arms. We don't need the curtain quite yet." Then Fiona systematically cleaned the red mask from all the exposed areas of his head and neck — forehead, eyelids, cheeks, nose, lips, chin, neck. She spent a lot of time on his ears, eyebrows, lashes, and nostrils. "Was your mouth open?"

"No."

"Are you sure?"

"I'd remember getting a mouthful of … that."

Fiona sighed. "All right." She turned to the techs. "We're ready." They lifted the tarp to block the media's view. Then she nodded at Chelsea.

They spent the next fifteen minutes slowly peeling the shoes, pants, shirts, and hat off him. Starting with his skin had made the most sense from evidence-gathering and temperature-suffering perspectives. But as her partner stood in the clearing behind a small plastic blanket, she realized their error too late.

It had given the media time to wonder what they were doing then shift their position for a clear shot behind the tarp. Now, as she and Fiona bagged the last of Jim's clothes and he — with goosebumps rising on his flesh and teeth chattering behind blue lips — fought with trembling fingers to step into cold joggers while his body shivered, lights from five different cameras shined down on them from various spots and angles around the bluffs, and reporters started shouting down questions.

At least they were so busy competing with each other, they were cancelling each other out.

"Well, I can expect a call from my parents as soon as this hits the news." He pulled a hoodie over his head.

Chelsea heard her name. She heard Fletcher's name. She heard "Grimm Reaper."

Now, her teeth started chattering. Her body started to shiver. She couldn't see her skin, but she had no doubt goosebumps had broken out on her flesh, too.

Fiona handed Jim a pair of socks from his bag.

"Chels?"

She saw everything he was doing in crisp detail, yet it was detached from her, like she was watching a movie.

"Damn it." He crammed the socks into the pocket of his shirt then jammed his feet into his sneakers. "I need to get her out of here."

"She okay?" Fiona asked.

"Sullivan has problems with the press getting too close. She doesn't like the attention. Especially when it comes to Fletcher. They can be … invasive. She'll be okay. She just needs space. Which is why I need to get her out of here."

"Well, I got what I need." Fiona held up the evidence bag of Jim's clothes.

"Let us know what you find."

"I will." He took the emergency blanket from the techs, wrapped it around Chelsea's shoulders, grabbed his empty bag, then started guiding her to the car. Closer to the road where the emergency vehicles parked, the police tape was unguarded, and one news crew had been emboldened by the absence of a sentry and had violated the sanctity of the barrier. As Jim pulled his partner toward his SUV, a reporter and cameraperson ran up to them, lights in their eyes, mic in their faces.

"This is the first time the Grimm Reaper used an explosive device. Detective Sullivan, is it a personal message directed at you because of your failed sexual relationship?"

Jim wheeled around, back-fisted the camera right out of the guy's hands so that it crashed on the ground. The light popped and the area blinked into darkness.

"Hey! You can't silence the press!"

Chelsea wasn't sure if the reporter or cameraman said that.

"And you're gonna have to pay for that!"

That one was probably the camera operator, so the first one was probably the reporter.

Jim opened the passenger door for her. "You're behind the tape. I was startled to hear a sound where I didn't expect one and spun around to see what the noise was. Your equipment bore the brunt. If you hadn't been in a restricted area, that wouldn't have happened. I suggest you get out of here before we arrest you."

"For what?" the first one said. "Freedom of the press, man."

"For hindering an investigation and failure to obey an officer of the law."

"Nah, dude."

"You're new to this, aren't you?" Jim sighed. "You better talk to your producer."

"Producer? We're a podcast."

"With that equipment?"

"Top of the line. Cost a fortune. And you destroyed it. That's why you're gonna replace it."

"Guess again. It's illegal to cross the barrier. Maximum sentence is two years of jail time. And don't think I won't be happy to testify and recommend you both get the max. Now get out of here." He closed Chelsea's door then rounded the bumper to the driver's side of the car. Instead of putting his bag in the trunk, Jim tossed it in the back seat. He got behind the wheel then started the engine.

Chelsea cranked the heat

The two so-called reporters were still complaining about their camera before Jim shut his door. "Do I need to cuff you?"

They walked away, but one of them flipped him off.

"Amateurs." Jim executed a three-point turn then headed down the mountain.

An officer moved barrels at the base of the ridge to let them through the barrier. When he hit the highway, he floored it.

She didn't have the energy to complain. Of course he had a lot of pent-up stress, too. He just had a different way of dealing with it than she did.

The longer she sat there, the indigo landscape whooshing past and bleeding into the stygian sky, the sicker she grew. She was appalled at what she'd witnessed that night, but even more disgusted with her behavior.

When her teeth had stopped chattering enough for her to form coherent words, she said, "I'm really sorry."

Jim glanced at her. "For what?"

"For freaking out like I did."

He scoffed and shook his head. "Chels, you've barely been sleeping, which makes it difficult to deal with people and situations to begin with."

"I slept last night."

"My guess is you passed out last night. Regardless, the media harangued you when you put Fletcher away the first time, more than once they crossed the line, and tonight they were in your face. *After* we came upon what was probably the most gruesome crime scene we've ever dealt with."

"We've had some pretty vile crime scenes."

"Can you name one that's worse than this?"

"The tire iron might tie it."

"It ranks in the top ten, but I don't think so."

"You're probably right. Certainly not after Boundy …"

"No, not after. I can't wait to get to the station and take a hot shower. For about an hour."

"I'm surprised you don't want to go home. I just want to go home."

"You think I want that in my bathroom?"

"Good point."

"First, though, I'm worried about you. There's nothing unusual about you being triggered. But I am concerned."

"Tonight was an anomaly. The brutality of the victim. The explosion. The press. It was a lot."

"We're going to catch Fletcher."

"I know."

"And this isn't even him. This is Boundy, a pale imitation."

"I know that, too."

"Then this will all be behind us, the press will forget all about us, and things will go back to normal."

"Thank God."

"You'll be okay."

"I know, Jim. We'll both be okay."

He gave her an awkward pat on the shoulder.

"Really. I'm fine."

"You sure?"

"Yeah. While you shower, I'll get a warrant to search Boundy's house."

"Shit. Get a warrant for his arrest."

"I'll see what Davenport can get for us."

He pulled into the station parking lot. "Maybe you want to sit this one out, Sullivan?"

She frowned. "Maybe you want to …"

"What?"

"I don't have anything. I'm too tired and frayed to come up with a snappy insult. But no, I don't want to sit this out. I can do my job, Jim."

"I know. But I'm your partner. It's my job to worry about you."

"No. It's your job to have my back. And my job to have yours. Go shower. I'll get the warrants."

Chapter Twenty-Three

PRESENT DAY
  Dad's Work Shed
  1:22 a.m.

HE WIPED the sweat off his brow with the back of his hand as he surveyed his handiwork. "What do you think?"

Prisoner 09301995, formerly known as Gwendolyn Cole, sat in the corner of the room, ankles duct-taped together so she couldn't run, left wrist duct-taped to the arm of the rusty lawn chair he'd unfolded for her to sit in while she ate. He'd positioned it so she'd be belly-up to Dad's old scarred workbench, and he'd thoughtfully left one hand free for her to feed herself.

Wasn't good enough for her, though. Nothing since he'd incarcerated her had been. She hadn't done anything but cry or scream or snivel since she'd gotten there.

By now, she should understand the rules of prison life. This wasn't a service industry where the customer was always right. She wasn't even a customer. That was her first mistake.

In here, he was always right.

She was lucky he'd provided her any nourishment at all.

When she didn't answer his question, he turned, surveyed her cooly, then pointed at her untouched plate with his paintbrush. "If you'd rather not use your fingers, I can cuff your other hand, too, and you can eat like an animal. Makes no difference to me."

"I can't eat that." Her voice was barely above a whisper.

Stood to reason. She'd spent the first two hours screaming at the top of her lungs. Didn't matter how many times he'd told her there was no one around for miles. Just kept screaming. And screaming. And screaming.

He dipped the brush in the paint thinner then wiped it dry on his rag, savoring the grind of the bristles under the pads of his fingers. Imagining the satisfaction of crushing her windpipe with a similar grip. Slowly squeezing her throat, quelling that incessant whine of hers. Her eyeballs would bulge. Her nails would rake uselessly at his knuckles, his wrists. Her feet would scrabble on the grit on the floor, searching for leverage she'd never find. Her cheeks would redden, her lips would blue. Then the windows to her soul would be vacant as her body grew limp, still. Lifeless.

As all criminals should be.

"Tell me, 09301995, what is wrong with the nourishment I provided you?"

"I ... I'm afraid it's poisoned."

He put his brush down deliberately. The soft *snap* of wood meeting wood echoed in the otherwise quiet of the cavernous room.

Her gaze darted to the door then back to him.

"You screamed for hours, 09301995, and no one heard you. Do you think that tiny tap will bring someone running in the middle of the night?" He picked up two bigger brushes then banged out a drum solo on the workbench. "I told you, my facility is secure. Isolated. No one is around for miles. More to the point, no one rescues the guilty. You are a *prisoner*. An *inmate*. My work is honorable. I'm to be commended. The sooner you learn that, the easier your sentence will be for you to bear."

Her head lolled to the side. A single tear trickled down her cheek.

"You need your strength, 09301995. You're in supermax. Do you know what that means?"

"Noooo." She was sobbing freely now, and her answer was one long moan that blended into her anguished wails.

"It means hard labor. Believe me, this is easier with a partner. I might be persuaded to knock some time off your sentence for good behavior if you work hard."

"My sentence? I never had a trial! I was never arrested, you freak!" She bucked in her chair and tugged at her restraints. "You're the criminal! You abducted us! You killed my boyfriend!"

"Settle down." He rose, then leaned across the worn table to loom over her.

She immediately stilled.

"Your so-called boyfriend was just using you."

"You killed him because you were jealous."

"Of a serial killer?"

"Of a Prince Charming."

"Here we go." His nostrils flared as he vented his breath. "Let's get one thing straight, 09301995, I'm jealous of nothing 08271993 has to offer."

"Because he's dead. But you couldn't stand that your ex-girlfriend chose him over you." She tried to cross her arms, but the cuffs prevented her from moving one of her hands, so she only managed to punch herself in the chest.

"Is that what you think?"

"That's what I know." She lifted her chin.

"Well, I'll tell you what I know." He took a knife from his pocket.

She recoiled from him, but she had nowhere to go.

"This is super-max, and you're going to work while you're incarcerated here." He sliced through the tape holding her legs in place. Then he took the key from his pocket and freed her from her cuff.

Again, her gaze found the door.

"Don't even bother. It's locked. My legs are longer than yours, I'm faster than you, and I have no qualms with using force to keep you here."

Her lower lip quivered, but she didn't run.

"Now, eat your damn food. I told you, this is hard work, and you need your strength. It's not poisoned." He grabbed one of the pieces of meat and popped it in his mouth.

She stared at him for a moment, then analyzed then contents of her plate. Finally, she nibbled at a morsel of food. "This isn't bad."

"I'm a good cook."

After finishing that piece, she ate another. Then she picked up a third. "These aren't chicken nuggets. Are these beef? Deer? It's some kind of wild game, right?"

"Carry the last one with you. This is going to be a long night. I want to give you a tour."

She took the last piece from the plate.

He grabbed her by the elbow, squeezing her a little more forcefully than necessary. Her bones rubbed together under his fingers, reminding him of his earlier fantasy, and he released her before he gave into the urge to squeeze harder.

In the very back of the large pole barn, he gestured to a bank of metal doors. "These are our walk-in freezers. Left side is where we store the animals before we work on 'em. Right side is where we store the meat after."

"You're a butcher?"

"Butcher, tanner, taxidermist. I live in the middle of the woods. Come from a long line of survivalists. Dad taught me to waste nothing of the animal. We eat the meat of what we kill and tan the hide into leather or use the pelts. Unless, of course, the customer wants his catch to be mounted on his wall. Then we turn it into a proper trophy for him. Or her — we're not sexist. So, we learned to make the forms and … don't worry. I'll show you on the tour. Anyway, if I send you down here for anything, know the difference. Left is what?"

"What people bring to you."

"And right?"

"The meat you butcher."

"Good. You're a fast learner. That'll serve you well here. Moving on." He led her twenty feet away from the freezer. There was a long sink against the wall and a table off to the side. He pointed at a hook directly above them. "This is where we do the butchering and skinning."

She blanched. "Skinning?"

"Kind of hard to get someone's trophy mounted for them if you don't skin it first. Note the drain on the floor. This process is messy. If the animal is too big for the table, we hang them from the hook. We make our incisions, peel back the hide, then remove the innards."

"Innards?" She gagged.

"If you're going to throw up, do it there." He gestured to a drain on the floor. "We've installed a garbage disposal in it for easier clean-up. There's a hose on that wall." He pointed to the sink." When we're done, it's just a matter of a quick spray down, a once over with bleach and a mop, then another pass with the hose. It's a very efficient operation."

"You want me to work here?"

"You *will* work here. There's nothing wrong with what we do."

"It's barbaric."

"It's state-licensed. And we're the best at what we do. We've done specimens for museums. Government agencies. Stars and athletes. Movies being filmed right in the city. You can act all high and mighty, but a lot of people — famous people you probably idolize — have purchased our work."

She started to cry again. "Why won't you just let me go?"

"Because you're guilty, and this is your sentence."

"You aren't judge and jury!"

He squared his shoulders and stepped closer so he looked taller and broader than he already was.

She cowered under his imposing form. "I'm … I'm sorry. I'm just scared."

"You should be, 09301995. I won't continue to tolerate your outbursts. Do you understand?"

"Yes."

"Yes, what?"

"Yes, sir."

"Very good. Moving on." He guided them to a large, triangular piece of wooden furniture with different sized PVC forms propped against the wall. Each had a notch at the bottom and a hole drilled into the center.

"This is an interesting bench," she said. "But you left a nail sticking out of it."

"It's not a bench. The nail catches the hole on this piece of PVC and holds it in place."

"If it's not a bench, then what is it?"

"It's a fleshing beam. After I have the hide off the animal, I need to get all the fat off the skin so it doesn't rot. Nothing worse than a putrid smell coming from a preserved trophy. Then you know you screwed something up. So, you put the hide here and scrape it clean."

She covered her mouth. "I might need to go back to the hose room."

"Better get used to this."

He pictured her hide there, pinned to the nail and stretched to the board while he scraped her flesh. Would it ever come to that? Would she ever be found guilty and sentenced to death at his hands? To "life" in his prison?

A groan escaped her. It snapped him out of his musings.

"When that's done, we take it back to the wash room to clean it. Soak the whole thing in the big sink and gently wash it with soap and water."

"That's the first almost normal thing you said. Can that be my job? I think I can maybe handle that."

"You're going to be part of all of the processes."

"I don't think I can scrape fat off an animal."

He looked down at her. A grin played at the corners of his mouth. "Don't worry. I won't make you start by scraping fat off an animal. Let's move on." They walked to another door. "In here is our drying room. I just took down a hide yesterday, so there's nothing to see. But if there was, the fires would be blazing and fans would be circulating, and you'd see a hide hung and stretched in the middle of the room."

"What would I do in there?"

"You might be asked to help me hang the hide."

"I guess I could handle that."

"In this next room, we de-hair the hide. It is scraped off the now-supple skin with a rounded blade or an elk antler. Here, we use the antler. I've already done that, too, so you don't need to worry about that."

"Wait, de-hair it? I thought in taxidermy, you stuffed the creature so it looked like itself. Why would you de-hair it?"

"Because in this case, we're doing a leather application."

"We're making leather?"

"I told you, we waste nothing here. Moving on." He led her to the next room. "Tanning can be done with chemicals, but we prefer a natural process. An animal's brain contains natural tannins, and it is exactly the right size to tan its entire hide. You boil the organ with a cup of water, blend it until it's perfectly smooth, rub it into a clean, damp hide, then roll it up and store it in a bag in the refrigerator for at least twenty-four hours."

"You just made leather with an animal's brain? Now I really might need the hose room."

"Don't act like it's disturbing. It's natural. Far better than a chemical treatment. People have been doing it for ages."

"I think I might prefer serving my full sentence."

He dragged her back to the workbench where the night had begun then threw her into the rickety, rusty lawn chair she'd been restrained in. It collapsed under the strain, and she fell to the floor.

"Get up," he spat.

She struggled to untangle herself from the bent aluminum and frayed cloth strips.

By the time she'd gained her feet, he'd returned to his art project. He spun it to face her.

Her knees buckled, and she almost hit the floor again.

"This is what I spent the last few days tanning. When you taxidermize a human, you run into all kinds of problems. They don't have fur or feathers to camouflage your mistakes, you know? I thought maybe turning him to leather would help. But the coloring is all wrong. Supple, though. Feel how soft." He tipped the body toward her.

She scrambled backward. Tripped over the detritus of broken chair parts. Slammed into a support post and rubbed her head.

At least it held her upright.

"Now, Nell, she's a damn fine artist. She'd be able to paint this son of a bitch to look like himself. I've been trying, but I think he looks more like the Joker than the Grimm Reaper. What do you think?"

He hadn't put in the artificial eyes yet, so maybe that was the problem. Right now, there were just two empty sockets, not staring back at him. Kind of reminded him of Michael Myers, but with more charm. Maybe he'd gone a little too white on the skin, a little too red on the mouth. The cheeks might be too pink, the smile might be too broad. But for his first attempt at a model paint job, he was kind of proud. Probably wouldn't get hired at that French lady's fancy wax museum, but it was just fine for his Hall of Prisoners.

When he found Nell, she could fix it for him.

"Th-th-tha … that's Sc …" She closed her eyes, swallowed, took a deep breath. "Is that my beloved Scott?"

"Well, it's 08271993's skin. The rest of him's in my freezer. Except for the part you ate for dinner."

09301995 vomited. Her legs finally gave out, and she fainted into her mess.

"Damn it. If that happened in the skinning room, I could have just hosed her down."

Chapter Twenty-Four

AFTER THE LONGEST shower Jim had ever taken at work — the water hotter than he usually used it, which was saying something — he dressed in the spare set of clothes he kept at the station then started back to the bullpen to meet Chelsea. Then he doubled back and glanced at Thompson's locker. Someone had shoved everything back inside it and put a new combination lock on it. His buddies had new locks on theirs, too.

Wonder what Davenport would say if he knew. He wouldn't be too happy knowing he couldn't access station property if the occasion necessitated it.

Then again, the captain would just cut through the locks if he deemed it necessary.

Either way, he wasn't going to rat out the three punks.

Would have been nice to see Thompson's shoe size, though.

Jim headed out to the bullpen.

Chelsea waved papers at him. "Judge Radcliffe came through with search warrants."

"Couldn't get the arrest warrant, huh?"

"This is a start."

"You said *all* Boundy's properties?"

"Yeah. House, detached garage, and a storage unit on Jackson. Davenport said if we find anything, we'll have enough to get the judge to get the arrest warrant."

"Let's hit the house first, then."

"Captain said to take uniforms, in case he's there."

"He won't be there."

"I know. Still." She shrugged.

"See if Rafferty and Giadone are here or on a call."

"I already checked. They were just about to go out on patrol, so I snagged them for our job. They'll meet us there."

"And if Boundy is home, their black-and-white's going to tip him off."

"They know not to approach the house. They just didn't want to sit at the station and risk being pulled into a less desirable detail. We'll catch up with them when we turn onto Boundy's block."

Jim made record time driving to Boundy's street. As Chelsea promised, Rafferty and Giadone were waiting at the corner. He liked the two of them working together. She was a much better partner for him than Thompson was.

He slowed, rolled down Chelsea's window, then bent to talk to the officers.

Rafferty lowered his glass.

"Sullivan and I don't expect Boundy to be home, but you're our backup, so we need you to be alert. Once we clear the house, I want one of you posted at the front door, the other at the back. You see him coming, you call us. Understood?"

"Yeah." Rafferty nodded.

"Yes, sir!"

Everyone looked at Giadone. She still felt responsible for Nell Thompson getting away and clearly wanted to make up for it.

Chelsea reached out the window and patted the officers' car door. "Relax, Sophia. We trust you."

"We'll see you down there." Jim started rolling up the window as he drove.

"Hey!" She snatched her arm back. "My arm was still out there."

"Chill. I didn't close the glass on your arm."

"What's with you?"

"I just don't think you should let up on her. It's good that she wants to redeem herself. It'll keep her frosty."

"It'll make her nervous, which will make her more likely to make another mistake. We have enough people on edge already."

"You mean me?" He whipped into the only spot in front of the house.

Rafferty drove past them. There were two more spots four houses down.

"You have been a little brittle lately. But I meant me."

"Let's just table this discussion. We have work to do." Jim got out of the car then approached the house. Chelsea followed. When Rafferty and Giadone caught up, he directed them around back in case Boundy was inside and tried to run. "If you hear us enter forcibly, do the same. Then start clearing rooms."

"Yes, sir."

"The waiting's the hardest part," Chelsea said as they counted off the seconds for Rafferty and Giadone to get into place.

Jim knocked on the door. When no one answered, he

kicked it in. He and Chelsea breached the living room as they heard their backup break into the back of the house. They cleared the first floor together, then he sent the officers upstairs while he and his partner checked the basement.

The hinges screeched as the door swung open. He groped the wall for a switch, but there wasn't one. Fucking old houses. His police-issue jacket was in evidence with Fiona Abbott along with his flashlight, so the only light he had was on his phone — too difficult to hold while he had his weapon at the ready. Jim turned around and whispered, "Sullivan. Flashlight."

"I'll take point."

He just stuck out his hand.

She sighed and passed him the torch.

The first step protested louder than the hinges did. The second also groaned under his weight. Worse, he also yelped like an old lady walking into a spiderweb — which he thought he did.

She gripped his shoulder. "What?"

He swiped at it. His fingers snagged it, his hand tugged it down and away from him. Turned out, his face had bumped into a pull cord for a bare bulb in the stairwell.

Chelsea smirked.

Jim pocketed her flashlight then continued down the stairs, each one creaking as he stepped on them. A few times, he wondered whether the treads would bear his weight. When he reached the floor, he found another cord in front of him. He pulled the string. The bulb was very low wattage, just enough to light the bottom of the staircase and a few feet of the basement floor.

"We need more light," she whispered.

"Maybe there's another pull cord or a lamp in the next room." He took her flashlight from his pocket, held it with his weapon, then rounded the corner. The odor of mildew lingered in the damp air. The beam of light danced around the room, floor to ceiling, as he searched for Boundy, any signs of danger, or an additional light source.

He found the third first — another string hanging from the ceiling. This time, when he pulled it, the bulb was bright enough to illuminate the whole basement, at least well enough to see Boundy wasn't in it. The area they were standing in was very bright and looked like every typical unfinished Western Pennsylvania basement — cement floors, cinder block walls, first floor wooden joists exposed in the ceiling. There was a washer, dryer, and laundry tub with a few clothes lines at the far end of the room. The light didn't reach there as well, so that end of the basement was mostly in shadow. Chelsea headed down there to check out the dark corners. Jim, on the other hand, steeled himself to look in the refrigerator. He envisioned jars with severed heads and feet in them and braced himself before opening the door.

Beer. Lots and lots of beer.

Also typical for Western Pennsylvania.

The freezer had frozen pizzas and more venison than he thought one man could eat in a lifetime. And it wasn't deer season yet, so either it was a year old or he was poaching.

"Nothing disturbing down here," Chelsea said.

"You checked in the washer and dryer?"

"I did." She sighed. "Sad that we have to say that."

"Nothing left to check but his pantry." Wooden shelves had been erected along one wall, and makeshift curtains of cheap muslin panels had been tacked to the top of each frame.

"There better not be jars of body parts behind the material."

"That's just what I thought about the refrigerator."

"What was in there?"

"Beer. Pizza. Typical bachelor stuff."

She wrinkled her nose.

Jim grabbed the edge of one of the cloth panels. Chelsea grabbed another. They each pulled aside their fabric sheets.

He shook his head. "This guy has way too many cans of fruit cocktail and nacho cheese than a person should have."

"This bank of shelves is all chili. Literally five shelves of cans of chili. I don't know what to say about that. Other than my stomach hurts thinking about it."

"Want to take bets on what's behind this curtain? My money's on SPAM and pineapple."

"That almost sounds gourmet after the wall of chili."

"What's your guess?"

"Half canned ravioli, half boxes of mac and cheese."

"Oooh." He shook his head. "I'll take that bet, Sullivan. Odds are in my favor. You made a bad call, moving into boxes. Cardboard won't hold up. It's damp down here."

"I want to switch to jars of olives and pickled pigs feet."

"Too late. All bets are final." Jim grinned at her as he pulled the fabric aside.

Her complexion turned whitish-green, and the first smile that he'd managed coax out of her since Spruce Bluffs — tiny though it was — melted off her face into a mask of horror.

"We're all clear up here," Giadone called from the first floor. "Boundy isn't here, but Rafferty found something of interest in one of the bedrooms. You guys find anything?"

Jim didn't know what they found up there, but he'd bet

his inheritance it wasn't as freaky as what he and Sullivan uncovered.

"Yeah, we found … something."

What they'd found were jars. Trophies of his kills, soaking in colorless liquid. Each labeled with a white sticker with black block letters.

Ariel's tongue.

Cinderella's foot.

Jasmine's hand.

"Damn it." Jim ran his fingers through his hair and let the curtain fall closed. He turned from the jars and paced the tiny basement as Giadone walked down the stairs.

They didn't creak nearly as much under her weight.

"Want to come see what we have, or do you want us down here first? Or should we guard the doors while you catalogue what you found? Or do you want me to call the mobile crime unit for you?

"Easy, Sophia." Chelsea held up her hands. She'd also let her side of the curtain fall. "Just give us a second to process … this."

"Okay. It's just … well. Wait. What did you find? If you don't mind me asking."

"Body parts. The tongue from our Ariel victim, the foot from our Cinderella victim, and a hand from a Jasmine victim we don't even know about yet."

"But that's not even a Brothers Grimm story."

"Neither was *The Little Mermaid*," Chelsea said.

"What did you guys find?" Jim asked.

"Bomb making materials."

"Well, that's to be expected."

Chelsea vented a breath. "Jim, we got what we need. These jars plus the stuff they found will be enough for the arrest warrant. Radcliffe has to issue it now."

"Giadone, you and Rafferty watch the doors. We need to get MCU in here. You guys did great work."

"Uh, thanks, but you don't understand. We didn't find the remnants of one explosive device. There's a lot of material up there. I don't think Boundy intended Cinderella to be his only bomb. There could be more out there."

Chapter Twenty-Five

JIM PULLED into the parking lot at the station. It had been one hell of a long night, and it felt like it was never going to end. He couldn't believe Davenport was still there. Or was already there. It was that weird hour of the morning where it was either really late or really early, and as he didn't know if the captain had been to bed or not, he didn't know which way to call it for him.

Nor did he care.

He and Chelsea hadn't been to bed yet, so for them, it was late-o'fucking-clock, and as he hadn't had a good night's sleep since that bastard Fletcher had broken out of Black Meadow, he felt it hard in his bones. Whatever Davenport wanted, he hoped it was quick, because he just wanted to deal with it then get home and get some proper shut-eye. At least for a few quality hours.

As he climbed out of his car, he heard voices somewhere in the lot. It wasn't time for a shift change. The place should be dead.

"Jim—"

He shushed Chelsea with a finger to his lips. Tipped his

head toward the noise, which was now silent. But he knew he heard it.

She raised her eyebrows but didn't speak.

Someone was there. Multiple someones. And they shouldn't be. It was a secured lot. He unholstered his weapon.

So did she.

Sticking to the edges of the bumpers and the cover they provided, he crouched low then started slinking along, checking between each vehicle. When he neared the end of the lot, he noted long shadows stretching beyond the end of the last sedan. He turned and pointed them out to his partner.

She nodded.

He reached the last car, with Chelsea at his hip. Then they rounded the bumper as one unit.

"Freeze!" she yelled.

"Hands in the air!" But he'd barely finished the last word when he recognized who he was shouting at. Jeremy Berger. Ethan Miller.

And Oliver Thompson.

"What are you doing here, Thompson? You're on leave."

"Lower your weapon, McPherson."

"I don't think so."

But Chelsea's hand on his arm made him feel like a petulant child, so he did.

"My buddies and I were getting together for an after-work drink."

"You don't currently work here."

"They do."

"Their shift ended hours ago. Or doesn't end for another few."

"It did end hours ago. And that's when we met up. Just walking back to their cars now."

"Bars are closed."

"Not the private club on Wilson."

"You expect me to believe you three went out for drinks all the way down on Wilson but you walked there?"

"Didn't want to add a DUI to my growing list of offenses."

"Could have called a FASTr."

"You know what, McPherson? I'm on leave, so I don't fucking answer to you." He took a step closer.

So did Jim.

His buddies came up on either side of him.

Oh, well. One against three. He'd had those odds before. With these exact morons before. And came out on top. Jim liked his odds.

Thompson swung his car door open — hard — clipping Jim in the temple.

"You son of a—" He lunged. Shoved the car door closed, trapping Thompson's arm inside.

Thompson thrashed. "Hey! Let up!"

Miller tried to pull him free while Berger yanked on the door.

"Okay, fellas." Chelsea pushed Jim until he moved away from the car, releasing Thompson. "This is getting out of hand."

"You did that on purpose!" Miller said.

"We'll tell Davenport!" Berger added.

"See who's suspended then." Thompson rubbed his bicep. "Hell, I'll sue your ass."

Jim stepped forward again.

Chelsea grabbed his arm and pulled him in the opposite direction.

The three stooges snickered as she manhandled him away.

"No offense, Sullivan," he growled, "but this is one time when it's not a good idea for you to have my back. Not if it means getting between me and them."

"I do have your back, idiot," she said under her breath. "That's why I'm putting a stop to this." She shoved him back a few more steps. "Davenport's already pulling strings to keep you out of trouble. He said he's not going to do it again. Don't put him in a position where he has to decide whether to let you hang or not."

Jim scowled down at her.

The door behind him banged. He wheeled around.

Norm and Charlie burst out of the exit.

"Isn't anyone working normal hours tonight?" Chelsea asked.

"Davenport called us in," Norm said.

"There a problem here?" Charlie asked.

"No," Miller said.

"Just out with a friend," Berger added.

Thompson tipped his chin toward Jim. "He took exception to it."

"That's probably because you're on suspension and aren't supposed to be on the property. Get out of here."

There was more laughter as they piled into their cars. Thompson leaned out Miller's window and called, "See you soon!"

"What was that about?" Charlie asked.

"Are you bleeding?" Norm studied Jim's face in the harsh parking lot lighting.

He touched his eyebrow. His fingers came away red. Fucking perfect. Probably leave a scar.

"Let's go upstairs." Norm nodded at the door. "Captain has something."

"Guys? About what happened here," Chelsea began.

"I didn't see anything," Charlie said.

Norm covered his eyes for a second then he walked inside.

Before they got to Davenport's office, they found Devani at their desks with a pile of papers in her hands.

"Seriously, doesn't anyone sleep anymore?" Jim said.

"Why? What time is it?" She glanced at her watch. Her eyes widened, and she looked up at him.

"How long have you been working on Nell Thompson's desktop?"

"What day is it?"

"Devani!" Chelsea guided her to her chair then lowered her into it.

She looked up at Jim. "Are you bleeding?"

He snatched a napkin from his drawer of unused take-out napkins then pressed it to his temple. "What do you have for us?"

"Sorry I asked." She opened the top folder, glanced inside, then passed it to him. "These are all the possible disguises we think they could be traveling under."

"Yeah, we already have the fake IDs."

"No. Not the IDs. What they might actually look like. Remember in high school when you got a fake license?"

Chelsea's brows arched.

"I mean, when some kids got fakes. They got caught because they looked exactly like the pictures on the IDs, right? Same hair, same makeup, sometimes even the same shirt — usually because they were using it the same day they bought it. Or because they just had favorite clothes they wore over and over."

"IDs are much harder to fake now," Chelsea said.

"You can buy 'em online from people like Nell Thompson." Jim tossed his napkin into his trash can. The bleeding seemed to have stopped.

Norm slung an arm around each of their shoulders. "I don't think that's her point."

Devani shook her head. "It's not. Point is, the kids looked too much like their fake ID for it to be believable. If you look at your license or passport right now, you'll resemble it, but you won't look like it."

"That's true," Charlie said. "I think I'm five pounds heavier now. My face is fuller."

"Try ten," Norm said.

Charlie snatched a rubber band from Jim's desk and shot it at him.

Devani sighed. "Anyway, that's what makes it more authentic. And that's what the second part of Nell's plan was. She worked up a variety of looks in Photoshop for each of them. Fletcher was a master at stage makeup. Remember, he made Detective McPherson look similar to Detective Sullivan's father."

"Don't remind me." Jim shivered.

"I'm sure they planned on using at least subtle prostheses, probably wigs or hair dyes. So I wrote a program to have every combination of all the layers rendered, then I printed them out. And I sent them to the cloud for you to access."

"Why every layer?" Chelsea asked.

"Because Fletcher doesn't have to do the whole transformation. Maybe he'll only do the cheekbones. Maybe he'll only do the beard. Or the brow. Or a combination of six of the thirty layers she added to one of the fake identities she made for him. Or to her. She made multiples for both of them. This was the only way to make sure we covered all our bases."

"That means there are hundreds of potential looks in this folder," Chelsea said.

Devani shook her head. "There are four potential faces per page."

"Thousands." Jim sighed. "That means thousands."

"That's not all."

Chelsea leaned on her desk, closed her eyes, and squeezed the bridge of her nose. She didn't see Devani try to hand her the other folder, so Jim took it.

"Tyler and I went through all the emails. The top sheet is the printout of her inbox. Legit art clients are high-lighted in green. Knockoffs in yellow."

"She dabbled in blackmarket forgeries?"

"Looks like she was just starting. Someone contacted her about replicating a Monet. I don't know if it was for their pleasure or to pass off as the real thing, but she took the job. Then there are the fake ID forgeries. And someone even contacted her about whether she could do counterfeit money plates. Those are all highlighted in pink."

Charlie shook his head. "That doesn't make sense. Most artists have one specialty. Seems Nell Thompson is a dabbler in all the fine arts."

Norm leaned over to look at the list. "That's how someone gets caught. Unless she's a modern day DaVinci, she can't be good at all that stuff. Unless she's still trying to find what she's good at."

"Or she got in with a bad crowd and is trying to earn her way out," Chelsea said.

"Big mistake." Norm sighed. "You can never earn your way out."

Charlie nodded. "These kids never learn."

Jim pointed at the colored stripes. "What are the orange and lavender highlights?"

"Lavender are emails between her and Fletcher. Orange are between her and her brother. I've also saved all these to the cloud for you, but I printed them out and sectioned them off."

"I want Fletcher's." Chelsea stuck out her hand.

"I want Thompson's." Jim started rooting through the folder.

"We have a case that points to counterfeit bills. Can we look at that email exchange?" Norm asked.

"I don't know if she ever completed that job," Devani said.

Jim pulled it from the pile.

Charlie took it. "Doesn't matter. The sender might be a good lead."

Davenport stormed out of his office. "Why the fuck am I sitting at my desk by myself when I summoned you all half an hour ago?"

"If you need anything else, call me. I'm going to bed." Devani crouched low to avoid the captain as she wove through the crowd toward the door.

The rest of them headed toward his office.

There were only two chairs in front of his desk. The sofa off to the side felt too far off to the side. But it didn't feel to Jim like a "sit down and make yourself comfortable" kind of meeting, so he opted to stand.

Everyone else must have felt the same, because the rest of them stood beside him in a semicircle behind the chairs.

Only seemed right. Davenport was standing, too.

"McPherson, you want to tell me why I just got off the phone with Thompson's attorney?"

"I don't know. Why did—"

"Don't fucking finish that sentence. He called me from the hospital. Said you damn near broke his client's wrist. They put him in a splint and a sling. Now he wants your ass in a sling. And not just yours. All of you." Davenport glared at each one of them.

"Us?" Charlie looked at Norm.

Norm looked at Davenport. "What did we do?"

"Sir," Chelsea said.

She was the last person Jim expected to speak up at the moment.

"Not now, Sullivan. I'm not done yelling."

"Well, sir, before you work yourself up—"

"I'm already worked up."

"He's lying."

"I wouldn't put it past a lawyer to lie, but doctors seldom do."

"Check the security cameras. Thompson hit McPherson with his car door and cut his head."

"You're not helping," Jim muttered under his breath.

"So he shoved the door back on him and pinned his arm."

Jim sighed.

"It'll all be on tape."

"And the tape'll bury McPherson."

"No, sir. You don't understand. When Jim pinned Thompson's arm, it was his bicep, not his wrist. And that's all he did. I stepped between them then. Then Norm and Charlie came out right after. It never escalated past that. So Jim couldn't have broken his wrist. Or even sprained it. I don't know what happened to his wrist. Maybe he's making up a phantom pain. Maybe he had an accident. Maybe he had his friends hurt him on purpose to get McPherson in trouble. Maybe he found or paid a doctor to lie for him. But you don't have to take my word for it. Or any of ours. The tape will prove it."

Davenport lost his bluster. As his yelling died down, he seemed to physically deflate. He melted into his chair, leaned on his desk, and sighed. "I remember when the boys in blue were a unit. A brotherhood. When we stuck together, no matter what." Then he looked up at Chelsea. "No offense. There just weren't any women on the force back then."

"None taken. Dad always talked that way. That camaraderie was one of the reasons I wanted to be a cop."

"I don't like the changes I'm seeing."

She stepped around the chair then sat across from him. "You can't let one bad cop color your perception of the whole unit."

"Why not? Everybody else does."

"You're just tired."

"Aren't we all?"

"Why'd you really call us in, sir?"

He sighed and looked up at them. "To talk about the press. I got a tip that they're about to run related stories. They're convinced the current vics are the work of the Grimm Reaper. I told my source we're running down a copycat but wouldn't give him any details, so he won't change his story. I even promised him an exclusive. Best I could get was that he'd float the idea that we were looking at someone else, too."

"Why?" Jim asked.

But it was Chelsea's gaze he met. "Because they'll sell a lot of papers by making you guys look incompetent. Practically unhinged. Like you're coming unglued under the stress."

"Unhinged?" she cried.

"Reaper isn't even officially our case," Jim said.

"No, but the two dead vics are. Sherick and Stack haven't been at either of those crime scenes, so you two look like you're the ones in charge. And nothing looks like it's getting accomplished. Not with bringing in Fletcher and not with stopping Boundy, which the press thinks is the same thing. Compounding problems? There's footage of Sullivan melting down at the last crime scene—"

Jim jumped to her defense. "The media was out of control, sir."

"And you stripping down to your skivvies at the same scene."

"I was covered in the vic's DNA!"

"I know that. But you can see how it doesn't look too good. I'm turning the case over to Anderson and Paxton."

"You can't do that!" Jim said.

"Captain, no!" Chelsea yelled at the same time.

"We've already solved this one," he continued.

"Yeah. We found enough to get an arrest warrant."

"Come on, Captain." Jim leaned on the desk. "It's almost over. When we bring this guy in, that'll shut the press up."

"We're already so busy," Norm said. "We can't take on more right now."

"Wouldn't be right to get a collar like that, anyway," Charlie added. "Not when they did the work. You trying to make us look like glory hounds? After you just got done saying this isn't a family anymore?"

Davenport sat back and sighed. "You're all driving me to drink. I'm trying to get the heat off these two. Don't you get that?"

"We can take it," Chelsea said.

"You have it worst of all."

"I'm fine."

He muttered something under his breath that was more vile than even Jim would usually say in mixed company. "Fine. If this is what you want, finish it out. McPherson, assuming the tape backs you up, then I will, too."

"It will."

"You and Sullivan keep the copycat case. Find Boundy and bring him in. I want to put this bastard away today and shut the press up for a fucking minute."

"Roger that, sir," she said.

"Anderson, Paxton. Sorry to drag you in here so early for nothing."

"Wasn't a total waste, sir," Norm said.

"Yeah, if we hadn't been here, we would have missed out on a lead for our counterfeit case, so it all worked out."

"How the hell did you … never mind. Everyone back to work. I need coffee."

They all filed out. In the bullpen, they headed for their own desks. Chelsea turned to Jim. "I could use some coffee, too."

"Hell with that. I need sleep."

"We need to get the arrest warrant from Radcliffe."

"He's going to be thrilled to get up at four in the morning to sign that. Especially when we don't know where Boundy is. We'll ask for it at a decent hour."

"But what if we find him before then?"

"I doubt he's in my bedroom. But if someone finds him from the BOLO, they can arrest him. We have plenty to hold him without the arrest warrant."

"That's not procedure."

"If you want to wake the judge to sign a piece of paper we can't use right now, feel free. I need a few hours before I face plant in the parking lot. Tomorrow — or later today — we need to find this asshole. And I also want to go through these emails. I feel like that's going to be how we find Fletcher."

"Go home, Jim. I'm calling Judge Radcliffe."

"You need me to tail you? We still don't know where Fletcher is."

"No. I'm sure Davenport has my babysitters waiting in the parking lot."

"Meet back here at ten, then?"

"Sure. Goodnight."

"Don't stay too late."

"I'm five minutes behind you."

Jim planned on waiting in the parking lot, but he saw the tail the captain had ready to follow her home.

Saw the one ready to follow him, too, so he decided not to wait.

He might actually get some sleep tonight.

Chapter Twenty-Six

CHELSEA WAS surprised that Jim beat her to the station. She thought for sure he'd sleep more than five hours. But there he was. And looking fresh as a daisy, too.

A frown pulled down the corners of her lips. What made daisies so fresh, anyway? Were they more sprightly than any other flower? She thought not.

She, on the other hand, looked like sleep was a distant memory. Like, from seven years ago or so.

Clearly she didn't get enough rest. And was in a mood.

"Coffee?" Jim held up a cup from Hill of Beans.

"You got in early *and* had time to stop for good coffee?"

"I got a good night's sleep."

"You barely had time for five hours."

"How about you try, 'Thank you, Jim.' then take this cup?"

"You're right." She sighed and reached for it.

He pulled it out of her grasp. "I'm right, what?"

"Thank you, Jim." She said it in a sing-songy tone.

"You don't sound sincere, but you look miserable, so I'll let it slide." He handed her the coffee.

Chelsea sipped the drink and instantly understood what "nectar of the gods" meant. She closed her eyes and let the beverage warm her soul. "Bless you."

"Well, I didn't think you'd have a religious experience over it or anything."

She dropped into her chair.

"You didn't sleep last night, did you?"

"Well, it took longer than five minutes to get the warrant. That got me wound up. Then while I was waiting, I started going through the early news reports."

"That was a mistake."

"Tell me about it. By the time I got home, it wasn't Fletcher keeping me up. It was the local media."

"They're vultures."

She took another sip of her drink. "We need to get Boundy."

"And Fletcher."

"Then take a nice long vacation. Somewhere warm and sunny. Preferably without a local news service."

"You mean a deserted island?"

"Your family has connections. Do you know of any? Or anything close?"

"Fantasy Island. But a wish there is like the monkey's paw."

"Only until the end. And it was fictional."

"Then no. I don't know of any deserted islands."

"That's too bad." She took another sip.

"I can probably hook you up with a kick-ass beach vacation at a private beach house, though."

"When you say it like that, it sounds like a monkey's paw."

"It was an honest offer."

"No. I can book my own vacation if I want to. Besides,

we have to solve this crime first. Or crimes, I guess. Any hits on the BOLO for Boundy?"

"No."

"You start looking through Nell Thompson's emails?"

"I honestly just walked in before you did. I don't know how we missed each other in the parking lot."

Chelsea unwrapped her scarf, unbuttoned her coat, tossed the whole ensemble over the back of her chair, then dropped onto her seat. "Let's get to it, then."

The two of them started poring through Nell Thompson's emails — Chelsea through her messages with Fletcher and Jim through her correspondences with Oliver. Jim grunted a lot, but she didn't take that to mean anything. He hated Oliver since the first day they met. He was bound to grumble over anything he found. So, she insisted they switch.

"Why?"

"Because you're looking to crucify the guy. If he ends up involved in this, we can't make it look like you targeted him. I want to take point on this. You look through Fletcher's messages. Besides, it's kind of icky. I used to date him. I don't want to read his love letters to someone else."

"I'm sure they aren't love letters. Besides, you don't still have feelings for the guy."

No, she didn't. But Jim had nothing but negative feelings for Oliver Thompson, and she didn't want that contaminating their case. "I just don't want to read these. We're switching."

"Fine." He traded her files.

Some of the emails turned out to be nothing more than regular sibling messages. Or what she assumed would be regular correspondences. Without a brother or sister, she couldn't be certain, but they were little jokes, complaints about family members, reminders about upcoming events it didn't sound like either wanted to attend. Those were easy enough to discard. It was unlikely they were hiding secret messages while discussing Aunt Clara's hip replacement.

But others were more interesting. Oliver sent her a series of messages over the course of the last year begging her to stop seeing the monster, the creep, the lech. There was only one person that could be. Why did she start visiting him to begin with?

Chelsea read on, hoping to find out.

No such luck.

She found other emails talking about the family bunker. These weren't from Oliver, though. These ones originated from Nell. Questions about the exact location — the woods had changed since they'd been there as a kid, and when she went looking as an adult, she couldn't find it. She asked questions about trail markers, booby traps, security alarms, and provisions.

Booby traps? That couldn't be good. And why did that ring a bell?

"Hey, Jim? Check this out. Nell Thompson was asking her brother about a family bunker in the woods."

"Yeah?" He barely looked up.

"Sounds similar to what the Warren family was talking about. I mean, I'm not a woodland expert, but she was asking about trail markers and provisions and stuff. She couldn't remember where it was, though. And she was asking about booby traps."

"Booby traps?" That got his attention. He put his pages down and turned toward her.

"Yeah. I was thinking we could run a search for property the Thompson family owns. If we can find where his bunker is located, then maybe we can find Nell."

"And if we find Nell, maybe we luck out and find Fletcher, too."

"But the booby traps concern me."

"Yeah." He tipped his head from side to side, cracking his neck. "If Oliver has that place rigged, God only knows what we'll find. Or what will find us."

"It's not that. Something's tickling my brain about that word. I just can't quite remember what."

"What is it?"

She sighed. "If I knew that, it wouldn't be out of reach of my memory, would it?"

"I was trying to help you remember."

Chelsea rolled her eyes.

"Hey, if it worked, you'd be thanking me right now."

"I suppose." She took a sip of her coffee. Had to tip the cup almost upside down to get the last of it. "Too bad. I was enjoying that. Haven't had such a good cup since — that's it!"

"What?"

"My dad made me coffee the other night."

"He must make good coffee if it rivals Hill of Beans."

"Anytime anyone makes me coffee, I'm happy. Except the swill they try to pass off as coffee here. But yes, his is really good. Anyway, I was falling asleep on his couch when he was babbling about his prepper meeting. He was talking about booby traps people install. He might be able to tell us about this. Or be able to introduce us to people who can talk to us about it. If we find the Thompson bunker, we may not have to go in blind, after all."

"That would be a big help."

"Let me give him a call."

"Bribe him with coffee."

"He doesn't need coffee."

"Bribe him with pastry."

"He doesn't need a bribe. He'll help because it's the right thing to do."

"Can we still stop somewhere for pastry? I'm starving."

"Would you shut up? It's ringing."

Jim shrugged then walked toward the coffee pot for a refill he would be disappointed with.

Chelsea smiled when she heard her father's voice, gruff with lack of use in the early morning hour. "Hi, Dad. I need a favor. What can you tell me about booby traps and bunkers?"

"I can give you some ideas, but you'd be better off talking to one of our resident experts. I'll text you some names and numbers."

"Thanks, Dad."

"No problem. Just give me five minutes to put a list together."

Jim came back, grumbling about the station's coffee.

"Dad's going to put us in touch with his local bunker buddies."

"Great. I'm going to pull property records on the Thompson family. Hopefully we'll both have answers soon." He got to work searching through public deeds.

Chelsea considered refilling her own coffee when she decided to just close her eyes, instead. She wasn't sure how much time ticked by before Jim woke her with a nudge. "What?"

He held his phone in front of her. A map was on the screen. "The Thompson property. It's not far."

"I don't think we should go until we hear from my dad." Just then, her phone dinged with a text.

"Hopefully that's him with the info we want."

She looked at the screen. "Well, you're not going to believe this."

Chapter Twenty-Seven

HE TURNED his back on her and counted silently to ten, though he suspected counting to ten thousand wouldn't help.

"You hear me?" she rasped. "I said I'm thirsty."

Slowly, deliberately, he turned around. "Maybe if you hadn't thrown up your dinner, you wouldn't be dehydrated."

"Maybe if you didn't turn me into a cannibal, I wouldn't have thrown up." She gagged. "I might be sick again."

"Vomit and you lose your clothes while I wash them. I'm not hauling you back up to the skinning room."

Her teeth started chattering, and she clutched her clothes closer to her. "You wouldn't. I'm already freezing."

"Then I suggest you don't give me a reason to take them."

"But they're still damp, and they smell."

"So, you want me to take them?"

"No!"

"Listen, 09301995, you have a lot to learn about the prison system."

"This isn't prison!"

"This is prison. Moreover, this is *your* prison. And the sooner you learn to follow the rules, the sooner your life will be easier here."

She started crying. Again.

Because that never got old.

"You're just going to kill me, anyway."

"The jury's still out."

"That's not even how prison works! You don't lock someone up and then decide her sentence later! What if you decide I'm not guilty?"

"Oh, you've already been found guilty. And plenty of prisoners are imprisoned before their sentencing hearing."

She collapsed to the floor, slumped into a heap only invertebrates should be able to achieve, and wailed, "I'm not guilty of anything, you sick prick."

"For that perjury alone, you've just added years to your sentence."

Her head snapped up. The whites of her eyes stood out in the dim lighting of the underground cell. Her nostrils flared, her chest heaved, and her body quivered not with cold, but with fury. Spittle flew from her mouth as she screamed, "You just said I didn't have a sentence yet!"

Some prisoners simply couldn't be reasoned with. They took time to settle into their new surroundings. A few required months of counseling, but he was no therapist and wasn't about to hire one.

Maybe he could make one. Fletcher once had a medical degree. He could pose 08271993 with a notebook, possibly give him glasses. If he only knew how to paint a thoughtful expression on a specimen's face, 08271993 could be the therapist the prisoners needed. And bonus, 09301995 was already comfortable with him.

He really needed Nell. Her artistic talents could fix him right up.

"Are you listening to me?"

He hadn't been. She'd been screaming the whole time, but he was good at tuning out his prisoners' tirades. There were plans to be made, and he couldn't let her rants and raves interfere. But then she started coughing, and it reminded him he had a rule he'd broken. One he needed to rectify, or he was no better than the inmates he imprisoned.

The polymer cup for her cell.

She'd accelerated his timetable. He hadn't been ready to take her to her permanent unit. That's how she'd ended up in the holding cell last night. When she'd thrown up in the workshop then passed out in her own mess, he'd had no choice. She was supposed to be stay in the shed for a while, but that obviously wasn't going to pan out. Her permanent cell hadn't been ready yet, so he had to prepare it while she was unconscious. He'd hauled her to the skinning room, hosed her off, then carried her down here and left her to dry while he prepared her permanent quarters. Cot, sheet, blanket, pillow … that was all she needed. Better than she deserved.

But he'd forgotten the polymer cup.

Much as he didn't feel like returning to the house for it, he went. He was all about doing things by the book. Rules were to be followed. Without rules, what did society have?

He checked her cell door. It was secure. Of course it

was. Because he followed the rules, and prisoners were to be in locked cells. Satisfied she wasn't going anywhere, he headed down the hall.

When he closed the door behind him, her screams instantly cut off. A blessing to his ears. Nothing, again, but the sound of his own breath. If he listened hard enough, he bet could hear his own heart beating. He closed his eyes and proved himself right. Then standing there, counting the steady *rump-thump, rump-thump, rump-thump*, he was almost lulled to sleep on his feet. It had been such a long night. But he still had a few things to do before he could rest.

It was a good thing he had called in sick. He needed the time to get his prison operating at optimum efficiency.

One more deep breath, then he opened his eyes. He deactivated one of his security measures so he could exit the prison, then stopped to reset it before heading up to the house.

He didn't bother disarming the rest of them. They were avoidable — if a person knew where they were and how to get around them, which he did. And he wanted to leave them all active. It was unlikely 09301995 would break free — and even more unlikely she'd avoid any of the traps — but on the off-chance she did, he didn't want her escaping. Leaving every measure active increased the odds that she wouldn't get away.

In his kitchen, he stopped to make himself coffee. And while he'd waited, he'd turned on the television for company.

That's where his day went from bad to worse.

Maybe it was just the one channel. So he tried another. And another.

It was on them all.

Though he could have used the caffeine, he didn't wait for the brew to finish. The polymer cup he did retrieve, because, after all, rules were rules. Then he stormed back to the prison, avoiding all his traps. Because he was in such a rush, he almost forgot to disarm the last security device. Thank God he dropped the cup just shy of the door. After retrieving it, he stood and came face-to-face with the release mechanism, reminding him to slow down. He deactivated it, stepped inside, reactivated it, then went to holding.

"Did you see the news?" He unlocked her cell, flung open the door, then stormed inside.

She stared up at him, brows raised. "Of course I didn't. How could I?"

He threw the cup at her.

"This is all your fault!"

"What is?"

He paced back and forth, rubbing the back of his neck. "It's all over TV. People are in a frenzy, worried about it."

"About what?"

"About you!" He wheeled toward her. "About … him!"

She grabbed the cup, clutched it to her chest like a child with her teddy bear, first twisting it in her fingers, then holding it tight.

"Isn't it good the people are upset that he's out of prison?"

"Of course it's good … not that. They're upset because he's killing again!"

"I don't understand."

He squeezed the bridge of his nose. "The Grimm Reaper killings have begun again. The public is in a frenzy because the police haven't caught him and he's accelerating."

"But he's … you … it's not …"

"I know! And it's all your fault!"

She climbed to her feet, put her hands on her hips. "How is this my fault?"

He wheeled around, strode into the hall, then began to pace. Some of the media were speculating that the Grimm Reaper was not known to have partners, and once he was free, any of his helpers were likely to end up victims. Because he'd already killed two women who had yet to be identified — which he hadn't — and because the only missing persons in the area were his suspected accomplices, the newscasters were speculating the victims were possibly Gwendolyn Cole and Nell Thompson.

Now, he knew 08271993 wasn't killing again. He was locked up, safe and sound.

But that meant there was a copycat out there doing terrible things.

And he knew Gwendolyn Cole wasn't a potential victim. She was 09301995, waiting to be sentenced.

But what about his darling Nell?

"What about my darling Nell?" he roared and spun around.

09301995 beaned him in the head with her polymer cup.

He blinked.

She grabbed the cell door, swung it as hard as she could. It bashed him in the side of the temple.

He saw stars before he fell to one knee.

She ran.

"Wait!" He cried. "09301995! Don't go that way!"

"Fuck you!" she screamed as she ran.

"You'll be sorry." But he didn't yell the words. Barely said them above a whisper. He had no idea whether she heard him or not, and he didn't care. Because it was time for her to be sentenced. And her sentence was death.

The bloodcurdling shriek came before he pushed to his feet. In fact, it was what gave him the strength to stand. He wobbled down the hall until he reached the doorway she'd run through without the release code.

Just on the other side, she lay on the ground, two crossbow bolts through her at opposite angles, one through her thigh, one through her side. Another was embedded in the floor just beyond her. "Look at that. Sixty-six percent accuracy. That's not bad. You're a tiny thing, after all. But I think I want to improve my odds. Probably add a few more crossbows, just to be on the safe side. What do you think?"

"What ... did you ... do ... to me?"

"I didn't do anything. You crossed the motion sensor without disarming the devices. You did this to yourself."

"Help ... me."

"Tell me where Nell is."

"I ... don't know." She took a shuddering breath and grabbed the bolt sticking out of her abdomen. "Please. Help."

He crossed the small space in a few strides, put his hand over top of hers. "Tell me where Nell is."

09301995 shook her head. "Don't ... know."

He squeezed, crushing her fingers under his, then he twisted the bolt.

She screamed, dropped to her knees. Shrieked and clutched her thigh with her free hand. Sweat rolled down her temples as tears streamed down her cheeks and blood dripped from her lips. "Please!"

"I guess you don't know where she is."

"I don't." 09301995 panted. "I don't."

"Then I'll help you."

"Thank you," she sobbed and reached toward him as he stepped near. "Thank—"

He snapped her neck and watched dispassionately as she fell to the floor. "Wonder how noticeable those bolt holes are going to be when I taxidermy her?"

Chapter Twenty-Eight

CHELSEA STARED AT HER PHONE.

"Who is it?" Jim asked.

She turned her screen so he could see. "Your biggest fan."

His eyebrows shot up. "Milo Hartman?"

Her phone dinged again. She looked at her screen then started laughing. "I was wrong. *This* is your biggest fan."

"Now who?"

Again she spun the device for him to read it.

"Fucking Oliver Thompson. Are you kidding me?"

"Well, given the choice of the two, I'm guessing Oliver isn't going to want to help us disarm any booby traps he might have installed on his property. So I think we'll be going with option number one."

"I'll call Black Meadow. I'm sure the warden's gate keeper will be as happy to hear from me as Hartman will be."

While he called the prison, she texted a note of thanks to her dad.

"Hartman's not in today."

"Well, we can't try Thompson. Did they say if Hartman's sick, on vacation, just not on the schedule?"

"Of course not."

"We could try his house."

"Beats sitting around here. No one's seen Boundy at any of his usual haunts. I've got units watching the homes of Gwendolyn Cole, Nell Thompson, and even keeping tabs on Ainsley Edwards. No signs of the missing women. No sign of Fletcher. If we don't have any leads on the people we're looking for, we might as well try Hartman. Maybe he can help us not get hurt trying to track down Nell Thompson — and maybe Fletcher, too — at the Thompson family's hidden bunker."

"All right, Jim. Just let me do most of the talking."

"You've got a deal. Let me look him up."

She could sense his frustration. She felt it, too. They were crossing the same paths — and the same people — but just tying themselves in knots instead of simplifying things.

They rode out to the Hartman homestead in silence. Jim didn't even insist on music. He seemed to be stewing about something.

That was fine. She was mulling something over, too, and didn't want to make small talk or argue over music or discuss the seven thousand open cases they were trying to solve.

Cases that all linked back to the Grimm Reaper.

Which meant they all linked back to her.

It chilled her to the core.

She'd thought she could relax when the judge pounded the gavel that last time and Fletcher was sent away. It was over. Done. He was going away, never to return.

But he got out. Wasn't supposed to, but he did.

And she felt him coming for her. Saw him in every

shadow. Heard him in every house-settling creak and crack. When she closed her eyes at night, she could smell his cologne in her bedroom. Feel his breath on the back of her neck.

Yet he wasn't there.

So, where was he?

And why, in the light of day, did he feel farther away? Maybe gone altogether?

Was it because she knew about Boundy being a copycat? And speaking of the acolyte, why was he trying to make people think Fletcher was active again? Was he trying to give him time to escape? Trying to add to his fame? Hoping to eventually hitch his own name to the Grimm Reaper's reputation?

They were missing something. A vital piece to the puzzle. Once they found that, she'd be able to see the whole picture. Until then, there was a hole where the crucial detail would be that would make everything come together.

She was staring out the window while working through her thoughts, though she wasn't paying attention to where she was. But something caught her notice, and she turned toward Jim. "Where are we?"

"Looks familiar, huh?"

"Yeah."

"It should. The turn to the Warren cabin is about two miles ahead."

"Hartman and the Warrens are neighbors?"

"Well, I wouldn't say that, assuming the GPS is accurate. Probably about ten miles apart. But the closest thing each other has to a neighbor."

"Am I the only one who finds it odd that all these people and places intersect as much and as often as they do?"

"If you think this is more than a coincidence, then you're really going to have trouble with this next bit of trivia."

"Yeah? What's that?"

"Just past the Warrens' place, we'll be coming to a fork in the road where we're going left. Want to guess what happens if we take the right path?"

She shrugged. "We end up in Sherwood Forest?"

"Nope."

"Narnia?"

"Wrong again. Going for three?"

"It's not Middle Earth. I give up. What's to the right?"

"The Thompson land."

"They're all just one big happy family out here, aren't they?"

"I doubt that." He turned left at the fork.

They rode another ten minutes until they came upon a driveway leading to a small white farmhouse and a giant white pole barn. The paint was just starting to peel on each, though someone had put a fresh coat of gray paint on the stairs to the house before the first autumn frost had put an end to outdoor updates until spring. A scarecrow with a garishly painted face stood guard over several bales of hay, and mums spilled out of wooden buckets on and around them. Nestled into the empty spaces were pumpkins and gourds of various colors, shapes and sizes. And on the bottom step, on each edge, sat a jack-o'-lantern, both carved with macabre grins.

Grins very much reminiscent of the one found at the Cinderella crime scene.

Chelsea's hand twitched above the butt of her weapon as she got out of Jim's car. She nodded at him then tipped her head toward the porch. "You see those?"

He turned his head toward the pole barn and drew his

gun. "Don't worry about those. I'm more worried about them."

She had her piece drawn based on Jim's reaction before she had her attention trained where he indicated. Not that it mattered. The two of them had three things going for them — their training, the high ground, and the element of surprise.

Two men were sneaking out of Hartman's outbuilding, and they had their hands full. Of what, she wasn't sure, as it was covered with a tarp, but they clearly didn't have Hartman's permission to be taking it, because they were hissing at each other to shut up, to be quiet, to tip-toe, and in so doing, generally making more noise than if they'd have just walked out of there as boldly as possible. Just before they reached their truck, Jim and Chelsea — approaching using the men's truck as cover — reached them and stepped out into the clearing.

"Police," Jim said. "Freeze."

The man with his back to them jumped.

The other man's eyes widened. "Oh, shit."

"Put the contraband down slowly, then get your hands in the air," Chelsea said.

"That'll ruin it," Backward Man said.

"What?" Jim glanced at Chelsea.

She shrugged.

"May I?" Backward Man asked over his shoulder.

Jim nodded. "Slowly."

He turned around, awkwardly shifting the giant bundle so his half was cradled in front of him like a baby. The tarp covering it started to slip, and two hooves poked free.

"This is Delbert."

"His name's not Delbert," Forward Man said. "Name's Clyde."

"Ain't no one never heard of a buck named Clyde."

"But a buck named Delbert's fuckin' famous?"

"Delbert 'cause it starts with D for Deer."

"But he ain't a deer."

"Well he ain't a fucking penguin."

"He's a buck, genius, not a deer."

"A buck is a deer!"

"But not all deer are buck."

"Did I say all deer were buck?"

"Well, what did you say?"

"I said Delbert's a buck."

"Delbert's a dumb name for a buck."

"Well, there's a B in Delbert, too. So, D for Del and D for Deer. B for Bert and B for Buck. C doesn't stand for Deer or Buck. It only stands for Clyde and what else? 'Cause the only other C-word I know is—"

"Okay, fellas," Jim said. He glanced at Chelsea, gave her a wide-eyed apology look that was almost as funny as the two guys were, then he turned back to them. "Who are you, and what are you doing at the Hartman residence?"

"Oh, this isn't his residence," Backward Man — who she would forever think of as Delbert — said. "This is the workshop. The Hartmans live up there in the house. Well, just the boy now, I think. Haven't seen the parents in a while. Heard tell they retired to Myrtle Beach."

"I won't ask again. Who are you and what are you doing here?"

"Oh. Sorry. Name's Bubba Harris," Delbert said. "That's my brother, Jackson."

"Nice to meet you," Clyde added.

Was it? Her money was on no.

They all stood there for a moment, staring at each other, not speaking.

"You realize you're not done explaining yourselves, right?" Chelsea prompted them.

"Oh. Sorry. Say, you mind if we put Delbert in the truck first? He's getting heavy."

"Name's not Delbert," Clyde said.

"Yes, we mind," Jim said.

"Can we at least put him down, then?"

"Thought you said that would ruin him."

"It can mat the fur. But if we put him on his hooves, it should be okay. Besides, my arms are hurting."

"Go on."

It took them a minute to balance that poor animal, whatever its name was to be. Chelsea was glad they left the blanket over it. Both men shook their arms out when it was done. They were red-faced and sweaty. When "Delbert" noticed they still had their weapons drawn, his face paled. "What's going on?"

"That's what we're asking you," Jim said.

"We hired the Hartmans to mount Delbert for us almost a year ago. They're the best in the business. Figured it was worth the price and the wait. But we've been waiting for a long time. Couple weeks ago, Milo said it was done and we paid him online. But every time we asked him about picking up Delbert—"

"Clyde."

"We're not naming him Clyde, Jackson. Now will you shut up about it?"

"Not calling him Delbert," he muttered.

"Anyway, any time we asked him about picking up the deer, he said he was working. That's when I found out his mom and dad were gone. Probably why it took him so long to finish it in the first place, if it's only one of him now. Anyway, Jackson and me was down at the Rusty Nail, and after we had a few … fries and burgers and completely non-alcoholic sodas with our meal, we figured we'd already paid for it, so it was our property. Technically, it wasn't stealing if we came to get it."

Chelsea looked at Jim. "The Rusty Nail?"

"Private club on Wilshire."

"There sure seem to be a lot of those around."

"A throwback to an earlier era." He holstered his weapon.

She did the same. Then she looked at the Harris brothers. "Wait. You were at a bar at ten a.m.?"

"We worked the night shift. We didn't get off until seven."

"So, let me get this straight. You got drunk at the club, at which point you had the brilliant idea to drive here under the influence, trespass on private property, then break into the Hartman's workshop to retrieve a stuffed deer."

Delbert shrugged. "Technically, taxidermy isn't stuffed. It's mounted."

"That's the part you want to take exception to?" She looked at Jim.

He shook his head.

"Are we free to go?"

She rolled her eyes.

"When did you leave the Rusty Nail?" Jim asked.

"Around nine-thirty."

"And how many drinks did you have?"

"Just a couple."

"By a couple, do you mean two or twelve?"

"Two."

"You driving or is Clyde?"

"The deer?"

"Ha!" Clyde said. "You called him Clyde."

"Only because the cop did."

"No, I didn't," Jim said. "I meant your brother."

"His name's Jackson."

Chelsea chuckled. Seemed Jim thought of them by what they wanted to call their deer, too.

"Sorry," Jim said.

"You know the deer can't drive, right," Delbert said.

"Just close your eyes and touch your nose."

"With the deer?"

"With the tip of your finger!"

Delbert — she really should call him by his actual name, but now she couldn't remember what it was — stood in the clearing at attention, eyes closed. He extended his right arm out to the side then brought it in to touch his nose, no problem. When he flung his left arm out, he hit the deer, which wasn't properly balanced on the rutted rock driveway. It teetered for a moment.

The Harris Brothers both lunged for their prized possession, but they were too late. The poor thing toppled onto the stones, the tarp flapping into the air above it as it fell. It landed fur-down in the gravel.

Both men caterwauled like toddlers whose ice cream cones hit the ground at the summer fair. Their commotion was enough to raise the dead.

Or at least it got the attention of the not-at-work-today Milo Hartman, who came running around the corner of the pole barn, rifle at the ready.

Chapter Twenty-Nine

JIM DREW HIS WEAPON AGAIN. "Freeze! Hartman! Drop your weapon!"

"Who's there!" Hartman yelled.

"Shit, Bubba! I done tole you this was a bad idea." Clyde's hands reached for the heavens. "

His brother struck the same pose. "Shut up, Jackson. Let the nice police people deal with him."

"Mr. Hartman," Chelsea called. She also had her gun drawn. "It's Detectives Sullivan and McPherson. I need you to lower your weapon."

He stepped closer but took his finger away from the trigger and held the weapon out to the side to show he was no longer a threat. "You know I'm within my rights to have this. I've got a permit for this weapon. Plus, they're on my private property, they broke into my pole barn, and they stole something."

Jim stepped forward to take the rifle.

Delbert — Bubba — grew braver once Hartman was disarmed. "Can't steal what you own. We paid you for it. And you had it a long time. You been holding it hostage."

"Hostage?" He stalked across the driveway.

Jim reached for his arm, but missed.

Chelsea jumped in front of him. "Mr. Hartman, did you make that stuffed deer for them?"

"Mounted. Taxidermists don't stuff animals anymore."

"But did you make that for them?"

"I did. And it was a damn fine piece of work, too. Before they tossed it in the rocks."

"We didn't throw it there. It fell over," Bubba said.

"Yeah," his brother said. "And we wouldn't have had to try to sneak it out of here in the first place if you'd just let us pick it up when we asked."

"And is it paid for?" Chelsea continued.

Hartman sighed. "It is."

"It would save us a lot of paperwork if you'd just let them take it and go. But if you want to press charges, we can haul them and the deer in to the station. You'll have to come down and file a report."

"I don't have time for that. And they did pay for it. Besides, I was going to call them today, anyway. They can take it."

She looked at Jim and tapped her nose.

Jim walked up to Bubba. Stood closer than he would have liked to so he could check his breath and eyes. The whites were a little bloodshot — probably from working the late shift — but otherwise clear. He smelled like fried food, but nothing like a distillery. "Walk a line for me."

"Jus' so you know, we're on rocks, and I have an inner-ear condition."

"You want me to call a patrol car and get someone to administer a breathalyzer?"

"I'm walkin'," He said and heel-to-toe'd it across the driveway and back, mostly in a straight line.

"Load Bambi, then take off."

The two brothers bent to pick up their deer.

"You know, we could call him Bambi," Bubba said.

"Nah. That's the name of that one dancer at the Triple-X place on Potomac. I can't have this in our man cave looking at me if I'm thinking of her."

"Good point."

They heaved the animal into the bed of their truck. Without even so much as a nod or a wave, they scurried into the cab of the vehicle then hurried down the driveway, leaving a trail of dust behind them.

Chelsea waved her hand in front of her face and coughed.

Jim turned to Hartman and looked at the rifle. "I trust I can return this to you and there won't be a problem?"

"I'm a lawman, same as you."

"That's not exactly an answer to my question."

Hartman scowled. "I only brought it out here to defend my property. As you're not a threat, there won't be a problem."

That still wasn't an answer. But Sullivan was giving him her patented *stop being such a dick* look, though she didn't swear, so she'd probably say *jerk* instead. Besides, he didn't think he was being a jerk. Hartman always set off warning bells in him.

Then again, who at Black Meadow didn't?

Jim passed him the rifle.

"So, I'm guessing you didn't come all the way out here because you suspected I might be the victim of a break-in this morning."

"No," Chelsea said. "We called the prison, but they said you were off today."

He held out his hands. "Obviously. If this is about

work, I'd appreciate it if we could discuss it when I'm back on duty."

Jim hitched his thumbs in his front pockets. "You, more than most, know criminals don't care about office hours."

Hartman sighed and started walking toward the house. "Follow me. I'll put on a pot of coffee."

"You don't have to go to any trouble." Chelsea felt into step alongside him.

Although Jim didn't contradict her, he wouldn't have minded a cup.

The stairs weren't just freshly painted, they were freshly repaired. Or just very well maintained. They were solid underfoot and didn't squeak or groan as the trio climbed onto the porch. The doors, however, were another story. Both the screen and the six-panel pine creaked on their hinges when Hartman opened them.

Just as the outside was a quintessential farmhouse, weathered with age and just beginning to be refreshed and repaired, so was the inside. There were touches everywhere of the senior Hartmans — old gingham couches, doilies on the tables, a threadbare recliner — then that one sign of Milo remodeling the inside.

A giant flatscreen television.

But they weren't staying in the living room. Hartman led them to the kitchen, which was also outdated but immaculately clean. He gestured for them to sit at the table while he started to make coffee. With his back turned, he said, "So, what brings you all the way out here?"

"My dad gave us your contact info."

He glanced over his shoulder. "Your father? I thought you were here about Fletcher."

"I am. We are. Sort of. Well, you see—"

"Fletcher had help escaping," Jim cut in. "Inside help.

You know that. We suspect it wasn't just someone at Black Meadow, but maybe one of our own. There's a cop we think might be dirty, and it turns out his sister was one of Fletcher's girlfriends. She's MIA and he's off the grid."

Hartman's eyes narrowed.

"We just found out they have a bunker out in the woods," she said.

"Not far from here, actually." He couldn't help himself. The guy might like Chelsea more than him, but she was moving too slow for his tastes. "Seems he's into the prepper scene, just like Detective Sullivan's father."

"Cormac Sullivan?"

"The one in the same. When we talked to him about the best way to find and approach the property, he warned us about potential security measures and said he was no expert. So we asked who was. He told us the two people in his group who he'd recommend were Oliver Thompson and you."

"Isn't Thompson a cop in your Zone?"

"He is," Chelsea said.

"He also happens to be the officer we're trying to track down," Jim added. "So, we're hoping you can tell us how to spot a hidden bunker. And how to find and disarm any booby traps he might have set."

"You know booby traps are illegal."

"Doesn't mean he didn't install any."

Hartman nodded. "You know survivalists keep the location of their bunkers secret so they aren't overrun by people who didn't prepare for emergencies. It's against the code to reveal the location of another person's shelter."

"And it's against the law to help serial killers escape from prison," Jim said. "Which do you think is the greater offense?"

Hartman plunked three large mugs and three spoons on the table beside a bowl of sugar. He went to the refrigerator, yanked open the door, slammed it closed, stomped to the table, then banged a carton of cream next to the flatware.

"Why don't you let me get the coffee?" Chelsea jumped to her feet then hurried across the kitchen. She returned with the carafe and a hot pad. "Shall I pour?" But she didn't wait for an answer. After the mugs were all filled, she put the hot pad on the table the placed the coffee pot on it. She added a splash of cream to her mug.

Jim took his black.

Hartman loaded his up with cream and sugar. "Hypothetically, if you were to come into possession of a hand-drawn map of Thompson's bunker, would he ever find out where you were standing when the wind blew it out some random person's window and into your hands?"

"We already know where it is," Chelsea said. "What we want to know is—"

Jim kicked her under the table. "When good luck falls in my lap, I tend not to question it."

"Really?" Hartman asked. "Because cops are supposed to fine people who litter."

"Hard to fine a person when I don't know where it came from. And that was the whole point of this hypothetical situation, right?"

He stared at Jim for a long time. Finally, he got up from the table and went into the living room.

"Are we supposed to follow him?" Chelsea whispered.

"I don't think so. He would have told us to if he wanted us to." At least, Jim thought he would have.

The front door banged.

"Are you sure about that?" she said.

No. "Yeah. How about this coffee? It's pretty good, huh? Wonder what kind he buys."

"You're changing the subject."

"Just drink." Jim had drained his and added half a mug more. Where was that big, bald bastard, anyway? He got up and was about to go looking for him when the front door banged again, so he hurried back into his seat.

Hartman strode into the kitchen, blueprints in hand. Upon seeing Jim hustling back into his chair, he gave him a hard stare. But he didn't say anything. He just went to the far end of the table and spread out the plans. "Come down here."

Jim and Chelsea joined him while he smoothed the pages.

"This first page is a bird's eye view of the land." Hartman looked at Chelsea. "The closest thing I have to a map. It's kind of like a map-blueprint hybrid." He pointed at the thickest line on it, which looked like the base of a letter Y. "I assume this is the road you drove in on. When you came to the fork in the road, you went this way." He touched the left branch. "It brought you here. If you had gone right, you'd have ended up on the Thompson property. That's what the next page is for." He started to turn the page.

Jim put his hand out to stop him. Hartman looked up — irritation clear on his face, a retort obviously on the tip of his tongue — but Jim took his cellphone from his pocket, waved it at him, then took a picture.

Hartman looked to him for confirmation that it was okay to turn to the next page. After receiving a nod, he flipped to the second one. "Follow this road exactly 7.3 miles. Don't go far enough or go too far, and you're liable to set off his security protocols."

"Which are?" Jim snapped another photo.

"Here, let me show you." Hartman turned the page.

"What are all those markings?" Chelsea pointed at the plans. "None of them are in the key."

"Remember, this is all hypothetical."

Jim started to put his phone away.

Hartman grabbed his hand. "You might want to take notes."

Chapter Thirty

CHELSEA STARED AT THE ODOMETER. She knew Jim was keeping track, but he was also watching the road, and Hartman had been adamant that they travel exactly 7.3 miles from the fork — no more, no less — or the other measurements would be off and they'd risk tripping some sensors.

That wasn't what worried her the most, though. Her biggest concern was Hartman's warning as they were leaving.

Just make sure you keep your head on a swivel and your eyes wide open. I told you what I — hypothetically — installed for him, but I can't tell you what upgrades he's made since.

She didn't want to stereotype Oliver. If their theory was right and he and Nell were hiding there — in a bunker outfitted with security measures to keep trespassers away — then when the story ultimately broke, the press would have a field day with the details. People like her father would be ridiculed. Some would go so far as to vilify them as part of a fringe group. Radicalized. The reason Fletcher got out in the first place.

But the evidence was right in front of her. In two-tenths of a mile, anyway. He was dangerous and needed to be stopped. "Now!"

Jim slammed on his brakes. "Yep, 7.3 miles exactly. I guess we walk from here."

She got out of the car. "I still think we should call for backup."

He closed his door and popped the trunk. "The more people we bring out into the woods, the more chance we have of someone triggering a trap."

"We have Hartman's specs." Chelsea hefted her vest from the trunk then struggled into it.

"Of what he installed. But you heard him. Thompson could have upgraded. We have no idea what else might be out here. What if someone triggers something we didn't see? Something we didn't prepare them for?" Jim put his on with a lot more ease and grace.

She hated to admit it, but he was right. It was dangerous for them to be going in alone, but it was more dangerous for them to bring a bunch of people in with them. "I should have at least called my dad."

"He's a civilian."

"He's a former cop with survivalist training."

"I don't think IA would approve of him being out here. And he obviously wasn't comfortable enough with his knowledge of the subject earlier, as he sent us to Hartman, and that was just for a discussion. You really want him working with live rounds?" He shut the trunk.

"No, you're right. I'm just uneasy out here. I don't like the unknown." Gnarled trunks reached skyward, branched outward, obscured her view. Her gaze scanned the web of boughs above her, the limbs interlocked like arthritic fingers holding her inside their ancient embrace. She shook off a shiver and turned her attention to Jim.

His focus was on the screen of his phone. "We need to get off the road now. Thirty paces, due north. We should come to a security camera. Hartman said to go around the trail cam to the east to bypass the first of his monitors."

"You lead. I'll follow. Your stride length is probably closer to his than mine."

"Shit. I didn't consider that. You're probably right, but still. Do you think he meant his stride or Thompson's stride?"

"He installed it, so I'd say his stride."

"He's a couple inches taller than I am, so I'll take bigger steps."

"That's very scientific, Jim."

"Do you have a better idea?"

"We should have brought him with us."

"Hartman was barely willing to give us the plans. No way was he coming with us. Plus, he's a civilian. We can't bring him out here."

"He could probably walk right up to the door without notes or a map. And he works for law enforcement."

"He's a corrections officer at a prison."

"Black Meadow. It's a super-max."

"That doesn't make him a cop."

"Just walk thirty paces north."

He sighed and started walking. Chelsea kept her eyes peeled for a hidden security camera. When Jim had taken twenty-eight steps, she grabbed his arm and pointed at a hole in the tree right beside them. Nestled in it, partially hidden behind an oddly-bent dead branch that should have fallen long ago, was the glint of glass and a bit of matte black plastic.

The security camera.

Just as they were about to circle around the camera, the report of a gunshot echoed through the woods. Like a synchronized dance, they grabbed each other's arms, pulled one another down, then drew their weapons, their movements silent, fast, and fluid.

Her head was on a swivel, her gaze even more agile. The brisk autumn wind rustled the tree canopy overhead and the brush on the ground, even this deep in the woods. Every flutter of dappled shadow caught her eye. Every skitter of a squirrel's foot or fall of an acorn echoed in her head.

"A hunter?" she guessed.

"Not quite rifle season yet. Besides, you see any flashes of orange?"

Three more shots rang out in quick succession.

"That's not rifle fire," he said. "That's a handgun."

"Then that's no hunter."

He shook his head.

"Where's it coming from?"

Jim looked around. "I fucking hate the woods. It's hard to tell out here. Sound bounces around … I'm not sure, but I think that way." He pointed back toward the road. "If I'm right, that means it's probably not Thompson."

"Is that good news or bad?"

"Is gunfire ever good news?"

He had a point.

"So?" She raised her eyebrows.

Jim turned so he could watch their six.

"What do you suggest we do? Do we go back toward the shooters, assuming they're by the road, continue on toward the bunker, or split up?"

But he didn't answer.

"Well?"

"Listen."

She cocked her head, held her breath.

Silence.

"Shooting's stopped."

He nodded.

"You think it was hunters?"

"That would be poachers, since it's bow season. And since they were using handguns, even that's not likely."

"So, where are they now?" She left her real question unvoiced. What — or who — were they shooting at?

"Probably a bunch of rednecks shooting at cans. Just target practice in their back yard."

"We're in the middle of nowhere. This is no one's back yard."

"There are cabins out here. When you go to your hunting cabin, you shoot at stuff."

"And you're Mr. Duck Dynasty now?"

"I might not be a wilderness expert, but I know a few things."

"Are you saying this to make me feel better or you?"

"They're done shooting now, right? We can only work one problem at a time. Right now, we're here to find the Thompson bunker, and hopefully Nell and/or Oliver Thompson. Maybe get lucky and find Fletcher, too. Keep alert for whoever's out there — if they're still out there — but we need to stay on our mission."

"Our *mission*? Who are you? Rambo?"

"Come on. We go this way to avoid the camera."

They circled around the trunk to the east, then continue north ten more paces. From there, they turned west. Jim stepped off another forty.

Chelsea's pulse pounded in her ears, but that was the only sound she heard. Even her panting breath was drowned out by the rush of blood in her ears. But no more gunfire rang through the woods.

She didn't know if that made her feel better or worse.

He turned around. "This is where Hartman said there

could be a net. Look for a rope. Or a blanket of leaves. We don't want to trip that and end up dangling from a tree for the next three days."

God, no, she didn't want that. They'd be sitting ducks, for sure. She analyzed the branches, the tree trunks, the ground, and every dead leaf that had fallen on it, but she didn't see any rope or net or indication of a trap there. "Maybe your stride length was off and we're at the wrong tree."

"I don't think so. But maybe." He looked behind them, then ahead of them, then to each side. "Or maybe we veered a little north or south of due east. I fucking hate the woods. Give me a metropolis any day of the week."

"Should we back track?"

"Um …" Jim glanced down at his phone. "Assuming we can avoid this trap, the entrance to his bunker should be dead ahead twenty yards. The entrance is between two flat stones."

"So, why don't we try to find it?"

"Because if I step forward and we haven't found the trap or the trigger, we end up dangling above this tree."

She peered past Jim through the woods. "Or we duck behind this tree trunk and wait for Oliver and his sister to come to us."

"What?"

Chelsea grabbed Jim's elbow then tugged him behind the tree trunk. It wasn't much cover, but hopefully Oliver Thompson and his sister didn't expect anyone to be out in the middle of the woods and didn't look too closely for anyone to be around. Because they were currently climbing out of an underground bunker about fifteen yards away.

Her heart pounded. Blood rushed in her ears. Her chest heaved as she struggled to modulate her breath.

Jim stood erect against the trunk of the tree, reminiscent of a bulky cartoon character trying to hide behind a slender pole. He drew himself in, looked down at her, and held his finger to his lips.

She nodded, like she needed to be told.

"Come on," Oliver said. "The boys are picking us up at the Y."

"It's too far."

"Would you rather walk to Mom and Dad's? That's ten miles."

"I'd rather you leave me here. I can't believe you're doing this to me."

The brush rustled. It sounded like it was right on the other side of the tree Chelsea and Jim were hiding behind.

Jim tipped his head toward her holster.

She nodded and pulled her weapon.

He reached for his.

"Doing this to you? Do you have any idea what you've done to me? You probably cost me my career. Hell, you may have cost me *my* freedom. And for what?"

The rustling stopped. Chelsea didn't dare move because she didn't want to draw attention to herself, and she suspected the Thompsons were too close for her to risk exposure. If they noticed her or Jim now, they would likely stop talking, and they seemed poised to reveal something pertinent to the case. So, she held her breath and waited.

"I couldn't go to college because there wasn't money for us both to go, and Mom and Dad sent you because they said I could always rely on my body to make a living with a physical trade."

"You could have worked your way through school."

"You didn't even want to go to college! You partied for four years and majored in art. Art! You didn't need a degree for your career. Especially since you make most of your money illegally."

"Why do you hate me, Ollie? You're supposed to be my guy. You and me, since the beginning."

"Oh, no. Don't play the twin sister card."

Twins? She didn't realize that. Not that it mattered. Did it?

"I'm not playing. I love you. And you're betraying me."

"Betraying you? I'm *always* there for you. When dirtbag after dirtbag broke your heart, who set you up with a good guy? An honest, hard-working, good man who would care for you and protect you and treat you right. And what did you do?"

"I moved on. What did you expect me to do? He was boring."

"Why? Because he had a job? Paid taxes? Didn't kill people and dress them up like Disney princesses for grins and giggles?"

"Scott didn't dress them up like Disney princesses. He paid homage to the Brothers Grimm fairy tales."

"That doesn't make it better, Nell."

"That's art, Ollie."

"You left a law man for a serial killer!"

"He's pure. He's real. You aren't an artist, so you don't understand the passion that he puts into his work."

"I understand he's a homicidal maniac."

"You're not even trying to see my side of this."

"Your side is on the wrong side of the law. I'm a cop, Nell!"

"Which are you first? My brother or a cop?"

"I'll always be your brother first."

"Then take these cuffs off me and let me go."

"The best thing I can do for you is to keep these cuffs on you and bring you in."

"I'll never forgive you for this. Mom and Dad will never forgive you for this."

"Nell, so far, you helped Fletcher escape, but you haven't helped him kill anyone yet. You stay with him, and you will. He'll make you cross a line that you can't come back from. I'm taking you in. Throw yourself on the mercy of the court, cooperate. Tell them where to find him. They'll be lenient. They'll get you help. You could end up with parole, community service. Practically a slap on the wrist. This doesn't have to ruin your life."

"No, it doesn't. But it will. *You're* ruining my life, Ollie. And I'll never speak to you again if you do this to me."

"Not to you, Nell. *For* you."

"Screw you, Oliver. I won't tell the cops anything. I'll do extra time before I betray Scott."

"Then you're a fool. And I feel sorry for you."

"I don't want your pity."

"You have it, anyway."

The rustling began again. They came abreast of the tree as Jim and Chelsea stepped out from behind it.

Oliver stopped in his tracks. His grip on his sister's arm fell slack.

She elbowed him in the side then broke into a run.

"Damn it! Nell! Wait!" He glared at Chelsea and Jim as he chased after her.

"Freeze!" Chelsea called, even though she knew it was pointless.

The girl was fast, and she obviously knew where she was going. She reached a path while they were still high-stepping through brush, then she broke into a sprint.

Oliver was the next to reach the trail. His sister's speed was impressive, but it was no match for him, and he ran her down in under ten seconds. Jim wasn't far behind him.

"What are you doing here?" Oliver snapped.

Chelsea, however, wasn't a fan of the woods to begin with, and Milo Hartman had amped her fear because of hidden booby traps, so she brought up the rear by a good twenty seconds. She had no trouble hearing them from a distance, though, and she could see the hatred in everyone's eyes long before she reached the group.

"We were looking for you. And her. And Fletcher."

"Fletcher's not here," Oliver spat. "And I'm taking her in. If you guys arrest her, the DA will throw every charge he can at her. If she comes in of her own volition, he'll go easier on her."

"But I'm not going in of my own volition. You're dragging me in. Makes no difference which of you does the dirty deed. A pig's a pig."

"What's the matter with you?" Oliver said. "Who taught you to talk like that?"

She spat at him.

He sighed. "I'm taking her. Jeremy and Ethan are meeting me about seven miles past the intersection of the Y. They're giving me a ride to the station. My parents are meeting us there with our attorney."

"That the same attorney who's lying about the sprained wrist you obviously don't have?" Jim pointed to Oliver's arm, which wasn't in a splint.

"Can we just let that shit go? My family's got enough to deal with. I don't need more beef with you."

"You were the one causing the trouble."

"I didn't st—" He sighed. "Maybe I did. I heard you were a dirty cop. It rubbed me the wrong way. I take my job seriously. I don't like people disrespecting the badge." He lifted his sister's arm. "Obviously. I'm arresting my own sister."

"I'm not a dirty cop," Jim said.

Chelsea shook her head. "He really isn't."

"If I don't end up in jail over all this," Oliver said, "maybe I can buy you a beer and hear your side of the story."

Jim's jaw ticked. His nostrils flared.

"Or maybe I'll just believe you and buy you a beer as an apology. But I'm guessing I won't get the chance, so it's probably not going to matter one way or another."

Jim tipped his head toward the road, and they all started walking. "We'll see about that."

"Isn't this nice?" Nell sneered. "Bunch of pigs, kissing each other's asses."

Oliver bristled, but Jim waved him off.

She oinked and laughed.

"You know since the mayor lost the election, you probably lost your protection," Jim said. "He still has connections, but not like he did. And not enough to sweep something like this under the rug."

Chelsea shook her head.

"What'd you have on him, anyway?"

"I didn't *have* anything on him. He was a family friend. And he liked me. You have family friends all over town, Richie Rich. Don't act like you're offended that I have one." He sighed. "Had one."

"Poor baby," Nell said. "I'd play the violin for you, but my hands are otherwise occupied."

They reached Jim's SUV, but no one was waiting to give Oliver a ride.

Oliver looked around, frowned, swore.

Chelsea said, "This is where Miller and Berger should be, right?"

Nell broke into a bitter laugh. "Guess they aren't the good friends you thought they were."

"Ride with us," Jim said. "You can call off your boys once we get cell service."

"Or we'll pass them as we drive out of here." Chelsea headed for the front seat, but Jim gave her a subtle shake of his head, so she climbed into the back of the car with Nell. "Protocol," she said to Oliver then shrugged before she closed the door.

Nell looked her over, head to toe. "I don't get what the big deal is."

"What big deal?"

Jim started the engine.

"Scott always gushes about you like you're some kind of Belle or something."

"Bell?"

"Yeah, Belle."

"Like, ring-ring?"

"Wow. Clearly not as well read as the character."

Chelsea rubbed her head. Fairy tales. Fletcher was talking about her with his adoring fans. And apparently comparing her to Beauty. It was beyond gross.

"Belle?" Nell continued. "With an E?"

"I know what you mean."

"So, what is it?"

"What is what?"

"Why are you so special, Belle-with-an-E?"

"He didn't think of me as Belle. He thought of me as Aurora. And he tried to put me to sleep for good."

"You're so lucky." Her voice was breathless, her eyes wide. A rapturous smile crossed her face as she stared into the distance.

"Are you kidding me? It wasn't make believe, Nell. It wasn't fancy gowns and happily ever after. He tried to kill me. He wanted me dead. Do you even understand the permanence of that?"

"He was giving you an honor."

"You're insane."

Oliver turned around. "That's my sister you're talking about."

"It's probably the best defense she can mount at this point."

"Sullivan." Jim glared at her through the rearview mirror.

Oliver scowled and faced forward again.

They came to the fork. Jim turned onto the main road. Less than a minute later, he rolled to a stop. "Found your ride."

Chelsea leaned forward to see what was going on. He had been talking to Oliver, who had already exited the vehicle, Jim right behind him. She turned to Nell. "Wait here."

"Aw, gee. Can't I go stand in the woods, too?"

When she got out of the car, Jim pointed to it. "Go keep an eye on her."

"Where's she going to go?"

He stood halfway between the stranded vehicle and his own, frowning at her. But he didn't argue.

"What happened to you guys?" Oliver said to his friends. "You were supposed to meet me fifteen minutes ago."

"Someone shot one of his tires," Berger said.

"What?" Oliver looked down at the car.

"Yeah," Miller said. "I was driving slow. These roads suck as it is, and I'd only been here a couple of times in the summer. It looks different in the fall with no leaves on the trees. Didn't want to miss the turn."

"You have GPS." Oliver frowned.

"I was fucking driving slow. You want to hear the story or not?"

"Fine."

"Someone shot at us."

"You and the car look fine to me."

Miller bristled. "You calling me a liar? After we came out here to help you and nearly died for it?"

"He just got done changing the tire," Berger said. "Donut's on the front passenger side."

Oliver's jaw twitched.

"Look if you don't believe me. Like I'd make up a story like that."

"It would take a hell of a shot to take out someone's tire while they're on the move."

"I was practically at a standstill, dick."

"We fired back, Thompson," Berger said. "I can't believe you didn't hear us."

"Can't hear anything in the bunker. That's the point of a bunker. It's cut off from the outside world."

"I heard them," Jim said. "Sullivan and I both heard them."

Oliver stared at his two friends for a long while, then he said, "You need a ride, or you need me to call AAA or something?"

"Call—there's no service out here, jackass," Miller said. "If there was, we would have called you."

"Drive in front of us," Chelsea said. "If that tire gives you trouble, we'll see you."

"You want to ride with us?" Berger asked Oliver.

"He stays with me and my partner," Jim said.

Berger looked at his buddy. Even Miller looked ready to fight if Thompson wanted him to.

Oliver shook his head. "They have Nell. The plan's still in effect. I'm going to walk her in. Hopefully I can get some leniency for her."

"Okay." Berger nodded. "We'll see you at the station."

Miller nodded at Jim. "Thanks for following us."

On the way back to their car, Berger and Miller pulled

out. Thompson snuck a glance at the spare tire as they drove past. Only then did his shoulders relax a little.

Chelsea shook her head.

Jim whispered, "I saw it, too." Then to Oliver, he said, "It must be hard to not even be able to trust your friends."

"I don't trust anybody. And you're a fool if you do."

"Why? You think because your family let you down you shouldn't rely on anybody? Thompson, you can't pick your blood. You can pick your friends, though. Your partners came through for you. And, strange though this situation is, the three of you seem to be trying to do the right thing. You were right to trust them. And you're right to trust me and Sullivan, too." They reached the car. He grabbed the handle. "We're—"

"Jim!" Chelsea cried and flung open her door.

Nell lay in the back seat, both wrists slashed.

Chapter Thirty-One

Jim RACED DOWN THE ROAD, wincing as he hit another hole. The road had more divots than smooth spots.

Miller and Berger signaled at them as they sped by, but there wasn't time to stop and explain.

Still wasn't cell service to call them. And they didn't have a patrol unit, so they didn't hear the radio call he'd made to dispatch. There wasn't time for a bus to reach them. By the time an ambulance found them, he'd already be at a hospital. So, he had the ER on standby.

They'd used rubber gloves to tie tourniquets around each of Nell's arms, and Chelsea was in the backseat, applying pressure to her wounds with Oliver's coat. And probably saying every prayer she knew under her breath. Lord knew, he was, too.

Oliver, however, was white as a sheet. And praying aloud. "Please, God, don't let her die. Not now. Not like this. Please, I'll do anything. Just … not now. Not here. Not like this. Please …"

When Jim hit paved road, he flipped on the red-and-blues. There was no traffic yet, so there was no need for the siren, but he'd need it soon.

"How long?" Chelsea asked.

"Please …" Oliver continued.

"Ten minutes, I think."

"No …"

"How's she doing?" He pressed harder on the gas pedal.

"I think the bleeding has slowed, but I don't want to lift his jacket to see." She met his gaze in the mirror. "You might want to drive faster, though."

"I'm already driving a lot faster than is safe."

"God, please. Not my sister …"

"I don't know this area that well, and we're in the middle of nowhere."

"I'm just saying sooner is better than later."

"No kidding."

"Please …"

Jim took a deep breath. They were finally approaching civilization. He flipped on the siren. Maybe it was closer to seven minutes, though it would all depend on traffic at this point. After easing onto the highway, he began to weave through traffic. Thankfully, most people were courteous and law-abiding and got the hell out of his way.

Chelsea jammed her leg into the back of his seat. He looked in the rearview mirror. Her eyes were wide, and she gave him a small shake of her head.

"Oh, God, please. Not my sister."

He floored it. They reached the hospital three minutes later. ER staff was waiting with a gurney at the door, and they had Nell out of the car and whisked away before he even had the gearshift in park. Oliver was out of the car just as fast, following right behind them.

Chelsea just sat in the backseat, dumbfounded.

"Shut the door. I'll go park."

"My arms are numb."

"I'm not surprised."

She reached for the door. It took two tries before she successfully pulled it closed.

After he parked, they sat quietly for a moment. Then both climbed out at the same time. Without either of them speaking, they fell into each other's arms. He held her while she cried for about a minute, then she stepped back. Just before she wiped her face, she stopped and stared at her hands, crimson with Nell's blood. Then she glanced down at her body. "I look like I've been through war."

"Probably feel like it, too."

"I can't go in there like this."

"I have a spare jacket in my ... no, I don't." He sighed. "The nurses can probably give you scrubs or something."

"Probably an ugly Christmas sweater in lost and found."

"It's October."

"Ugly clothes know no calendar day."

"That's likely true." But neither of them moved.

She looked up at him. "You don't want to go in, either?"

"If she didn't make it, Oliver's going to be inconsolable. And he already hates me. I'm not looking forward to the backlash."

"He'll blame me. I was the one who left her alone in the car."

"How'd she do it?" he asked.

"I don't know." Chelsea opened the car door. Before searching for the weapon, she turned back to him. "God, Jim, your car."

He didn't want to think about it, let alone look inside. His car was his baby.

It wasn't long before she took a glove from her pocket to retrieve the weapon in question — a hunting knife.

"Is it engraved?"

She turned it in her hand. "Yeah. E. A. T."

"Eat? That's kind of sick."

"I'm sure it's not the word. I'm guessing it's her initials."

"Nell Thompson?"

"Eleanor. Her middle name's probably Anne or Abigail or something with an A."

He'd forgotten her name was Eleanor. It wasn't exactly a common name for the times. Not that Nell was, either.

"You have a bag?" she asked.

Jim checked his pockets. "One. Not sure if it's big enough with the blade open."

"Not sure we want to bag it unless we fold it up. That blade is sharp."

"We fold it, we lose evidence."

"Jim, this isn't a crime. We know who did it and with what." She snapped the knife closed then dropped it into the evidence bag.

"You're the one with the glove and the bag."

"I know. I'm … I'm just at a loss. If she does die, there will be an investigation. I'm just glad she didn't get the weapon from one of us."

"Why do you think Oliver didn't frisk her after he cuffed her?"

"Why didn't we?"

"Because I assumed he did," Jim said. "He's a cop."

"That's his sister. He obviously wasn't thinking clearly."

"Were we?"

"I don't know." She sighed. "I hate this case. These cases."

"Me, too." They started walking toward the hospital. "That blade is sharp."

"I know. That's what I said."

"No, I mean, it's *sharp*."

"Yeah."

"If she wanted to kill herself, I mean really kill herself, she could have shredded one of her arteries. But she didn't."

"You don't know that."

"Yes, I do. If she had, there would be a lot more blood in my car." He stopped before entering the hospital."

"There's a ton of blood on the seat and the floorboards. And on me." She gestured to herself. "I look like a butcher."

"No. I mean puddles. And she'd have died before we got in the car, let alone before we reached the hospital."

"I don't know …"

"She grew up with a hunting family. She probably knows about anatomy."

"Of deer, maybe."

"Her bedroom is a shrine to taxidermy."

"Again, that's animals, not people."

"Her boyfriend is a doctor."

"That doesn't make her one."

"I'm telling you, Chelsea. She knew what she was doing."

"To what end? What purpose did it serve?"

"It got her out of going to jail."

"For now. This was nothing but a brief reprieve."

"Maybe you gave her the idea."

"Me?"

"You said it yourself, she's nuts. She already has a cop saying so. Now she's supposedly tried to kill herself. She's going to be on suicide watch. It's everything she needs for an insanity plea. You handed it to her on a silver platter."

"This is my fault now?"

"Not your *fault*, per se. We're all culpable to some extent. We didn't frisk her. We didn't watch what we said around her. But she's definitely got a defense now. And her attorney's never going to let us near her. We have to talk to her the second the doctors let us. Before her family gets the lawyers involved. Or we'll never get a bead on Fletcher."

"I can't believe you think this is my fault."

"I just said it wasn't *just* your fault."

She shook her head and stormed inside.

He followed, shaking his head, too. Chelsea was already at the desk. He thought about waiting in the chairs and letting her update him, but a nurse buzzed her through a locked door. So, he approached, reaching for his shield. When he reached the window, he said, "Detective McPherson."

"Mm-hmm." She didn't look up.

"You just took my partner back."

"Mm-hmm." Her fingers flew a mile a minute on the keyboard, and her gaze remained fixed on the computer screen

"Can you let me in?"

"No." She continued working.

"Miss? Do you mind giving me a moment of your time?"

Finally, she stopped typing and looked at him.

"We brought in a suicide attempt. Her brother isn't in this waiting room. My partner was just taken somewhere. I can only assume they're both with the patient, who is an important witness to a very important case. I need to get back there, and I'd appreciate it if you'd stop stonewalling me."

She took off her glasses. "The patient in question in with her doctors. Her brother is in the waiting area because he is family. You and your partner are not. If a police officer needs to be posted there, then we can make that happen. But I assure you, your belligerent attitude is not going to expedite that process. Your partner is not with the patient or her family. She is changing her clothes because she looks like she just came from the Battle of Gettysburg. When she's presentable, she will join you in the seats over there." She nodded toward a waiting area where about twenty other people were seated. "When I have news about the patient you brought in, I or someone else will let you know. Is that all?"

"Other than police presence outside her door, I guess so."

"Are you sure?" She crossed her arms.

"I can be the police presence outside her door until patrol gets here."

"Anything else?"

"I suppose an apology is in order." He wasn't sure if he meant he owed her one or the other way around.

Her expression softened.

The door opened. Chelsea stepped out in a pair of scrubs. She was holding a bulky plastic bag, which likely carried her soiled clothes. She nodded at the nurse. "Thanks."

"Why don't the two of you come with me? The waiting room over there is pretty full."

Jim lunged for the door, but it closed before he could reach it, so the nurse buzzed them in. She gave them directions to the waiting room for the OR where Nell was being worked on, then returned to her desk before either of them could thank her.

As they walked down the hall, he said, "You look very medicine-y."

"Shut up. I'm irritated with you."

"I know. I'm trying to apologize to you." Not that he entirely understood why.

She sighed. "This isn't my fault, you know."

"I *know*. I said I'm sorry."

"You didn't, actually."

"Well, I am."

"What if she dies?"

"She won't."

"What if she did?"

"She didn't."

"You don't know that."

"I do."

"How?" Chelsea looked at him.

"Oliver would have found us if she had. Or the nurse would have told us."

"Should we call his friends? His parents? The captain?"

"Let's see what we're dealing with first." They walked in silence the rest of the way.

In the waiting room, Oliver was alone, perched on the edge of a chair, rocking back and forth and muttering to himself.

"He's still praying," Jim said.

"Wouldn't you be?" Chelsea asked.

They walked over. She headed for the seat nearest him, so Jim planned on taking the one on the far side.

But Oliver stood before they reached him. "What do you want? Here to finish the job?"

Chelsea recoiled.

"We're here to see how your sister is," Jim said. "And how you are."

"Bullshit. You're here to make sure she doesn't make it."

"You don't believe that. Cops don't take lives, and you know it."

"No? She tried to kill herself on your watch. On *her* watch." He tipped his chin at Chelsea. "You left her alone on purpose. Hell, for all I know, you slit her wrists yourself before you got out of the car. I was already out of the vehicle. You were right beside her. It wouldn't have taken anything for you to run a blade right up her arms before climbing out. I'd never have known."

Chelsea gasped.

"Why would she do that?"

"Get rid of my whole family, right?" Oliver stood then started to pace. "Yeah, it all makes sense now. You're a dirty cop. Her dad's a dirty cop. Only makes sense she becomes one, too. It's in her blood, in her training."

"How dare you?" she said.

"How dare I? How dare you? My sister is fighting for her life because you tried to kill her. And why? Because you're jealous that your ex picked her over you?"

"Are you kidding me?" Chelsea's face paled. "He tried to kill me. Why would I want him? Why would your sister want him? Why would *anyone* want him? I want your sister alive. I tried to save her. She's our best chance of finding Fletcher and putting him away for good this time."

"Liar!"

Jim took the bagged knife from his pocket. "Look familiar?"

"Where'd you get that?"

"My car. Where your sister dropped it. You never frisked her when you found her at the family bunker, did you?"

Oliver ran his hand through his hair.

"Yeah, you're the pot calling the kettle a bad cop, but you might want to look in the mirror."

"You're mixing metaphors," Chelsea whispered.

Jim glanced at her. "I don't give a rat's ass." He turned back to Oliver. "You've been calling me a dirty cop since the day we met. Now you're throwing those accusations at my partner and her dad, too. All because you don't want to admit that your sister is a criminal and you made a few mistakes. You want to take the moral high ground? Then admit when you're wrong."

A doctor stepped out of the OR door. "Oliver Thompson?"

He jumped to his feet. "Yes?"

"Come with me. We need to talk."

Chapter Thirty-Two

"THE SUSPENSE IS KILLING ME." It was Chelsea's turn to pace back and forth.

"She made it," Jim said.

"You can't know that."

"Do you hear him wailing?"

"No."

"Then you should know I'm right."

"Most men are stoic."

"He was falling apart in the car when he thought she was dying."

"That's different than being faced with the certainty of it."

Jim sighed.

But she knew she was right. He might have more experience in the field than she did, but she'd bet she had more experience trying to figure out men than he did. They were all enigmas, but one thing remained consistent across the breed — they tended to hide their emotions. At least, they did when they had a chance to prepare themselves.

Like Oliver did with the doctor.

"Maybe I'll go ask a nurse," she said.

"Just wait a minute. He'll come back."

But he didn't. Five minutes later, Chelsea said, "I'm going to find a nurse."

"Fine."

She walked down the hall to the nurses' station, but no one was there. On the way back, she saw the doctor who had come for Oliver stepping out of a patient's room. "Excuse me?"

He looked up. "Yes?"

"I'm Detective Sullivan. You were the doctor who worked on Nell Thompson, right? The attempted suicide?"

"Oh, yes."

"Did she make it?"

"Weren't you with her brother?"

"We were, but after you spoke with him, he never came back out to tell us what you said. We don't know if he's with her or in the chapel or calling his family …"

"Ah." He nodded. "I suppose it could be any of those things. She did make it."

Chelsea sighed with relief. "Thank you."

"She's going to have a long recovery, but it's not her physical scars that concern me."

"Psychological?"

"Yes. It's not always the horizontal cuts that are a cry for help. Sometimes the vertical cuts are, too. Her cuts weren't deep enough to hit the arteries. She lost a lot of blood, sure, and she took a big risk, but—"

"But it was a calculated risk."

"Yes."

"She didn't hit any arteries?"

"Not even a nick. It was like she knew what she was doing."

"I see." Chelsea nodded. "So, what happens now?"

"Well, she may have nerve damage. There will be rehab. And counseling, certainly. Once she's out of post-op, we'll have a psychiatrist talk to her. In cases like hers, there's a mandatory seventy-two-hour evaluation."

"No visitors."

"No."

"What about police questioning?"

"Are you here as a friend of her brother's?"

"More like in an official capacity."

"What's going on? Is she a danger to our other patients?"

"In her current state, I doubt it. But her associates could be. We'd like to position a guard at her door."

"Oh. Okay. Um, well. That's new to me. I don't know what protocol is for that. I … well. Uh. Okay. Well, do what you need to do, I guess, and I'll talk to the chief of staff. Or the administrator. Or, well, I'll talk to people. In the meantime, get your people here."

"We're on it. Thank you. And you said you don't know where Officer Thompson is?"

"If he's not with his sister, I'd try the chapel."

"Which room is his sister in?"

"Room four-one-two."

"And the chapel?"

"Third floor. Get off the elevator and turn right. You'll see the signs. You can't miss it."

"Thanks. One more thing."

"What?"

"Your name?"

"Oh. Right. Sorry. Lane. Dr. Lane."

"Thank you, Dr. Lane. Here's my card." She went to produce one from her pocket only to realize she was in scrubs. "Sorry. I had to change. I was covered in … well, long story."

"I heard."

"My partner has cards, if you'd come with me, I can give you one of his so you have our contact information."

"Please leave it at the nurses' station. I have to make arrangements for the guard."

"There's no one at the nurses' station."

"What?" His eyes widened and he ran down the hall.

Chelsea followed him.

"Where is everyone?"

She shrugged. "I don't know. I tried here before I tracked you down."

He frowned, picked up the phone, then spoke into the receiver, "Code forty-seven. Code forty-seven."

"You have a code for nurses to return to their stations?"

"We have a code for everything. I just never heard this one called before. There's always someone at the desk."

A few minutes passed, but no one returned. They exchanged worried glances. Jim sauntered down the hall.

"You're not a nurse," she said.

"Not that I know of. What's going on?"

"We can't find any of the staff on this floor," Dr. Lane said.

Chelsea nodded at the phone. "Page them again."

"Code forty-seven." His voice was taking on a desperate tone. "Code forty-seven."

They stood there, staring at each other, for about thirty seconds, with no movement in the hallway.

"Is this just for nurses to come," Jim asked, "or is it for any medical staff? I haven't seen any doctors on this floor, either."

"It's just me and one other doctor right now. We're short-staffed today. But we should have seen someone by now. I haven't seen a hospital this dead since *Halloween II*."

"I hated that movie," Jim said. "It was so unbelievable. No hospitals are like that."

"This one is right now," Dr. Lane said.

"True."

"Really?" Chelsea raised her eyebrows. "That's your problem with that movie? Not the un-killable monster, but the quiet hospital?"

"Well, you have to suspend belief in a slasher film."

She shook her head.

A nurse ran down the hall toward them.

"Liz!" Dr. Lane said. "Where is everyone? What's going on? Are you crying?"

She nodded and wiped tears from her eyes. "It's Dr. Norrick. She had a heart attack. We tried, but …"

"Oh, my God. Excuse me." He turned and started jogging down the hall. "What room?"

She ran alongside him.

Chelsea turned to Jim. "This day just keeps getting better and better."

"And now you know why I didn't become a doctor. They lose too many patients."

"Dr. Norrick wasn't a patient. She was a colleague. And we deal in death every day."

"But we don't know them or work on them first. And we get justice for them."

"Speaking of, Nell did make it. And you were right. Dr. Lane thinks she knew what she was doing when she cut herself. He's going to hold her for a psych eval. If we want to talk to her, we need to do it after she wakes from the anesthesia but before they put her in the ward."

"Small window."

"Yep."

"Do we know where she is?"

"Room four-one-two."

"Let's head there now. Maybe she's up."

"Leave your card for him at the nurses' station. I didn't have one on me."

Jim took one from his pocket. He placed it by the phone, then they headed down the hall.

They found Nell's room with ease, and as luck would have it, her brother wasn't there.

"Wonder where Oliver is," Jim said.

"Dr. Lane said he might be in the chapel or calling his family."

"I'm guessing if he's talking to his family, they'll be here soon. And if they're on the way, their lawyer isn't far behind them. That means our window is closing fast."

"Well, there's not much we can do about that. She's not lucid yet."

"Do you think a nurse can give her something to rouse her?"

"No. And even if they could, they wouldn't. Besides, they're all busy with Dr. Norrick."

He sighed.

"Wouldn't matter if they did. She'd be loopy with drugs if they gave her some kind of speed to wake her. And it couldn't possibly be good for her."

"We need a lead."

"Not at the expense of her health."

"She clearly wasn't concerned about her health earlier."

"That doesn't make your suggestion right."

"I know." He kicked the chair. "I'm just tired of all the dead ends."

"If it makes you feel any better, she probably wouldn't have talked to us, anyway."

"It doesn't." But he chuckled.

"What are you doing in here?"

Chelsea looked at the door as Oliver stormed in.

"How are you doing?" Jim asked.

"How the fuck do you think I'm doing? My sister is fighting for her life. No thanks to you."

"I'm not doing this with you again."

She stepped between them before things got out of hand. "Oliver, Dr. Lane told me he thinks your sister will make a full physical recovery."

"Oh, he did, did he? That's quite the HIPAA violation."

"He was answering my questions, doctor to police detective. He didn't break any laws."

"We'll see what our lawyer has to say about that."

"I thought you were trying to get your sister a reduced sentence," Jim said. "Why are you suddenly making life harder for all of us?"

"I'm doing what's best for my family."

"What's best for your family is making sure you do everything you can to put Fletcher back in prison."

"What's best for my family is making sure my sister lives through this ordeal. What's best for my family is making sure my mother and father don't have heart attacks from the stress. You think you know me, you think you have a handle on my family, but you don't know jack. So, just leave me alone. Get out of my sister's room. And don't come back."

Chelsea laid her hand on his arm. "Oliver, if Nell told you anything that will help us, we can talk to the DA—"

He flung her hand off of him. "Get. Out."

"If you change your mind, you know where to find us," Jim said as he exited the room.

"I'm glad she's going to be okay," Chelsea said, then she followed her partner. Out in the hallway, she turned to him. "Now what?"

"Back to the station, I guess. Least we can do is fill in Davenport."

"On the way, I'll try calling Miller and Berger. They have to be wondering what the hell happened."

"Assuming their spare held and they got out of the woods."

They didn't talk the rest of the way to the car. Jim shook his head when he climbed behind the wheel. "Smells like copper in here. I don't think the best detailer in the city will be able to fix this mess."

"Do you know the best detailer?"

"Of course." He backed out of his spot then headed toward the station.

She called dispatch and asked for Miller's cell number. They gave her his info for future reference, which she typed into her contacts list, then they transferred her. He answered the call and screamed at her for a full two minutes before she had a chance to tell him what happened. After she filled him in, he asked which hospital, thanked her, then hung up on her.

"Just as pleasant as his buddy," Jim said.

"Kind of can't blame him," she answered. "You'd probably have done the same thing."

"Don't compare me to them."

"Am I wrong?"

"Just … don't compare me to them." But the corner of his lip ticked up.

Her phone rang before she could answer. "It's Rafferty. Wonder what he wants."

"Bet I know one way you can find out."

She stuck her tongue out at Jim as she hit the green button. "Hey, Neil. What's up?"

"Where are you?"

"On the way to the station. Why?"

"Good. Giadone and I will meet you there."

"What's going on?"

"We got him."

Her pulse picked up. "Him who?"

"Boundy."

Chapter Thirty-Three

As JIM SAT across from Phillip Boundy in the interrogation room, he considered investing in aluminum. With as many nut jobs as they'd been dealing with lately, the price of aluminum had to be on the rise. If it wasn't, it should be. Or would be soon.

Jim thought back to his first day as a patrol cop. A disturbed man was causing a scene at a park. There were young kids everywhere, and the situation was dicey. He and Dom were trying to defuse the situation but weren't having much luck. Two other patrol units showed up and had similar results. They were about to surround the man, weapons drawn, but were worried about potential casualties. *Young* casualties. Then a grizzled detective pulled up in a beat-up old sedan. The guy looked like he was a day from retirement and couldn't wait for his gold watch. As soon as he got out of his car, he told all the young, foolish unis — Jim and Dom included — to stand down and get out of his way. He put on a rumpled fedora as old as he was, then opened his trunk. After rooting around for a moment, he came out with a roll of Reynolds Wrap then ambled over to the guy. Said, "I hear 'em, too. Put this on." The guy just stared at him for a moment. The detective tapped his hat. "Foiled lined." He offered the Reynolds again. The man yanked the box from him, ripped a sheet of foil from the roll, made himself a beanie, stuck it on his head, then sighed with relief. The detective cuffed him, no problem. Crisis averted without anyone drawing a weapon. The man followed the detective to his car with a smile on his face. While he climbed into the back of the sedan, the detective returned the box to his trunk and said, "It pays to keep this stuff with you. They think it shields 'em from whatever they think's buggin' 'em."

Jim and Dom laughed at the time. But it had worked for the old detective.

Now he was thinking he should definitely invest in the stuff. Or at least start carrying it with him. Because people in Steel City were bat shit crazy.

At least the fucker sitting across from him was.

Boundy looked at him, stuck his finger in his ear, then licked it. "Yum."

Chelsea gagged.

Definitely needed to start carrying foil. And probably invest in it, too.

Jim opened the folder of evidence they'd gathered against him, leafed through it, then went back to the beginning. "All right, Phil. Your only hope at leniency is to cooperate with us. Because we have enough evidence to put you away for the rest of your life."

He continued staring at his fingers, the chains of his restraints occasionally clinking against the ring they were threaded through on the table. "Will I be at Black Meadow? Can you arrange it so I'm the Grimm Reaper's cell mate?"

"Is that what all the killings were about?" Chelsea asked. "You bunking with Fletcher?"

"If you had the chance to cohabitate with him, wouldn't you take it?" Boundy slowly raked his gaze from his hands, across the table, then up her body until it bore into her eyes. "But you did have that chance, didn't you, Aurora? You had it, and you squandered it. Tell me, what makes you think tainted trash like yourself is too good for the master?"

"Get out of here, Sullivan," Jim said.

Her breath hitched. Her hands splayed on the table.

"Oh, he told me all about what a cold fish you were." Boundy leaned forward.

Chelsea's cheeks flushed. Her chest heaved as she breathed heavier and faster.

"At first, he thought you were chaste, saving yourself for him. But then he realized you were just a lousy lay. Not pure because of virtue but inexperienced because of inability. Simply lack of talent."

"Sullivan, out. Now."

Boundy placed his hands flat on the table, mimicking Chelsea's posture. His breath rate was also increasing. "But then, I thought to myself, maybe she's not bad in bed. Maybe she's just not interested in him. I bet I could show her a good time. I bet I could show her what a real man is like. Then I could tell Fletcher all about what she feels like. What she smells like. What she tastes—"

"That's it." Jim shoved his chair back so hard, it banged off the wall. He grabbed Chelsea's arm, hauled her to her feet, then dragged her from the room to the sounds of Boundy's maniacal laughter bouncing off the walls.

In the hallway, she rounded on him, planted her hands against his chest, and shoved him with enough force, he lost his balance and had to take a step back so he didn't fall. "What the hell?"

"That's what I want to say to you!"

"I don't get it, Chels. I was coming to your rescue."

"Do I look like I need rescuing?"

"Well, actually, yeah."

"I was acting, Jim."

"Could have fooled me."

"I'm pretty sure I did."

He rubbed the back of his neck. "I'm so confused."

"Clearly."

"What's going on?"

"Boundy let his guard down. He thinks he's getting me agitated. Thinks he's getting to me. He's bloating with self-worth and self-aggrandizement. It was loosening his tongue. I can't go back in there now. He'll see right through my charade."

"You mean, you really weren't upset?"

"Did you really think I didn't let Fletcher touch me because I'm cold? And that I'd care if he told people that? No. And no."

"Oh." He didn't know what to say to that. "Sorry. I wish you'd have told me that was your plan."

"I didn't know that was Boundy's plan, or I would have. Now, we're just two cops going straight at him."

"No. We don't have to be."

"What do you mean?"

"We keep your plan going."

"How?"

"Don't go back in."

"Like hell I'm not."

"Watch from the mirror."

"I have questions for him, too."

"I'll wear an ear piece. If you have any questions I miss, tell me. I'll ask for you."

"No. I want to be in the room, same as you. I deserve to be in there."

"You do. But you can't be."

She glared at him.

"Chels, you know this is the right move. I'm sorry I didn't recognize your play. But it was a good play. Let me finish it for you."

"This sucks."

"You've interrogated people without me before."

She rolled her eyes. "You better ask whatever I tell you to."

"Come on." He walked her into the observation room and put in an ear piece. After making sure the mic worked — and suffering one last dirty look from her — he returned to the interrogation room.

"Where's your partner?" Boundy licked his lips.

"After that stunt you pulled? I'm not letting you anywhere near her."

"Relax, Detective. I'd never touch her. I'm gay. I only have eyes for one man." His gaze traveled Jim's body head to toe and back.

"Knock that shit off."

He laughed. "You've got some sexy muscles, I'll give you that. But I didn't mean you. I meant Reaper."

Jim sat across from him. "Walk me through your thought process slowly, because I don't get it. If you wanted to bunk with him, why'd you help him escape?"

"Not saying I did, not saying I didn't. But don't you think I'd rather the two of us be free together than be incarcerated together?"

"All right. I can see your point there. Here's what I don't get. Once Fletcher was out, why the copycat kills?"

"Who said they're copycat kills?"

"They aren't Fletcher's MOs."

"They're fairy tale murders."

"You clearly aren't as big a fan as you claim."

Chelsea said, "That's not enough. Tell him he's not a good student."

"You certainly aren't one of Fletcher's favored students, or you'd know how to properly set a Grimm Reaper murder scene."

Boundy scowled. "I'm his best student!"

"Your copycat kills say otherwise."

"I'm not confessing to any copycat kills."

"You already did."

"No, I didn't."

"We talked to you at the scene of the Cinderella murder. You tried to blow me up."

"I didn't try to blow you up."

"You hung up on me when I called you by your name, then detonated the bomb."

Chelsea said, "Remind him Fletcher didn't use explosives."

"The Grimm Reaper didn't use bombs. He would never destroy his handiwork."

"Artistry," she added.

"His artistry," Jim continued.

"Sometimes you have to make a statement," Boundy said.

"Do *you*?" Jim asked.

"'You' in the generic sense."

"Phil, we've been to your house. We've been to your spare bedroom. We've been to your basement."

He looked up at Jim.

"Phil, it's like I said from the beginning, we have enough to put you away for life. We have the bomb-making materials that match the signature of the bomb at Spruce Bluffs Park. We have the jars of trophies from your basement. You have no leverage at this point. If you hope for any leniency, you need to identify your victims, tell us where the other bomb or bombs are, and help us bring in Fletcher."

"I'll need to see terms in writing. I want a guarantee that I'll be Fletcher's cellmate in perpetuity. Not just a day or a week or something, but forever. Unless I request a change."

"We can get that in writing. In the meantime, we need to know where he is."

"No. The guarantee first."

"I need something in good faith. The location of the other bombs and the identities of the victims."

"Not until I get the paperwork from the District Attorney."

"The DA isn't going to give you anything without some indication that you intend to work with us."

"You can build a failsafe into the contract specifying that I don't get what I want if you don't get what you want. I'm sure you will, anyway. You law types are tricky like that."

Jim's eyebrows shot up. "We're tricky?"

"Yeah. Can't trust you as far as a bomb can blow you." He burst into hysterical laughter.

"You're a real prince among men, you know that, Phil?"

"You mean that?" Boundy's eyes lit up, and he sat straighter in his seat. "Like, the actual Prince Phillip from the fairy tales? Do you think the Grimm Reaper would think so?"

Chelsea said, "Remind him Prince Phillip was Aurora's love interest."

"It's interesting," Jim said. "You picked the one prince Fletcher most identified with himself."

"I did?"

"Oh, yeah. When he role-played with Sullivan, he dressed her as Sleeping Beauty and wanted to be her Prince Phillip. Funny you bonded with that character yourself."

"You think I'm just like Reaper?"

"That's not what I said."

But Boundy was lost in his reverie. "I mean, I always knew we were simpatico about so many things. But this? I mean, you're basically saying we're the same person."

Chelsea said, "Tell him Fletcher gave up all the information he had the second we had him in custody."

The words were already half out of Jim's mouth as she was saying them. "You know, when we arrested Fletcher, he recognized his plight. And he knew the honorable thing to do — the thing an honorable prince would do — would be to share any and all information he had. Which he did. He gave us everything he had on all his … stories."

"He did?"

"Every last detail."

"Fine. I'll tell you everything. As long as I can be his cellmate. I'll give you the girls' identities, the location of the last bomb, all of it."

"Great." Jim slid a tablet and pen across the table. "Start by telling me Fletcher's location, then you can write down the rest."

Boundy grabbed the pen, wrote one word, then looked up at him.

"On my honor as a fairy tale prince, I had nothing to do with him breaking out of prison. And I have no idea where he is or how to reach him. In fact, I was kind of hurt that he didn't ask for my help."

He tapped the tablet. "Write what you know. Everything. Don't leave a single detail out."

Boundy resumed writing.

Jim left the room. He wanted to punch something. He wanted to punch some*one*. He wanted to punch that asshole sitting in there.

No, he wanted to punch Fletcher. Then put him back behind bars. Or put him in the ground.

But he'd do things by the book. He'd just have to find the bastard first.

Chapter Thirty-Four

HE PUT DOWN THE PAINTBRUSH, placed his hands on his back for support, then stretched into the deepest arch he dared. It wouldn't do to topple off the stool and crack his head open. Or pop a disc in his spine and have to try to crawl to the chiropractor.

Because if he didn't make it and someone had to come to his rescue, he'd have a lot of explaining to do.

Or he'd have more work to do.

And he was already operating in a gray area, which was something he'd never believed in before. The law was black and white. There was no room for gray. Right was white, wrong was black. Legal, illegal.

Except, more and more, he was discovering that wasn't always true.

Every day, criminals cut deals to lessen their sentences. Sometimes they went scot-free.

That wasn't right. Wasn't white.

It was a morally gray area.

These days, he seemed to live in a morally gray area. His life had become morally gray.

His mother would be saddened by that, though she would understand.

His father would not approve.

Funny … Dad was the reason the darkness had crept in. Not that he'd ever tell him so.

He picked up the brush, dipped it in the red. Touched up the lips on 08271993. They still didn't look right. Anger roiled through him, as bright and hot and brilliant as the color on the bristles. He snatched the paint from the table then threw it across the room.

The tiny pot impacted the wall with a thud then shattered into a dozen plastic shards. A crimson blot blemished the wall, and two drips of red trickled down from it like tears.

"See what you made me do?" he screamed at 08271993 and backhanded him.

The prisoner fell helplessly to the floor then lay there, motionless, giving him no response.

He pressed his hand to his forehead, closed his eyes, and took a deep breath. "That's going to leave a mark. And you're already a mess. What if I can't find Nell, hmm? What then? Are you just going to be sloppy in your cell? And what of the others? My prison is starting to fill up. Am I supposed to have inmate after inmate after inmate with discolored skin and odd expressions?"

The inmate didn't move. Didn't answer.

It took every ounce of willpower he possessed not to kick 08271993 in the ribs and send him sailing across the room. How he hated being ignored. It was the height of rudeness to deny someone a reply. Manners. His mother raised him with manners. Basic civility. It wasn't so much to ask of another, was it? He thought not.

"I asked you a question, 08271993."

Still nothing.

He bent down, got nose to nose with him to intimidate him into talking. Spittle flew from his mouth as he screamed in the prisoner's face. "You're supposed to counsel me, not give me the silent treatment!"

But the prisoner remained insolently silent.

He stood. Tipped his head left, then right, savoring the release of tension that accompanied the audible cracks. Did the same for each knuckle on both hands. Finally, a deep squat let him enjoy the popping of his knee joints. "You hear that, 08271993? I'm all warmed up. I could go fifteen rounds with you. You think you could go fifteen rounds with me?"

No answer.

"You think you could even last one?"

Not a peep.

"I didn't think so. See, you might think you're being disrespectful by ignoring me. But I choose to think you're too fearful of me to respond at all. In fact, I think you and the rest of the criminals in this joint are so intimidated by my formidable presence, that I deserve some kind of commendation."

The inmate still didn't move or respond in any manner.

"I see you agree."

He strode over to the wall then stared at the red blemish. "I expect you to clean this up while I'm gone. I'm going to go get myself a cake. For what, you ask? Thanks for finally inquiring. I'll tell you. I believe I've just been promoted to Grand Warden of this prison." He cocked his head to the side. "Did you hear that? Yes. No longer guard, no longer warden, but Grand Warden. This is cause for celebration. So, clean up this mess. When I get back, I expect this place to be spotless."

Then he stepped over the taxidermied remains he referred to as 08271993, still lying in a motionless heap on the floor, as he left to prepare a celebrational feast for his new promotion.

Chapter Thirty-Five

CHELSEA WAS ALREADY WAITING for Jim in the hallway, pacing. She rounded on him as he closed the door to the interrogation room. "We're right back to where we started. Which is with no leads on Fletcher."

"It's not all bad. We closed the copycat case."

"But that monster's still out there!" She ran her hand through her hair.

"Okay. That's true. But we're closing in on him."

She stopped pacing. Stopped fidgeting. Stopped arguing. Just stared at him.

"Well, maybe it's not exactly true. But we're no further from catching him than we were."

Chelsea started pacing again.

Norm rounded the corner. "Got someone here to see you. Want him in Interrogation Two, or you want to keep it more friendly and chat at your desk? Or in Davenport's office?"

"Who's here?" she asked.

"Thompson."

"Interrogation," Jim said.

"No." She shook her head. "Send him to Davenport's office."

Norm raised his eyebrows.

"You sure?" Jim asked. "Taking him to task in the boss's office?"

"I don't plan on taking him to task. Besides, the interrogation rooms are for criminals, and I don't want him to feel like one. I want him to be comfortable."

"I wouldn't be comfortable in the captain's office."

"Well, I'm not taking him out for drinks. Besides, this will save us from repeating it all for Davenport later."

"I'll tell him," Norm said.

"We're coming now, anyway." Chelsea started to follow him.

"Go ahead," Jim said. "We'll be along in a minute."

Norm waved as he walked away.

As soon as he was gone, Jim said, "Are you sure about this?"

"About meeting in Davenport's office?"

"About talking to Thompson at all. He blames us for his sister almost dying, and he wasn't trustworthy before he hated us. Whatever he's doing here, he probably has an ulterior motive."

"It's the only lead we have. Unless you know where Gwendolyn Cole happens to be?"

His jaw ticked.

"Let's go."

Chelsea led him to the captain's office. A bunch of files were on the sofa. Someone had pulled in a third guest chair from somewhere. She — wisely, she thought — took the one in the middle, keeping Thompson separated from her partner. Because the office wasn't very roomy, she was rubbing elbows with both of them once they were all seated. "Thanks for coming in, Oliver. How's your sister?"

"They won't let us see her for a few days, but they assure us she's recovering. Mom and Dad are at the hospital. They refuse to leave until they see her for themselves. I suspect by tomorrow things will get ugly if they don't see her with their own eyes."

"I'll see if I can arrange a camera viewing," Davenport said.

"I don't know if they'll accept that."

The captain took a deep breath as he leaned back in his seat. "It's probably the best the hospital will agree to. They're very strict with rules regarding … delicate situations like this."

"Well, I appreciate whatever strings you can pull."

He nodded. "So, I'm guessing you didn't come here for a favor."

Thompson shook his head. "I know you don't believe this, probably because I haven't given you much reason to, but I'm a good cop."

Jim scoffed.

Chelsea nudged him.

He turned it into a cough.

"No, it's okay. I get it. We got off to a bad start, and it was my fault. Now, with my sister mixed up in this mess, you think I'm involved, too. And I've been nothing but hostile and defensive this whole time. Except when I was on the attack. If I was in your shoes, I'd think I was a problem, too."

She prepared to elbow Jim again, but he remained silent.

"No fake cough this time, Detective?" Thompson asked.

"Why are you here, Thompson?"

"I told you. Because I'm a good cop. And I'm going to prove it to you."

But Jim didn't say anything.

Chelsea laid her hand on his arm. "Oliver?"

He looked up at her. "Huh? Oh. Sorry. I was thinking about Nell."

She gave him a soft smile.

"She's my only sibling. My twin. I've always looked out for her. Our parents gave her everything. I tried, too. But I swear, it was never enough. You know those people who seem to have natural gifts but can't see them? The ones who spend every waking second begrudging the one thing they don't have? The one thing that you do have? That's Nell."

"What did you have that she wanted?" Chelsea asked.

"That was the thing. She could have had it, too. If she'd just waited them out." He shook his head. "Freedom."

"I don't follow," Davenport said.

Oliver sighed. "Mom and Dad spoiled her rotten. I always had to work twice as hard for half as much. But I didn't care. She was their little princess. Mom wanted a girl, you see. There were boys in the family forever. Wasn't a girl on either side of the family. Boy cousins coming out of the woodwork. But our grandmother wanted a girl, and Mom delivered one. There were photoshoots and pageants and all kinds of nonsense. I was glad not to be part of it and to fade into the background. Nell — Eleanor, named after Gran, of course — hated it. So, she rebelled. The more she fought, the more Gran insisted on controlling her. And Mom and Dad let her. I, on the other hand, faded into the background. Nell both hated and envied me for it. I had all the freedom in the world. I'm not sure Gran knew my name. Had to work my ass of just to be noticed by my parents. It was a blessing and a curse. If I'd realized how much Nell was suffering, maybe I'd have helped more, but

I was a kid. I was only concerned with how it impacted me."

"Of course you can't be blamed for that," Chelsea said. "No one would expect you to be aware of the psychological manipulations your grandmother and parents inflicted on you and your sister."

"When you say it like that, it sounds bad."

"It was bad."

"You're making it sound abusive."

"Wasn't it?"

"No. They doted on her. Gave her all kinds of attention."

"Not the kind she wanted. And they ignored you."

"You're twisting things."

"And you're making excuses for them."

"Do you want to hear this story or not?"

She frowned. "Go on."

"When Gran died, Nell was in college. She didn't want to go to school, but our parents and grandmother insisted. So, she chose what she thought would be the most useless major, just to waste the tuition money. Art. Turned out, she liked it. She already knew she was good at it. You've seen her work. She has talent."

"She does," Chelsea said. "And she could have made a good living doing honest work. Why didn't she?"

"Because she lived under Gran's thumb for so long, I think she just became a rebel. Or something in her broke. I don't know. I tried to help her. But maybe she's beyond help."

"Help her how?" Jim asked. "By giving her contacts in the crime world?"

"Why would I do that?" Thompson asked. "How is that helping her?"

"You tell us. She met these lowlifes somehow."

He sighed. "Yeah, I guess it was through me. So it is my fault."

"See," Jim said.

"But not how you think!"

"What do you mean?" she asked.

Thompson rested his elbows on his knees and cradled his head in his hands. "I tried to help her by introducing her to one of my buddies. A survivalist guy, so I knew he could take care of her if shit ever hit the fan. And he's in law enforcement, so I trusted him to keep her on the right path."

"A cop? Someone from the crime lab or the ME's office? Not someone who works with the DA?" Chelsea wasn't overly fond the people over there. Most of them had chips on their shoulders.

"No. A prison guard."

She didn't like where this was going.

Jim leaned forward.

"My buddy really liked her. And I thought she liked him, too. They seemed to be getting along great. But Nell …" He shook his head. "Over the years, dealing with Gran and Mom and Dad, she became quite the schemer. She was just using him for information. Talked about his job all the time. He thought she was interested in him. You know, being polite and attentive. But she was mining information. That's how she found out about the criminal underworld. Who the players were in which organizations. She built a name for herself in the black market because of him. Then she started visiting him at work. He broke the rules for her. The one rule he ever broke, and it was for her. He arranged it so she could meet Fletcher. Said she wanted to paint his portrait. Told him she could make a fortune off it. He didn't understand why she'd want to, but he made it happen. And how did she repay him? She fell in love with the freak and helped him escape. Broke my buddy's heart in the process, too. He's barely talking to me. Took a leave of absence from work. Guy's a mess over it."

"This guard at Black Meadow?" Chelsea said, already knowing the answer. "He a big, bald guy?"

"Yeah."

She could see his hulking figure — which undoubtedly was supported with a size thirteen shoe. Heard his deep bass timbre extolling the importance of obeying the rules and his disgust with the people who refused to follow them. His special hatred for the Grimm Reaper.

Chelsea glanced at Jim, then she looked at Oliver. "His name wouldn't happen to be—"

"Milo Hartman."

Chapter Thirty-Six

Jim GLANCED at Chelsea as he turned off the highway. "Anything yet?"

"Did you hear my phone ding?"

"We need that warrant to search Hartman's property. He's not going to invite us in."

"If we have to, we'll sit on his place until it comes. We've done it before."

"We've got probable cause to breach. He could be torturing Fletcher as we speak."

She scoffed. "Like you care? If he killed Fletcher, it would be a dream come true for you."

"And it wouldn't be for you?"

"Police protect and serve. We don't root for the loss of human life."

"That's a non-answer." Jim turned onto the unpaved road.

Chelsea gripped the dashboard as he rounded the bend. She continued holding it as the car bounced over ruts. "You might want to slow down a little. This vehicle doesn't have the suspension your car does."

"Cop cars are sturdy. It can take it."

"My spine can't." She braced her hand on the ceiling as they bucked over a particularly large divot in the road. "I think I'd have preferred the smelly car."

"I don't even want to think about that right now."

She sighed.

"Maybe you should call Rad—"

Her phone dinged. "Warrant came through."

"Search or arrest?"

Chelsea scanned the document. "Search, of course."

"Damn it."

"He's being careful. We don't have enough to arrest Hartman. We barely have enough to suspect him."

"My gut says it's him."

She tapped out a text.

"What are you doing?"

"Letting Danny know what's going on."

"Sullivan, I appreciate your loyalty to him, but you do realize we've done a lot more notifying him than he's done in kind, right?"

"This tired argument again?"

Jim turned down the fork toward the Hartman property. "For it being Sherick's case that he gave us the *courtesy* of working on, we've done most of the work."

"They've been running down leads all over the tri-state area. We've been focused on this concentrated county. Really, a fifteen-square-mile tract of woodland, when you think about it."

"Yeah. And what's that tell you?"

"That the State Police have a heck of a lot of territory to cover."

"No. That we're the ones who did the real work on this case. They've been chasing shadows."

"So, we're back to looking for credit again?"

"That's not what this is about."

"Then I don't get it."

"I want your head in the game. Stop worrying about Danny and focus on us. On the here and now. For all we know, your boy's on the other side of the state. But I'm right here. I need to know you've got my back, and if I'm in trouble, you're not going to be looking at your phone sending status updates to your case manager."

She gasped. "Jim, how could you say that? Or think it? When we're in the field, I'm focused on the job, one hundred percent. I have your back. I *always* have your back. You have to know that."

"It really feels like I've been fighting for partner status this whole case. I'm not mentioning it now to start a fight. I'm bringing it up because I want to be sure you're focused."

Chelsea stuffed her phone into her pocket. "I am. Completely."

"Good. Because we're here. And I don't expect this to go smoothly."

"How should we play this?"

"Hartman has no reason to think we're on to him. Last time we were here, it was to ask for his help. Let's just approach him as colleagues, same as last time." Jim got out of the car.

She scrambled out after him. "Hey."

"Yeah?" He looked back at her.

"I'm sorry if I gave you the impression that—"

"No. We're not doing this now. Nothing that sounds like last words before going into a potentially hostile situation. That's bad luck. You trying to jinx us?"

"You drive me insane. You know that?"

"That's better. Let's go."

She rolled her eyes and shook her head.

He grinned and turned around. But as soon as his back was to her, the smile left his face. Just as she hasn't meant to push his buttons, he hadn't meant to push hers. It was important that they were in sync walking into this situation, and a little ribbing to let her know he wasn't angry was the best way he knew to make that happen.

Jim wasn't jealous of Danny. Not a lot, anyway. Not really. But she had been intently diligent about keeping the man in the loop. Made him wonder if she'd have been as careful to keep her own partner informed as she was her former colleague.

Of course, he knew she would have. He'd been unfair. But he needed to be certain her attention wasn't split, then he needed to put her in a good frame of mind.

Because evidence or not, he trusted his gut. From the beginning, he wasn't comfortable around Milo Hartman. Hyper-vigilant prison guard. Doomsday prepper.

Possible serial killer abductor.

And they were about to confront him on his home turf.

Chapter Thirty-Seven

THEY WERE ALMOST at the steps to the Hartman house when Chelsea grabbed Jim's arm. She pointed down toward the pole barn, where two men were sneaking out, both of them with a stuffed duffel in each hand. "Why are people always stealing from him? He's the last guy I'd want to cross. Are they stupid? Do they have a death wish?"

"To be fair, the last guys weren't technically stealing. They had already paid for their dead animal. And I don't know about these two, but I think we know the last two weren't Mensa members."

"Come on." She nodded at the men, who were about to round the corner of the barn. "Let's go see what they're doing."

The two of them jogged down the slope, silent in the grass. As soon as they reached the driveway, the crunch of the gravel underfoot made their presence known. The men turned, saw them, then broke into a run.

"Fuck," Jim said and sprinted after them, weapon raised.

Chelsea unholstered hers and followed close behind.

Whatever the men were carrying must have been weighing them down considerably, because she and Jim quickly caught up. She didn't understand why they didn't drop the bags. They'd have made it to their truck before she and Jim reached them, and by the time they got back to their unit, the two men would have been long gone. Instead, they slowed, stopped, and let go of the duffels.

"Police." She stopped about ten feet back. "Hands in the air."

They did as they were told.

Jim continued toward them. He frisked them both.

"We're unarmed," one of them said.

She couldn't believe anyone went to Hartman's without a weapon.

"Turn around." Jim stepped back. He kept his gun trained on them.

"Hey, man." The one on the left recoiled. "You know we're not packing."

"Who are you?" Chelsea asked.

"Cody Lawler." He eyed Jim's gun.

"Greg Finnegan," the other said.

"You can put your hands down." She tipped her head toward the duffels at their feet. "What's in the bags, Cody?"

"Venison."

"You stole deer meat from Mr. Hartman?"

"No! It's ours."

Greg inched forward. "You don't understand. It really is ours. Me and Cody got us a twelve-point buck last month, and Hartman butchered it for us. You know how much meat you get from a twelve-point?"

"You know it's not hunting season?" Jim asked.

"We weren't hunting. I hit the damn think with my truck."

"*Our* work truck," Cody amended.

"Yeah, yeah. *Our* work truck." He shrugged almost abashedly. "We're me and him."

"Obviously."

"No, I mean we're Me and Him Are Handy."

"The repair guys?" Jim asked.

"Yeah." Greg smiled. "You heard of us?"

"I did. You know it's 'he and I,' right?"

His brow furrowed. "She's a girl."

Jim looked at her. "Sullivan?"

"Pick your battles. This isn't it."

He sighed.

She turned to the two men. "So, you two hit a deer then brought the carcass here to be butchered?"

Cody nodded. "Yeah. Milo's a whiz with animals. Plus, he gave us a great deal because he wanted the head."

"I'm sorry?"

"He does butchering and taxidermy. Tanning, as well. His dad did, too. Taught him everything he knows."

"So we've heard." Jim holstered his weapon.

Chelsea did the same.

The men visibly relaxed.

"Anyway," Greg said, "he said he'd give us a discount on the meat in exchange for the head. Only the body got damaged when we hit the thing, so I guess he wanted to mount it."

"You can eat meat you hit with a truck?" she asked.

"It didn't all have road rash. Said he was going to see if he could get any leather from the hide. Depended on the amount of damage to the skin, of course."

"Doesn't matter," Jim said. "You can't just take meat from the premises. You don't know what's yours, you have to pay him, not to mention—"

"We do know what's ours. It's all labeled." Cody

pointed to the bag. "You can check for yourselves. We only took what was ours."

"And we paid in advance, so it really is ours already," Greg added.

"You should have made an appointment." But Chelsea had a feeling their story would sound remarkably similar to the Rink brothers'.

"We tried," Cody said. "If he answered the phone — and that was hardly ever — he always had an excuse why it wasn't a good time. Long story short, he was stalling us. I was starting to wonder if he ate our meat. Or maybe sold it to someone else."

"Yeah. It's our venison. We didn't do anything wrong."

Jim scowled at him. "You trespassed on private property and broke into his workshop."

"Well, that's a technicality."

"No, that's a crime."

"Two, actually," Chelsea said.

"We'll replace the padlock."

Cody nodded. "And whatever else Milo wants."

"Don't get carried away, Cody."

"You realize breaking and entering is a felony, right?" Chelsea said.

"What?" Greg looked from Chelsea to Cody to Jim then back to Chelsea. "We just wanted our meat."

"Did you see Mr. Hartman inside?"

"No. If we did, we wouldn't have cut the lock."

"Shut up, Greg!" Cody looked at Jim. "Do we need a lawyer? Are you arresting us?"

"No. Consider this your lucky day."

"Really?"

"You don't know how lucky," Jim said. "Now get out of here."

"Can we take our venison?" Greg asked.

Chelsea rolled her eyes.

Jim glared at him. "Yes. Now go."

The men snatched their bags, then hurried for their truck. They didn't look back.

She watched them go, shaking her head. "If Hartman has exterior surveillance cameras around — and as he's a prepper, we have to assume he does — he definitely knows we're here."

"He knew we were here the second we drove onto the property."

"Yeah, but we were here as friendly cops then."

"And we still can be."

Chelsea shook her head. "We caught criminals on his property and sent them on their way. No cops would release two B&Es unless they were after someone more dangerous. If Hartman is watching us, he knows we're on to him."

"You're right. Fuck." Jim kicked a rock across the driveway. It bounced into the woods then rustled in the brush. But the noise continued a couple of seconds longer than the rock's momentum would have.

She slowly drew her weapon, stepped toward him, and whispered, "You notice that?"

"What?"

"The lingering noise in the weeds."

He stared into the trees and drew his weapon. "I didn't hear any—" A twig snapped. "I heard that."

They advanced on the woods in tandem, him on the left, her on the right, both of them zeroing in on the spot where the noise originated from.

Chelsea's pulse kicked into overdrive. Her palms slicked with sweat, and she had to adjust her grip on her weapon.

When they were about five yards from the tree line, the branches of a bush wavered.

She breathed in, moved her finger from the side of her weapon to the trigger.

A rabbit hopped out from under the thicket. It stared at them for a second before scurrying across the driveway.

"Son of a bitch." Jim lowered his arms.

Chelsea chuckled and holstered her weapon. "All that drama for a little bunny."

"We're not out of the woods yet. Literally."

That sobered her. "True. So, back to the house?"

"If you were Hartman, would you be there? I wouldn't be."

"The venison guys didn't see him in the pole barn."

"I think he's in his bunker."

"We don't know where his bunker is."

"No, but he taught us a little about how to spot them."

"Wrong. He taught us a little about how to spot the Thompson bunker."

"The skills are transferrable, I'd assume."

She rolled her eyes. "Do you really think he'd teach us something that we could turn around and use against him?"

Jim stood in the middle of the driveway, looking all around — first to the house, then to the workshop, then into the woods. Finally, he faced her. "You're not going to believe this, and you'll never know how much it pains me to say this, but I think we need help."

"You're right. I don't believe it."

"Then you're really not going to believe this. I want to bring Oliver out here."

Chapter Thirty-Eight

JIM MARVELED that time could both fly and drag simultaneously. But as he sat behind the wheel in the very uncomfortable cop car in the woods, awaiting Thompson's arrival, it was doing that very thing.

He and Chelsea were staring at Hartman's house and workshop, looking for any signs of movement and expecting none. So far, they hadn't been disappointed.

And the clock indicated Thompson should be there any minute. When his partner suggested they call him in, Jim resisted even though he knew it was their best chance. As she spoke to the captain and made the request, he prayed they'd be denied. And ever since, while they'd been waiting for the man to show up, he'd been both dreading his arrival and in a hurry to get it over with.

"We should just go without him."

Chelsea sighed. "He'll be here soon."

"For all we know, he's on the way to Mexico and we're standing here holding our—"

She raised her eyebrows.

He cleared his throat. "Tempers in check, wasting time."

"Oliver's looking for redemption. And for a chance to prove himself. He's not running away. He'll be here."

"In the meantime, Hartman is probably fleeing to Mexico."

"No one's running to Mexico. Besides, he'd never get past us."

"You don't know that."

"We'd spot him. His bunker entrance is right out there in front of us."

"If we knew that for sure, we wouldn't need Thompson."

She didn't answer him.

And that's what was eating him. That they did need Thompson. Chelsea knew it. Davenport knew it. The whole department probably knew it. Jim, although it killed him to admit it, knew it.

Thompson fucking knew it.

He could just see the smug look on his face now when he pulled up. Shit-eating grin. Eyes dancing with glee. Arms crossed over his chest and one ankle crossed over the other as he leaned against his car — probably not a department ride, either — judging Jim requesting his assistance.

It was tantamount to eating crow.

That didn't set well with him.

"I'm going to explore."

She grabbed his arm as he grabbed the door handle. "That's the worst possible idea. Remember all the security cameras and booby traps Oliver had? His were harmless. What if Hartman has something more dangerous out there?"

"That's illegal."

"I doubt he cares about that at this point."

"He's all about the rules, Chels."

"No. He *was* all about the rules. Before he broke them. Now he's making his own rules. And we don't know what they are."

"We don't even know for sure he's guilty of anything. He's still just a suspect."

"I thought we were trusting your gut?"

Jim glared at her.

"Doesn't matter now. Here comes Oliver."

Wonderful.

She jumped out of the car.

Jim was slower to exit. Chelsea had already greeted Thompson when he joined them. He'd steeled himself for the I-told-you-so sneer or you-couldn't-do-it-without-me laughter at his expense, but there was nothing but grim determination in the set of his features and, unless he missed his guess, concern in his eyes.

Thompson nodded to him as he walked to the passenger side of the car. "Davenport has backup units on standby down where the road forks." He retrieved his body armor from the front seat then pulled it on. "Cell service is shit out here — you know that — but the radios will work."

"Thanks," Chelsea said.

"You two better get your vests on."

Jim looked at the car then at Chelsea. "Did you think to transfer your gear?"

She shook her head. "I'm guessing you didn't, either."

"No."

Thompson gaped at them. "You two have been out here for over an hour — planning a raid on a crazy, gun-happy man's bunker, might I add — and it never once occurred to you that you didn't have your protective gear?"

"When you put it like that, it sounds bad," Chelsea said.

"You called me out here," he continued. "I could have brought it to you."

"Now it sounds worse."

He ran his hand through his hair. "I'm familiar with his set up. Probably more than anyone other than him. But if he's guilty of a crime and thinks people are coming for him, the first thing he's going to do is reinforce his defenses. Especially knowing I'm a cop. So, all the knowledge in the world that I have is going to be next to useless."

"But you know where the entrance is, where his cameras are, what traps he has set."

Thompson shook his head. "I do know where the entrance and exit are. I know where the *original* cameras were and where and what the *original* traps were. But if he's planning on waging war, that knowledge is practically worthless. He'll have changed everything."

"What does that mean for us?" Jim asked.

"It means I'll keep a sharp eye out for pitfalls as I take you to his bunker, but I can't promise we'll make it."

"That's not comforting."

"Sorry. That's the best I've got."

"We appreciate it," Chelsea said.

"Before we go, let me sketch a couple of quick maps for you."

"A couple?" she asked.

"One to get you to the bunker, and one of the inside."

"But you're coming with us."

"I told you, he's going to have a lot more traps. There's a good chance all three of us won't make it there. And I'm taking point, so if I go down, you need to have a rudimentary understanding of where you're going and what you might be facing."

She shook her head. "No. You're the expert. We need you. One of us will take point. I'll do it. You lead from behind, tell me where to go."

"That's not happening," Jim said. "I'll do it."

"I hate to pull rank, and seeing as you both outrank me at work, I guess I technically can't, but when it comes to this, I'm the expert, so I'm in charge, and what I say goes. I'm taking point. Even if I told you where to go, you wouldn't know what to look for. And besides, I hate to beat a dead horse, but *neither of you has body armor*. Now, give me a couple of minutes to draw these maps, then we can get going."

So, Jim didn't eat crow when Thompson showed up, but he had to chew a few feathers now.

Chelsea pulled him aside while Thompson worked on his maps. "This feels wrong."

"He's not wrong, Chels."

"No, I mean, I know he's right. But it feels wrong to let him do this."

"We fucked up."

"Yeah, and he's paying the price for it."

"Beating ourselves up about it now doesn't do him or us any good. We need to focus. Besides, he's right. He is the best person to take the lead on this."

"We're the detectives. We're supposed to lead."

"And sometimes leading means knowing when to defer to others. Like when I didn't want to call him in the first place, but you knew it was the right thing to do."

"It was your suggestion to call him."

"Yeah, but I didn't want to."

She frowned, and a little crease appeared between her eyebrows.

He poked it with his index finger and rubbed it until she batted his hand away. "You're getting old before your time, Sullivan. Keep worrying like you do, and pretty soon, you're going to have wrinkles."

"Why are they laugh lines on men but wrinkles on women?"

"On that part of a face, they're wrinkles on everybody. Now, stop stressing out and put on your game face."

"You just rubbed away my game face."

He rolled his eyes. "Let's go. Thompson's ready."

They approached the car.

"Take pictures of these so you both have them." Thompson showed them maps. "This one is the route we're going to take through the woods. It's not the shortest or fastest, but as of the last time I was here, it was the safest." He started pointing out landmarks and routes. "Here's Milo's house, his driveway, and his workshop. We're going to enter his bunker all the way out here. I'm sure you're tempted to take this straight shot, but he's got cameras all over it. We'll never avoid them. I know he had two snares on that route. At one point, he talked about making a pit trap, too. Last I talked to him, he hadn't gotten around to it. But since then, I'd bet he did."

"That's illegal," Chelsea said.

"He wouldn't have activated it unless there was an apocalypse. Or, you know, he was being pursued by the police."

"Charming."

"This is the way we want to go. It's a hike, but there are fewer pitfalls."

"Probably literally," Jim said.

Thompson snorted. "Yeah."

Chelsea pointed at a squiggle on the map. "What's that?"

"There's a creek that winds through that part of the property. We'll have to cross it."

"How does it wind through that part and not this part?"

"Makes a dogleg turn and juts back out again."

"I only see one squiggle. How many times do we have to cross the water?" Jim asked.

Thompson scratched his head. "I'm not sure."

"Come again?"

"I was only ever here in the summer when the creek was practically dry. We talked about fishing in it when it filled in the fall, but one thing led to another, and it just never happened. I can't recall if he made his entrance inside the bend or outside it."

"I guess we'll find out when we get to it," Chelsea said. "Right, Jim?"

But Jim was less optimistic. If Thompson's intel was flawed about a detail he'd personally witnessed, then this operation was doomed before it started. Their so-called advantage might cause this whole thing to blow up in their faces. And there wasn't a damn thing he could do about it but follow him into the forest.

Chelsea looked at him for guidance, probably wondering if they should follow Thompson, make him follow them, or leave him behind and chart their own course. Lousy as all their options were, his slight bit of knowledge was still better than their complete lack of any, so he said, "This is your rodeo."

Thompson nodded. "Okay. The entrance will be camouflaged, but it's easy enough to find. The top is artificial turf, and the surrounding area is also artificial turf. The seams are so tight, they're almost impossible to see, and with all the leaves falling, you'd never notice. So you need to look for landmarks. You'll see a dead tree that's standing and another that fell beside it. They make an 'L' that points toward the entrance. Walk off twenty paces directly toward a rock across the clearing. Then feel around on the ground for a stone."

"A stone?"

"Yeah. It's not really a stone. It's camo. Hides a combination lock."

"What's the combination?"

"I didn't know it then, and I'm sure it's different now. You'll have to break it."

Jim gritted his teeth. "Probably on a sensor. He'll know we're coming the second we do that."

"I'm sure he'll know well before that."

"Then we're in?" Chelsea said.

"Then the hard part begins," Thompson said.

Her face blanched.

Jim nudged his arm. "Hey. You said entrance and exit."

"Yeah."

"So, there's more than one way in and out?"

"Of course. If there was only one way, it would be too dangerous. You could get trapped."

"Well, what's his other way? Maybe that's the better way to go."

"It's not."

"How do we know that?"

"Trust me."

"What is it?"

"A house of horrors. Literally. You think the traps out here are bad? Indiana Jones wouldn't want to deal with that shit."

Chelsea sighed. "We're losing daylight. Let's just go."

"Fine," Jim said. "Explain map two on the way."

They hiked for about an hour and were losing daylight. Fast. Thompson had pocketed their maps long ago and was intently scanning the woods for any cameras or traps

Hartman might have set. Chelsea and Jim looked, too, but their untrained eyes didn't catch anything. Not before their guide, anyway, who had pointed out a dozen cameras, five snares, three trip wires, two pits, and a steel-jawed bear trap.

They'd lost more time disarming everything, but it wasn't safe to leave them active. By the time they got close enough to the water to hear it, purple shadows from the trees stretched long and lanky across the dry, brittle brush while the indigo sky suffocated the last streaks of golds and corals on the horizon.

"There," Thompson said as he walked around a tree trunk. "I knew we were close to the—" He dropped to the ground.

"Oliver!" Chelsea rushed to him.

Jim beat her there.

Thompson was on his back, staring up at the first stars winking to life. The full moon cast his face in a sickly glow, highlighting how pale he'd already become — probably more shock than blood loss, though the latter would be a problem soon enough. A crossbow bolt was sticking out of his abdomen.

Chelsea reached for it. "Oh, my God."

"No!" Jim cried. He thought Thompson might have objected, too, but his yell was too loud to have heard the man.

She looked at him. "We can't leave him like that."

"If we take it out, he could bleed to death before we get him help. It's better to leave it in. Right now, the bolt is actually staunching the flow of blood."

Thompson nodded.

Chelsea grabbed her cell phone. "I don't have service."

"Radio," Thompson said.

Jim wasn't wearing a shoulder unit. All their tactical

gear was in his bloody car back at the station. He muttered, "Damn it."

"He's got one." Chelsea leaned over to grab Thompson's shoulder mic. When she pulled it free of his uniform, the cord wasn't attached to anything. It had become severed from the radio unit by the bolt.

"Fuck," Jim said. "What are the odds of that? One in a million? More?"

"Doesn't matter. We need to get him help."

"And we need to get to Hartman, too."

"There's a priority here, Jim. And Thompson's it."

"What if Hartman has Fletcher? Gwendolyn Cole? One or more other victims we don't even know about?"

"We don't know that he's escalated. We don't know that he's even got Fletcher."

Thompson grabbed Chelsea's hand. "We know." He took a labored breath. "And you have to stop him."

"No. We have to help you."

"Fletcher … ruined my sister. We have to … stop him. If Hartman … has him, great. But … where does it end?" He took another pained breath then looked up at Jim. "Go get him. End this."

Jim nodded. Then he met Chelsea's gaze. "My odds on my own were shit in the daylight. It's almost pitch black."

"All the more reason to give up and come back."

"No. Thompson got us this far. The bunker is just across the creek."

Oliver nodded.

"You go back the way we came. We disarmed all the traps."

"That we know of."

"Be careful. Get Thompson help. Then come back me up."

"I don't think we should split up."

"And I don't think we have a choice."

"Two against one," Thompson whispered.

"You heard him."

"Barely," she said.

"He agrees with me."

"Now you give him a vote?"

"He's one of us. Of course he gets a vote."

Thompson gave a lopsided grin. Or attempted one, anyway.

Chelsea rubbed the back of her neck. "I hate this."

Jim squeezed Chelsea's shoulder. "Be careful."

"You be careful."

"It's bad luck to say that."

"You just said it."

"Get going."

As Jim walked away, he heard Chelsea reassuring Thompson that he'd be fine. He flipped on his phone's flashlight app as he headed toward the creek, which was more like a small river. No way he wasn't going to be soaked up to his waist, easy. Which meant dripping and squeaking in the bunker.

A dead giveaway to his position.

He looked behind him. Couldn't even see Thompson anymore, and Chelsea was long gone. No one around to see him but the forest dwellers.

And any night-vision cameras.

It was worth the risk. Hartman knew they'd been coming for him for the last few hours. If he wanted a peepshow, so be it. A little humiliation now was better than a lot dead later. Jim stripped to his birthday suit, balled everything up inside his jacket, held the bundle over his head, then waded into the "creek."

The bottom was a disturbing combination of slimy and pointy — jagged rocks pierced the tender flesh of his feet and all kinds of disgusting microbes probably swam their way inside the tiny cuts. But his brain could barely process that fact because his blood flow grew sluggish. The swift flow of water was icy cold and stole his breath, which he could already see in the brisk October air. He sprinted and splashed his way to the opposite bank, threw his clothes clear of the water, then scrambled out of the burbling current.

The thicket was poor shelter from the biting gusts of autumn, and his teeth were chattering before he was done, but he eventually managed to get dressed. Jim found it most difficult pulling up his pants while his legs were still wet and his fingers were numb, but once he'd conquered that problem, the rest came easier.

His clothes did stick to him a little, but he wasn't dripping, and his shoes wouldn't squeak as he walked, so all in all, he knew he'd made the right choice.

It wasn't long until he found the L-shaped dead trees, just as Thompson said. After approaching them, he looked across the clearing for the rock. Then, heading right for it, he stepped off twenty paces.

Hartman must have been to the bunker recently — which they expected — because the hatch was easy to find. Most of the dead leaves had been cleared away.

In fact, the fake rock hiding the combination lock had been tipped up, and it hadn't been replaced.

And in a stroke of luck — or in an obvious trap — the lock had been left open.

Chances were, it was a trap.

His blood ran cold, and it wasn't from his unseasonal swim.

Didn't matter. Jim had to go in.

So, he did.

Chapter Thirty-Nine

JIM CLIMBED DOWN THE LADDER, expecting to find himself in a cement block room, or maybe a metal one. Admittedly, he knew next to nothing about survivalists and should have spent more time talking to Chelsea's dad or Thompson regarding his expectations of bunkers, particularly Milo Hartman's. He hadn't spent much time — okay, he hadn't spent any time — thinking about what bunkers should look like. If he had considered it, he'd have expected "military base austere," with beige everything and no frills.

He was no interior decorator, so he knew he didn't have the right words to describe what he was looking at, but all he could see was "*Green Acres* meets *The Green Mile*." The space he'd lowered himself into was reminiscent the decor in Hartman's own home — very appropriate for a farmhouse living room, with pine tables, plaid furniture, and woven rugs. An opening to his left led to a tidy galley kitchen painted in shades of blues and yellows. But on the opposite wall, where a door or archway in a regular room would be, was a gate made of iron bars.

Left open, of course.

Milo Hartman was no Grimm Reaper, but he might as well have thrown down a trail of breadcrumbs for Jim to follow.

And, dumb-ass that he was, he was following along. Probably going to end up like Hansel, shoved in an oven and turned into some witch's dinner. And he knew that wasn't exactly how the fairy tale went, but Sullivan was the expert, and she wasn't here.

Just more proof that he was a dumb-ass. Because she wanted him to wait for her and he insisted on coming alone.

He pulled his weapon, then walked through the gate.

Jim wasn't sure if he was more comforted or more disturbed by the fact that this part of the bunker looked more like what he'd expected — right down to the beige block walls, beige vinyl tile, and beige ceiling. What he didn't expect, however, were jail cells. Lots and lots of jail cells.

The first several he passed were empty, for which he could only be grateful. But then he came upon one that had a prisoner in it. Though the lights were bright in the hallways, the cells themselves weren't illuminated, and this prisoner was standing in the corner with his back to Jim, so he couldn't see his face. But, based on his hair color, height, and build, he thought it was possible it was Fletcher. One leg was propped on his cot and his arms were bent at odd angles. It looked like he was trying to run away and froze when he heard Jim so he wouldn't be caught.

He'd have been less conspicuous had he just stood at attention and risked the slight movement.

Funny. Now that Jim might have found him, he was finding it incredibly difficult to offer him help.

Yet that was his job.

Legal obligation, social justice, and moral principle warred inside him for … how long? An instant? A second? A minute or two?

It didn't matter. He had no idea how long he stood there, warring with himself, but he had a job to do. He could decide what was "right" later.

And on the off chance that captive wasn't Fletcher, there was nothing to decide. He really had to get the man out of there.

"Hey?"

The guy didn't answer him. Didn't move. Didn't acknowledge that he'd even heard him speak.

"Hey!" Jim said louder.

Still nothing.

"Hello? I know you can hear me."

Not even a hint of a reaction.

Was he catatonic? In shock? Drugged? Unable to respond?

Or unwilling?

"Is this some kind of game?" Jim tugged on the cell door. It didn't budge, but it rattled.

"Ah ah ah."

The deep bass came from speakers in the walls and echoed through the chamber. Jim easily recognized the voice as Hartman's.

"You've got me at a disadvantage, Milo."

"That's an understatement."

Jim clenched his jaw and took a deep breath. When he spoke, he managed to keep his tone even. "No, I mean, you can clearly see me, but I can't see you. Why don't you come talk to me face to face? We can discuss things like men."

"Are you saying I'm not a man?"

353

"Of course not." So, this was off to a great start. "I just like to look people in the eye when I talk with them. Don't you?"

"I am looking you in the eye."

"Don't you think I deserve the same courtesy?"

"You're trespassing on my property. You broke in. You set two criminals free who did the same. No, I don't think you're deserving of any courtesies."

"I have a warrant allowing me to be here. And I let Cody and Greg go so they didn't get in the middle of anything. We can always track them down later if you want to press charges. They have a business in town. They're not going anywhere."

"A likely excuse."

"It's the truth. You do business with them. You know that."

"I don't mean their business. I mean yours."

Jim scoffed. "I'm a law man. The truth is my business. That's why I'm here."

"Is that so?"

"My partner and I came to you for help more than once. You know that. You're the rule guy."

"That's right, I am. Warden Perry didn't care about the rules. Black Meadow is corrupt. All the people who work there, corrupt. That's why I had to take things into my own hands."

"By helping Fletcher escape?"

"No! That would be against the rules."

"And yet he's free."

"Is that so?"

Jim sighed. "Do you know where he is?"

Hartman laughed, the booming sound bouncing off the walls. "Oh, yeah. I know."

"Where is he?"

"Stone Cellar."

"Stone Cellar?" Jim's blood chilled. He had a bad feeling about this.

"Yeah. If a prison above ground is named after the black stripes we paint on the walls and those stupid grass plants that line the drive up to the place, then I figure why can't I do something similar?"

"I don't follow."

"Look around you. Everything's pained the color of sandstone. And this is a cellar. Of sorts."

"You're telling me you turned your doomsday bunker into a prison?"

"Welcome to Stone Cellar. Prisoners here serve life sentences. Originally I thought they could earn parole, but that didn't work out. So now, it's life or the beige mile."

"The beige mile?"

"My floor's not green."

"You execute your … prisoners? Don't you think it should be up to the state penal system to make that call?"

"They had their chance. I'm righting their wrongs."

Jim had to keep him talking. He didn't know how long it would take Chelsea to get Thompson help and then find the bunker, but he figured it would be a while. And he hadn't even drawn Hartman into the light yet. "Milo, how many people——"

"Criminals."

"Sorry. How many criminals have you incarcerated?"

"Not nearly enough."

"You know, Milo, I was thinking, with you having the inside scoop at the prison, you're in a perfect position to help us take down Ross Bradley and any other corrupt guards, Dr. Ellerby, even the big man himself. I'm sure you have dirt on Warden Perry, and probably his battle ax secretary and the accountant, too. Wouldn't it be great to know you were responsible for cleaning up the entire place? Making Black Meadow the facility was always supposed to be?"

"From the second I met you and your partner, I had you both pegged."

"What do you mean?"

"She's a straight-shooter, that one. Doesn't play games, doesn't manipulate people. I know exactly why the Grimm Reaper targeted her. She was pure, like all his victims."

"Fletcher targeted women he considered tainted. Women who should be pure but had recently become corrupted."

"That's right. And when he targeted her, I'm guessing he sensed her essence had become stained by working with you."

Jim scoffed. "I'm sorry?"

"You should be."

"I'm a cop. Non-corrupt is in my job description."

"You're talking to a guy who works in law enforcement. I know how much — or should I say how little — those job descriptions mean. And your reputation is public knowledge, so don't try to claim the moral high ground."

"Milo, you can't always believe everything you hear."

"Stop using my name!"

Jim backed up a step as the bellowed words reverberated around him.

"You think I don't recognize the tactics you're using? This is right out of the hostage negotiations handbook. Keep him talking, keep him calm. Use his name, find common ground. Give me a break, *Jim*. I'm not some rube off the street who's going to fall for your mental manipulations. You're in my house now."

"Okay, Mi—" He sucked in a breath, vented it slowly. "Okay. You're right. This is your house. Quite literally.

We're on your property. That section of the bunker back there" — he gestured over his shoulder — "is set up to be your home in the event of an emergency. You're calling the shots here. Is this an emergency? Or do you see a way out of this?"

"I'm a prepper, Jim. I always have a plan. You, however, don't strike me as someone who thinks ahead. You're more of a fly-by-the-seat-of-your-pants kind of guy, am I right?"

"I can be spontaneous, sure, but I'm more of a planner than you think."

"Oh, I doubt that."

"Come on, Hartman. You've had your eye on me since you met me. You said so. You know how I work."

"Yeah. You're a maverick."

"I have a reputation for thinking out of the box, sure. Never one to back out of a fight, and never one to lose a battle, either. But look past all that. I close all my cases. I put the bad guys away. And why is that? It's not dumb luck or rash decisions. It's because of carefully thought-out and well-executed plans."

"And yet you're down here all alone."

"Well, sometimes things go awry. That's why it's good that I know how to improvise."

A loud bang behind him made him wheel around. The barred door had swung shut. Jim rushed toward it.

"I wouldn't touch it, if I were you."

He reached out, anyway. A jolt of electricity raced up his arm. Jim yanked back his hand, shook out his fingers.

"Told you not to touch it."

"You can't keep me in here, Hartman."

"Oh, but I can. For now. Until your sentencing."

"My sentencing?"

"I'm the judge, jury, and executioner around here. So

watch your tone. If you expect any leniency from me, you'll show me some respect."

Jim tucked his tingling digits into his pocket then pressed them against his thigh for relief, hopefully away from Hartman's all-seeing eyes. "I thought you were the warden."

"Grand Warden."

"Grand Warden?"

"I'm all things in Stone Cellar."

"How about you open this door, the two of us go sit in your kitchen and crack open a couple of beers, and we can talk all this out?"

"How about you get to know the rest of your cellmates? You'll be spending a long time with them. I have some arrangements to make before your stay here is permanent. While I'm gone, feel free to get acquainted with each other."

Lights flickered on in some of the other cells.

"Hartman?"

He didn't answer.

"Hartman!"

Had he really gone, or was he watching in silence, waiting to see what Jim would do next?

One thing he wasn't going to do … touch that damn gate.

He turned toward the inmate he'd first seen upon entering the "prison" part of the bunker. "Hey, man. You okay? I think he's gone."

The guy still didn't answer. He was facing the corner, like a kid in "time out." But from what Jim could tell, he hadn't moved a fraction of an inch since he'd first seen him. Still in that same "run for your life" position. Was he somehow restrained? Surely his muscles would twitch or something …

"Buddy, you all right in there?"

When he got no response, he shrugged and gave up, deciding to continue on down the hall. "Hello? Anyone else down here?"

A steel door at the end of the hall was closed, and he presumed locked. And very likely electrified. That would be the last thing he'd try. So, he'd keep checking the cells. The next two were empty, but shadows stretched out of the next one, and the one across from it. Jim made his way down to them and first looked in the one to his left. A human skeleton was suspended with wire from the ceiling, posed near the foot of a cot with a book in its hands — Dostoevsky's *Crime and Punishment*.

He stumbled backward and turned away, bringing him face-to-face with the scene in the cell across from it.

Black shoes grounded the man's outfit — an orange prison jumpsuit covered with a dirty white straightjacket. He was propped on an upright medical gurney for transport. The scene was right out of *Silence of the Lambs*, but there was no fiberglass mask over the prisoner's face. That leathery-looking face cover was unnecessary.

Because the man's face was leather. Not old, weathered skin, but actual leather.

He seemed to have been preserved. Kind of like a mummy, but … less desiccated.

Literally like leather. Painted leather.

It looked like a child had been given a ten-pack of basic paint colors and a one-inch brush and told to design a clown. The skin was too white, the cheeks were too pink. The lips had been stained primary red and extended way outside the lines.

Jim started to hyperventilate. His stomach roiled. He fought to control his breathing and swallowed the bitter bile rising in his throat.

The butcher. The tanner. The taxidermist. Hartman had a whole shop of horrors right on his property where he could take an animal and turn it into meat, clothes, and a statue. Why not do it to people, too?

Except, people couldn't be taxidermied. Not only was it immoral and illegal — two things Hartman was against — it just couldn't be done. Without fur or feathers or scales, a body didn't look right preserved like that. You could see the incisions. The sutures. The discoloration. The skin would need to be …

Painted.

He looked again at the body, where lifeless glass eyes stared out at nothing, past him into the cell beyond. In a sociology in college, one of his favorite professors had told them about El Negro, a South African man who was removed from a fresh grave in the 1800s by French taxidermists and displayed in Europe for over a century before public outcry finally resulted in him being sent home for a proper burial. Only his skull and certain arm and leg bones were even sturdy enough to be returned to Africa. His skin had crumbled in Spain when they were preparing his body for transport.

That story had stuck with Jim for years. It had disturbed him greatly, and it took him a long time to lock it away. He still thought about it occasionally when he saw some human rights violation on the news, but usually he focused on the atrocities visited on segments of the population as a group. But now? The details of that particular barbarity came flooding back, and all he could remember from Professor Detterman's lecture was that El Negro's skin was repeatedly touched up with shoe polish to keep it presentable.

Humans couldn't hide the imperfections because they didn't have fur or feathers or scales. That's why they needed to be painted. The discoloration. As hideous as the clown-cover was, he hated to see what was under it.

Oh, my God.

Nell.

Eleanor Thompson.

That's what he needed her for. Sure, he probably did love her. If a sick, twisted fuck like Milo Hartman knew what the word meant. But that's not what he *needed* her for. She was an artist. And a masterful one, at that. Hartman needed someone who could make his prisoners look less like pre-school paper mâché art projects and more like people again. If anyone could.

Which, he suspected, was impossible. But a lunatic probably didn't realize that.

Jim's heart skipped a beat. It just occurred to him that he was Hartman's latest prisoner. And while he hadn't been sentenced yet, he already knew he wasn't getting off with a warning.

He zeroed in on a device in the upper corner of the cell.

Chapter Forty

CHELSEA PEERED through the bars of the iron gate, down the prison hallway. Jim stood at the end of the corridor, staring, dumbstruck, at something in one of the cells. She wasn't sure where Hartman was or how long he'd be gone, and she didn't want to wait to find out. "Jim."

He didn't answer.

"Jim!"

Still nothing.

"McPherson!"

Finally, he turned to her. His eyes widened, and he started running toward her with both hands out, fingers splayed wide. "No! Stay back!"

"I know." She waved him off. "Relax. I know."

"It's—"

"I *know*. I've been here for about five minutes."

"What?"

"I got here just before he locked you in. I'm lucky he didn't see me, or I could be in there with you."

"Or he did see you and separated us on purpose."

"I guess that's possible." Chelsea took a step back and

looked all around the door. "There's got to be a release mechanism."

"Why? There isn't one in prison."

"This isn't prison."

"Isn't it?"

She frowned at him.

"How's Thompson?"

"Rafferty and Giadone are sitting with him until the EMTs get to him, then they're coming in. And we called for more backup. Worst case, we wait out Hartman."

"Unless we can't."

"What do you mean?"

"He has more booby traps down here, Chels. And he said his contingency plans have contingencies. You need to go."

"Not without you."

"Get topside and wait for help. If I make it out, great."

"What do you mean, if?"

"He has nozzles in the cells, Sullivan."

"Nozzles?"

"I think this whole bunker is one big gas chamber."

"Probably for fresh air."

"No. He has vents for that. These nozzles are only in the cells. You need to go."

"Jim—"

"Chelsea, no. He's already been gone for five minutes. I don't know if or when he's going to turn it on, and when he does, I don't know what kind of gas it will be, how long it will take for the chamber to fill … It's best you're not down here."

She backed up again and studied the door.

"Sullivan, would you just listen for once?"

Chelsea took out her gun.

"You can't shoot the lock."

"I don't intent to." She pointed her weapon at the gate.

"Then what are you doing?"

After sighting the lock, she aimed about a foot right.

"Sullivan!"

She fired.

The lock clicked. The gate swung open an inch.

"What did you do?"

Chelsea tapped it, and when it didn't zap her, she pushed it wide. "Come on."

Jim stepped through the opening then looked back at the wall. There was a generous hole in the wall revealing fried electrical circuitry. "How did you know that was there?"

"I took a shot."

"Literally," he said.

"Come on." She pulled him toward the living room and the ladder to the surface. "Figured it couldn't hurt to try. He was controlling everything remotely rather than with a lock and key, so it had to be computerized." She started climbing the ladder. "There was a better than average chance there was circuitry in there."

A glass partition slammed to the floor between the living room and the hallway where the iron bar gate was. Gas started shooting from the nozzles in the prison corridor. The residential spaces were spared.

Chelsea hurried faster up the rungs, her partner right on her heels. When she broke into the clearing, she took in several lungfuls of fresh air.

Jim's breaths were even longer, even deeper. After three or five or a dozen, he grabbed her hand and met her gaze. "Thanks for not giving up on me."

"That's what partners are for."

He squeezed her fingers before letting go. "You think Rafferty and Giadone will pick up Hartman as he flees?"

"If he takes that route. Otherwise, hopefully a backup unit will grab him at the fork."

"Yeah." Jim took another deep breath. "Yeah."

Her eyes widened. "No."

"What?"

"No. Remember what Oliver said? Entrance and exit. Hartman didn't leave the bunker through the living room like we did."

"There was a door at the end of the cellblock. Thompson said there's always more than one way out. And the other way was a house of horrors."

"What if it's his actual house? What if this bunker is a giant tunnel filled with booby traps, but it comes out in his house? He'd know how to avoid or disarm all of them. He could navigate it in his sleep. But it would be a death trap for anyone else."

"Good thing we're already out of there," Jim said. "Let's go. Underground might be a labyrinth. Above ground on foot, we just might be able to head him off." He headed toward the creek.

"This way's faster." She pointed toward the direct route.

"Oliver said it was dangerous. Too many cameras and traps."

"Cameras don't matter anymore. And I already disarmed the traps when I came for you."

"You did?"

"I never would have made it, otherwise. Between my dad and Oliver, I knew what to look for."

"But it was dark."

"You were in trouble."

"Damn, Sullivan. You're my hero."

She was glad it was dark out, because her cheeks were

burning. "Well? What are you waiting for, McPherson? Come on!"

"Yes, ma'am. You better lead the way."

Chelsea led them away from the bunker and back toward their starting point, where they ran into Rafferty and Giadone.

"EMTs just left with Thompson," Giadone said.

"They think he's going to make it," Rafferty said, "but he's in bad shape."

"No sign of Hartman?" Jim asked.

"Nothing." Giadone shook her head.

"I need you two to stay here and make sure he doesn't get out this way," Chelsea said.

"We have no cell service out here. Rafferty, give me your radio so we can stay in touch." Jim held out his hand.

Neil passed it over.

"McPherson and I are going back to the house for Hartman. Hopefully we find him there and can either take him into custody or drive him your way. Stay alert."

"Roger that." Giadone nodded.

Chelsea and Jim headed toward the house.

Chapter Forty-One

THE SCARECROW WAS NOW an eerie reminder of what was left in Stone Cellar. An homage to the inmates of Hartman's prison and of what Jim nearly became. He tried to ignore it as he approached the house, but the glow of moonlight on its grotesque grin sent chills down his spine. Lowering his gaze didn't help much, as the jack-o'-lanterns leered up at him with maniacal smiles.

He could practically smell the gas from the prison under his feet.

Jim stole a second glance at the scarecrow to confirm it was burlap or duck cloth and not actual human skin.

"He lit all the pumpkins," Chelsea said.

"I noticed."

"Why would he do that?"

"I have no idea."

As they approached the front porch, he said, "I'll go around back."

She nodded and started to climb the stairs.

He ran around the side of the house, looking in windows as he went. The living room was dark, but the kitchen had a single electric candle burning in the window. Hartman was standing at the oven, holding a photo in his hands.

Jim darted to the back porch then climbed the stairs. Unlike the front steps, which had already been repaired, these hadn't been and groaned under his weight. Hartman had to have heard him coming. With the element of surprise gone, there was no point in trying to sneak in, so he burst inside.

The odor hit him like a wall. He hadn't been imagining the smell of noxious gas outside.

"What are you doing, Hartman?"

"I see you managed to break out of prison, McPherson."

"Well, technically, I hadn't been sentenced yet, so …"

"Another gray area." He put down the photo and picked up something small. Something Jim couldn't make out.

"I don't follow."

"No. I suppose you wouldn't. Cops like you live in the gray. I always believed in black and white. Lately, it's all been gray. I'm rather tired of it." He fumbled with the item he held.

Jim noted the box of matches in Hartman's left hand, the lone match in his right.

"Milo, I know what you're thinking about doing. And it's not the answer."

"But you think sending a prison guard to prison is?"

"We can figure something out."

"What's to figure out? I was a good man, a good son, a good employee. Then it all went to hell. Now I'm going to hell."

Chelsea stepped into the room. "No, Milo. It doesn't have to be that way."

"You … you're a good person. And a good cop. I don't want to hurt you."

"Then don't."

"You need to leave." He held up the box and the match.

"Put those down, Milo."

"Please go." Tears welled in his eyes, dampened his cheeks.

"Nothing is this bad."

"Some things are."

"I don't understand."

"You will soon enough."

"Tell me now." She stepped toward him, between him and Jim.

But Jim saw the look in Hartman's eyes. He didn't want to hurt Chelsea, but he didn't want to live with his own hurts more.

"You need to go, ma'am."

"Give me the matches, Milo." She held out her hand.

Hartman raised his.

Jim grabbed Chelsea around the waist then dove for the back door.

She screamed, "No!"

But her voice was soon drowned out by the sound of the explosion.

Chapter Forty-Two

Chelsea looked up as she sorted through the mail in her inbox. Here fingers trembled as she read the block handwriting on the envelope. "Jim. This letter's from Milo Hartman."

"Open it."

It was weird getting a letter from beyond the grave. Two days ago, he'd killed himself and nearly taken her and Jim with him. Now he was communicating with her? Talk about surreal. But these were technically the man's last words, and it was probably the only chance they'd have to get answers.

She slit open the envelope. A key fell out along with the paper.

DEAR DETECTIVE SULLIVAN,

By now, assuming all went according to plan, the worst is over. At least, it is for me. I know the ME will have my remains for a while. You might find this hypocritical of me, but I don't want to end up like my prisoners in Stone Cellar. Please give me a Christian burial with my parents.

You might be surprised to learn my parents are dead. I told people they retired to Myrtle Beach. In fact, Mom died of cancer two years ago. Dad and I buried her behind the work shed. He was never the same after that. Wasn't even the same when she was sick.

When Shane Warren escaped from Black Meadow, he accidentally ended up at our place looking for his old hunting cabin. Dad killed him. He was Stone Cellar's first prisoner. I judged Dad for that. It was my job, you see, upholding the law. I couldn't let his transgressions go unpunished. He's laid to rest beside Mom.

When your case is finished and my body is released, I'd like to be beside them. Then I can be at peace.

To that end, let's finish your case. My inmates will need to be transferred to another prison, now that there's no warden at Stone Cellar. In addition to Shane Warren, I've got Scott Fletcher and Gwendolyn Cole. Warren and Fletcher are doing time in Stone Cellar for escaping prison. Cole's sentence is for helping Fletcher escape. When their sentences are done at whichever institution you place them in, they can be extradited back to Black Meadow to serve out the remainder of their original sentences. Don't send them to Black Meadow for the time they owe me. That place is corrupt. Hopefully by the time they're returned to Black Meadow, the Board of Corrections has cleaned house and it's the institution it's supposed to be.

To that end, you'll note I sent you a key. It's to a safe deposit box at the Steel City Bank branch on Main Street. Safe Deposit Box 342. In it you'll find all the evidence I have against everyone at Black Meadow. It should be enough to put them all away. If it's not, you're on your own.

I sign this letter at peace with my decisions and with what comes next for me. I truly hope you don't get caught in the crossfire.

Sincerely,

Milo Hartman

. . .

"THAT WAS by far the weirdest thing I've ever seen at the end of a case," she said.

"Makes clean-up easier." Jim finished off his donut.

She sipped her coffee. "Nothing's easier. The Hartman property is a museum of the macabre. It'll take forever to clean that place out. We can't bury Milo there. Plus, we'll have to find and move his parents' remains. Oliver's still in recovery. His sister's still going to do time for helping Fletcher escape. So is Ainsley Edwards. Half the staff of Black Meadow is corrupt. And poor Mr. and Mrs. Warren."

"Okay. No more coffee for you." He leaned across their desks then took her cup.

"Give me that."

"No." Jim held it out of her reach.

"I'll just get another."

"You don't need more caffeine. What you need is a break. Weren't we going to go to the beach?"

"I wasn't vacationing *with* you."

"The house is big enough that we never have to see each other if we don't want."

"It's your parents' house, isn't it?"

"Does that matter?"

She sighed. "How can you even think about a vacation at a time like this?"

"Are you kidding me? It's snowing outside. Fletcher is dead. As in *never coming back*. And, in case you didn't realize this, we just put away our third serial killer. Most cops never take one off the streets. We've put away three — Grimm Reaper, the GS killer, and now Reaper's copycat, Boundy. Plus Hartman, who was turning into a serial killer himself. Frank Salerno only got the Hillside Strangler and the Night Stalker. When you and I first teamed up, I told you rookies always think they're onto a big case but it seldom happens. And look at our record. We're fucking legends, Sullivan."

"This isn't about fame, Jim. You know how I feel about fame."

"Most cops love it."

"It wigs me out."

"I know."

"And I certainly don't want my name to be forever associated with freaks like that."

"Too late."

"Well, I don't have to like it."

He sighed. "No, you don't."

"I have paperwork to do."

"You need to learn to relax."

"I can't imagine stepping away right now. There's too much going on. Our case load grew while we were working the Fletcher case. We're never going to dig out of this hole. My desk looks worse than Delfino's."

"At least it doesn't look like Davenport's."

"No one's is that bad. But it's a close second." She sighed.

"Speaking of." Jim nodded at the captain's door.

Davenport came out of his office. "Hey, you two. Press wants to do some interviews."

"Oh, gee, Captain. That's too bad." Chelsea looked across her desk at her partner. "We have vacation time coming, and we're both in need of a rest. Jim was just telling me about this gorgeous villa his parents have on this private stretch of beach-front property …"

~

The End

What to read next...

Emily Wyatt wants to save the world.

Or at least take some seriously bad guys down. But with a chip on her shoulder and betrayal in her past, she might be her own worst enemy.

Pick up your copy of A Simple Kill today.

A Quick Favor...

If you enjoyed this book, please take a moment to write a short review on your favorite online bookstore so other readers can enjoy it, too.

Thanks so much!
Nolon King

About the Author

Nolon King writes fast-paced psychological thrillers set in the glitzy world of entertainment's power players with a bold, insightful voice. He's not afraid to explore the darker side of human nature through stories featuring families torn apart by secrets and lies.

Nolon loves to write about big questions and moral quandaries. How far would you go to cover up an honest mistake? Would you destroy your career to protect your family? How much of your soul would you sell to get the life of your dreams? Would you cheat on your husband to keep your children safe? Would you give in to a stalker's demands to save your marriage?

www.ingramcontent.com/pod-product-compliance
Lightning Source LLC
Chambersburg PA
CBHW010523100726
47903CB00011B/2868